Paterson Jc   belov   B
seen on *Vigil* and *Noughts and
Peep Show and *Law & Order U*   ch
in the forthcoming *Wonka* mc   *arles
Ignatius Sancho is his debut r

'An absolutely thrilling,   nder of
a historical novel. I read with   cination, dread,
hilarity, admiration, sorrow   nph for a full life
rendered with such animation, brilliance and understanding.
Told in wonderful prose and with dazzling energy and
brilliant panache. Hugely recommended.' Stephen Fry

'A super talented actor but an even better writer.' Dan Snow

'Absolutely loving this . . . A great storyteller and a
fabulous actor. Well done, sir!' David Harewood

'Elegant, moving and vital, that this book is the
product of a deep interest and long study of one man's life
and times is evident. But what Paterson Joseph does – what
every writer of historical fiction yearns to do – is make
history fall away so that in every moment we are immersed
in a lived life. A stunning debut.' Jess Kidd

'Joseph breathes vivid life into the first Black man
to cast a vote in the England, but whose family ranked
higher in his heart than any others in his life. The novel
sings with the words of a man who survives his struggles,
and expresses himself through music, language, and love.'
Gretchen Gerzina

'I so admire Joseph's verbal imagination which seems
to effortlessly bridge the gap between our time and Sancho's.
In a huge, warm, real voice, Joseph makes us look at a past
world fro   lter

The
Secret Diaries of
Charles Ignatius
Sancho

PATERSON
JOSEPH

DIALOGUE BOOKS

First published in Great Britain in 2022 by Dialogue Books
This paperback edition published in 2023 by Dialogue Books

1 3 5 7 9 10 8 6 4 2

Copyright © Paterson Joseph 2022

The moral right of the author has been asserted.

A CIP catalogue record for this book
is available from the British Library.

ISBN 978-0-349-70237-7

Typeset in Berling by M Rules
Printed and bound in Great Britain by
Clays Ltd, Elcograf S.p.A

Papers used by Dialogue Books are from well-managed forests
and other responsible sources.

Dialogue Books
Carmelite House
50 Victoria Embankment
London EC4Y 0DZ

www.dialoguebooks.co.uk

Dialogue Books, part of Little Brown, Book Group Limited,
an Hachette UK company.

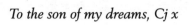

To the son of my dreams, Cj x

Author's Note

This book was written to tell Our Story. Yours and mine, whoever you are. I did not write this book to stir debate on the historical accuracy surrounding the presence of Black people in the United Kingdom in ages past. The numbers are disputed, naturally, the presence is not. This, only, is my goal: to depict that presence in the form in which I met Oliver Twist, David Copperfield and Jane Eyre. Very personally and movingly. I feel I know them, when in truth they were wholly fictional characters, their stories created by an author: typeface on a page. My material, on the other hand, springs from documented history, and not just of one man, but of a people.

I have taken a real person – Charles Ignatius Sancho – and performed an act of fiction on him. Why fictionalise the story of a real man? My aim was to avoid the lugubrious snares of a history-laden story, full of choice educational snippets. The paucity of documentation on his life was also an incentive, if his story was to be told in full. A dry history of what we know might be interesting to dip into, but let's face it, just wouldn't be as much fun – for any of us. I won't apologise for seeking first to entertain, with a by-product of enlightenment about the Black presence in the United Kingdom in the eighteenth century thrown in. Grand ambitions, soft intent. This is an imaginative telling of the life of a Black man who breathed London's air two hundred years before I walked its streets. I was once timid about my place here in the UK, but researching Sancho's story for the last twenty years – and more – has given me a deep sense of belonging, of a shared history with a nation that sometimes ignores, sometimes rejects, my people's right to an equal role in its storytelling. More than anything, this book is an attempt to add to the growing canon of Black Historical Fiction. The bonus might be that readers seek further study into this growing area of research, both historical and artistic.

I urge anyone reading this who has been caught in the maelstrom of anger and misunderstanding that surrounds debates of British and English identity, to momentarily lay those arguments aside with this book. It is right that we debate what have become divisive issues; the background whisper in every artistic or creative depiction of Black People in situations some find incongruous. But congruity is my aim. To correct the colour-balance that has allowed an historical distortion of British history to exist, leading to the majority of my generation presuming that Windrush 1948 was the start of Black British History on this island.

To the expectations of the reader who awaits a tale filled with whips and curses and rapes and murders of Black People by White People in every chapter, you will not find much to please you here. To others, who want pageant and a multicultural cast of larger-than-life characters, sashaying unmolested through London, likewise. Nothing is skirted, but neither is this an American or strictly Caribbean tale. This isn't slavery porn – the insidious desire for violence to suffuse all stories involving Black protagonists . . .

This is the tale of a lucky African orphan, who despite being born in abject slavery, rose to become a leading light of the early abolitionist movement. A hero. A man. An African. An Artist. Erudite. Wise. Grand. Flawed.

I want to tell a story by the fireside that will enlighten, but more essentially, delight you. I hope you smile, laugh, rage and cry. And in those sentiments assure yourself that whatever the truth of our origins and place in the world, we can all agree that no one should be denied their freedom to belong where they were raised.

Paterson Joseph

London

1 September 2021

*If you adopt the rule of writing
every evening your remarks on
the past day, it will be a kind
of friendly tête-a-tête between
you and yourself, wherein you
may sometimes happily become
your own Monitor; and hereafter
those little notes will afford you
a rich fund, whenever you shall
be inclined to retrace past times
and places.*

CHARLES IGNATIUS SANCHO,
1729–1780

PROLOGUE

1775

Forty-six years old

Time away from one's diary is as valuable as a little time away from one's lover. Absence not only softens the tender feelings toward the belovéd other, it also provides the benefit of perspective, that renders the object of affection so much more precious and beautified. So, too, with quill, ink and leaf – I reunite my body with my mind and the pleasure this act gives me has grown rather than diminished. For I speak and write to purpose, now. I seek to lay forth a history that speaks of all the truths of my life up to this present day. To survey – like the architect of my own life – the line I have followed that brought me here – my history. Not chaotically rendered – as in my earliest diary entries – no, as I see them now – put together – to make sense of the whole.

This, for you, my son – William Leach Osborne Sancho – born last Friday the twentieth day of October – exactly at half past one in the afternoon – my second son – my only living son. I will speak to you as you will be – as I see you in my mind's eye – when you will find these pages carefully concealed in my old room at Windsor Castle. I speak to Billy, the gentleman. The instructions for finding these will be given to you before I pass. I know with a certain knowledge that I will not live to see you at man's estate. So, here am I – addressing the man, Billy Sancho.

'Know thy father – and forgive him . . .'

I will not stint on necessary detail but have no time for flights of fantasy or anecdote not pertinent to my aim, neither. Which is no less than to render the truth of a complex web of a life – a life lived in many kingdoms – or so it seems to me presently. I am now a shop-owner. 'But hold . . . enough.' I gallop ahead and must grasp the reins of my memory more firmly.

Much of the following comes from my diary entries over the years – I will record my retrospective interjections – these may be useful in aiding my Billy to navigate the story of your father's life thus far.

This rendering may benefit Older Sancho, too – when time has eroded precision in recollection of even the most momentous twists and turns of a long life. I began writing a diary in earnest at the age of seventeen – those entries will appear in these pages as I see fit. For the present, I will begin at the beginning.

Book One

1729–1749

In which we meet the author –
Charles Ignatius Sancho relates his early life –
We meet Tilly Grant.

Chapter I

In which Charles Ignatius Sancho relates his early life.

1729

Origins

I had, on reflection, little right to survive. Born on a slave ship crossing the Atlantic Ocean on what is quaintly described as *the middle passage*. I now say a slave ship is neither in a *passage* nor does it navigate *the middle* of anywhere. It sails straight to the heart of hell.

My future articulacy would have astounded my master, standing a safe distance from the helpless African girl of unknown origin. A daughter of Eve, from somewhere along the Guinea Coast. Neither would it have occurred as a possibility to my terrified boy-father – traumatised by the last days' events and near paralysed – emasculated – by fear of the unknown. In contrast, his wife – my mother – is simply – *luckily* – lost in the bewildered agony of a painful breech-birth. Lucky to be together at all, these child-parents, captured and sold as slaves, I would guess, by a rival tribe's chief. The human spoils of war.

Lucky!

A charnel house of black flesh, this – cramped and rank with rat droppings and the spillage of a thousand filthy slop buckets. Filth – amassed over the fifteen years of this ship's barbaric life. A life spent plying its brutal, unfeeling trade between the pestilential slaughterhouses of the Guinea or Slave Coast, and the slow death of plantation life in the Americas which awaited the cursed souls who were doomed to never return home. Neither they nor their offspring. A permanently lost tribe.

Let us roam. Leaving the child-parents to their agonies for a moment, let us venture to the next deck down. No – not that lower, mezzanine deck, that one is for the piccaninnies. They can really pack them in there. Conveniently small, these little ones; they hardly complain at all but simply lie in stupefied terror. All the better. Much less trouble that way. Quieter. No, we need to look at the lowest deck.

We find the men's quarters, quite the largest space in the ship. Roomy. Or at least it would be, if three hundred men were not crammed head-to-toe so tightly that no room can be afforded for the slightest movement, without feeling the calloused skin of a stranger's feet – or the tangled, woolly roughness of the hair of one's neighbour – pungently ripe with sweat – and the acrid smell of fear and death. The rhythmic rolling of the ship, accompanied by the groans of hundreds of men who cannot speak or understand each other's languages. Divide and rule starts early in the *seasoning* process. That shameless word for the conditioning for a life of slavery, that the white and black traders along this treacherous coast give to the *slave apprenticeship*. An apprenticeship that starts in earnest once the enslaved soul has reached their destination. Usually, a plantation of one kind or another. Cotton, sugar cane, tobacco: crops that bring ready money. Commerce – where will your cruelty end?

Let us hurry back up to the birth cabin. Our young mother-to-be is about to bring our main subject forth. Past the mid-deck with the women and young girls' deck, half the area of that of the men, and made more uncomfortable for them by the fact that some are in stages of pregnancy akin to our lady above – who, now we see, has expired ... There is the dumb-struck master – the Surgeon charged with midwifery duties, guiltily sullen – the near-catatonic gaze of the frightened boy-father – now without a soul who knew him free ... He has the fleeting notion to bolt from the room – perhaps, to fling himself overboard – broken by the loss of his wife, his life's companion. Futile. He will be shackled below with the rest.

What of the *debris* left in the wake of this storm of grief? The mewling, puking infant boy – soon baptised Charles Ignatius, after the father of the Jesuits, and growing strong and round – always round – in New Granada.

On arrival, Billy, when first my father – your grandfather – saw that the colour of the majority of labourers on that benighted dock matched his own, he set his eye on a dozing overseer's unguarded scabbard – seized the man's sword – then swiftly slipped the blade from his own guts to his heart, before any had time to register the act. He died in merciful seconds and my world contracted, yet again.

This – the story I have pieced together from the fragments I harvested from servants' gossip – the indiscretions of my guardians – my own meditations – my nightmares. My story is just that – a story. Neither better nor worse than any enslaved orphan of Afric's.

I have few recollections of life on the plantation in New Granada. I have meditated on this over time, and now believe that my owner shielded me from seeing the worst of that hateful world. Guilt, at his part in my status as orphan, may have caused him to keep me in the house with him. I cannot tell. There was some affection there, surely, as his next was an act of undeniable kindness towards a little black child. When I was three years old, he took me to England. I know him as Mr Henry – though I cannot remember if that was his name, or the name my mistresses later gave him – possibly to prevent me knowing my true origins. But eavesdropping is the art of necessity for the alien. Fragments of information may be gleaned in this way that may later save a life . . . I was sent to live with my master's three maiden aunts in Royal Greenwich – near London. I will not name them, however, but give them false names.

Though these ladies were very particular about their household, they reckoned 'the black' would make a fine addition to their entourage. What household of any note was truly complete without a black *pet* to bring comfort and entertainment? And so, I quickly became *Sancho*, after a seeming likeness to the rotund servant of Cervantes' hero, Don Quixote. A sweet and affectionate compliment in their eyes. In mine, an early intimation that my name – indeed my life – would not be my own with any great alacrity. Sancho – for that was how I would be known for ever after this casual renaming – grew to be a polite and witty child, Tilly tells me. Dressed up in, say, the garb of an Arabian prince one day, topped with gold silk turban – a swarthy pirate the next. Docile and malleable. What child does not enjoy make-believe? I recall little of these very early days. Tilly – my only ally in this strict and watchful household – told me much when I came of an age to ask. Tilly Grant. Sixteen or seventeen years old, then? A girl who sometimes confused terror with obedience. Easily done, as it was tricky negotiating the contrasting but uniformly demanding natures of these Sisters Three. Abigail – the unofficial leader – tall, imperious with an air of great superiority; Beatrice, plump, pale and cursed with a persistent sniffle; Florence, painfully thin, uncompromising and didactic, a walking stick permanently in her hand; though Tilly and I privately guessed she used it more for effect and to stand out from the other two.

One of the Sisters' favourite turns was to have me play Sancho Panza in extracts from *Don Quixote*, alongside an aged, drunken buffoon of an amateur thespian, one of their acquaintances. This actor's trick was to bring a well-worn hobby-horse as a prop and use it, suggestively, as Rocinante – his ass; placing it provocatively between his legs and making riding motions. Quite tedious. For my part, I always felt myself fortunate not to have been named after the beast rather than the servant. Despite *panza* in the Spanish meaning *belly* – and despite my ready acknowledgement that I was – I remain, yes – quite roly-poly, I also knew myself to be lucky to not have one of those daft names the other black servant boys I rarely met had been burdened with: Pompey. Caesar. Hannibal. Or worse, Mungo. Besides, it's true to say that my appetite has been my Achilles heel, as well as stomach and legs, all my life.

Witness today: the Demon Gout, my constant – unwelcome – companion.

One momentous evening's entertainment at the home of the Greenwich Coven cannot pass without some detailed attention in these pages, for it changed my life forevermore. I was no more than seven years old, and my story takes a dangerous twist, now.

But I must leave off for the night – Anne Osborne waits for no man. To bed.

Chapter II

*In which Sancho – as a lad of nineteen –
continues the tale of his early childhood.*

1736

Seven years old

One night, when I was seven years old, the Sisters decided to turn theatrical impresarios, and had myself and that old, drunken fool of an actor – their acquaintance – play a scene or two before a group of select friends in their large, first-floor drawing room. The piano was pushed into the corner; the velvet drapes adorning the large window framed our stage (windowsill); the candles were lit. The guest-of-honour, newly arrived in London and known to few then: David Garrick. Soon to be, undisputedly, the greatest actor of our times, though I was only many years afterward told he was present – by the man himself. My part was conned by rote, naturally, hearing and repeating lines as Florence delivered them – they would not suffer me to learn to read.

Spoilage of Negroes through education is studiously avoided by many of our Enlightened European masters and mistresses,

Billy. You will not grow so ignorant as I, my lad: this I vow by heaven.

This night, our amateur thespian, already the worse for several glasses of port and a very large supper, tangled himself up in a Gordian Knot of curtain, cloak, limbs and scenery. His battle with the windmills he had short-sightedly mistaken for *giants*, turned out to be a very physical battle with scenery, costume and, finally, gravity. Professional that I was, however, I did not speak extempore but used the very words of Miguel de Cervantes Saavedra to express my dismay:

"'Did not I tell your worship, to mind what you were about for they were only windmills? And no one could have made any mistake about it but one who had something of the same kind in his head.'"

Strange thing. My genuine tears rendered the adults in the room pin-drop silent. Then, a wave of surprised and enthusiastic applause. Two strong gentlemen lifted me onto their shoulders – nearly tumbling over with me, as my bulk for such a small child caught them off guard – and paraded me in triumph around the salon, the crowd madly clapping. Coins were thrown at the stage, and even Mr Garrick raised his glass to me, he says. The Greenwich Coven were content to be lavished with so much unexpected praise and attention; they had 'bred the little savage well', I overheard several guests declare . . .

I found it impossible to sleep. The evening had been too exhilarating to embrace an abrupt ending. Tiptoeing, stealthily, from my room at the top of the house, I crept down the stairs. What was I intending? To stand in the window alcove, again, and relive my triumph? To find more of those coins thrown – against all social convention and, indeed, taste – by the enthusiastic crowd? A penny or two to add to my little box of *treasures*, perhaps?

In that precious old tea caddy, which I kept for many years under my bed, one would then have found a small, beautiful shell, from New Granada, my first home, its lapis lazuli-like surface a constant lure to my eyes; and the outsized ring Mr Henry took from his own finger to give to me – a memento, with a shining green gem set into it. Tilly had to palm it, like a cut-purse, for fear the Sisters would confiscate so valuable a thing given to a boy so young.

But I never reached the drawing room, or even the end of the staircase. For, on the landing, I saw a book. *Mother Goose's Tales*. A book Miss Abigail had read to me whilst I was ill in bed with a passing fever. An incongruously pleasant – maternal? – memory. Ordinarily, Miss Abigail would take me into her bed at night. I was not to tell the others, she had warned me, for they could be jealous. So, she would come and fetch me in those days – when she felt the need of me. Not every night, but frequently. Not to embrace me – simply for her own comfort. It seemed to me, at those times when I was lying nervously beside that granite-faced woman, as if this were my employment. In many ways, it was. To bring comfort to three lonely ladies. Strange to say, but that bout of fever was like a holiday from my daily life. A break from my usual treatment in the household. I often – without a trace of guilt – longed to be ill. But – damn it – was I not cursed with the most robust of constitutions?

The brightness of the outer shell of this precious book caught my eyes, as it sparkled, red and gold, beneath the flickering candlelight. I caressed the cover lovingly – turned it over and – 'words, words, words' – mysterious signs and hieroglyphs – indecipherable to me, naturally, but fascinating all the same. I thought: If only I had the key to unlock this knowledge. These stories. How far could I travel? What could I not achieve?

These thoughts had no sooner entered my childish mind, when they were violently expelled from my imagination. I felt a rough hand on my nightshirt collar, and someone boxed me on the ear – hard. Looking up – my ears ringing with the impact – I saw Miss Abigail's devil-eyes, in a face grotesquely deformed by rage. She threw me through the door of my room and slammed it after me. I leapt into bed and trembled beneath the covers, fearing that the Monster Sister would return with a switch – or worse. But despite my growing tension, I eventually fell into a fitful sleep, only to be awakened in the morning by Tilly shaking me, gently. The Sisters Three wanted to see me in the drawing room – immediately – for an interview . . . My trepidation palpable, I dutifully dressed and descended the stairs one by one, in a vain effort to postpone the inevitable haranguing.

The predictable gist of their jeremiad was one of patronage (matronage?) and general, false, racial thinking.

'You will lose that calm docility of nature all your kind are blessed with by the Creator, were you to fill this head with knowledge . . .'

I rushed from the house, that demon, Rage replacing my more familiar angel, Caution. I flew through the streets of Greenwich – a red-faced white man swung a cane at my head in anger at being brushed past by a 'fat little nigger'. My feet took me to the very banks of the Thames. I hid, Moses-like, among the thick bulrushes, and contemplated the water for so long that I did not note the time had passed from day till near evening. Every sound, every rustle in the undergrowth provoked terror in me. When I finally ventured to move from my haven, I found that my limbs had become benumbed, somewhat. I began to run once more, gathering energy that came more and more from a fear of capture; the consequences of which my childish mind imagined only the worst.

But something more unfamiliar than fear was also at war with the many emotions battling within my young frame. If I were to state now what I felt, it would be a strange, internal, fiery fury. A fury so strong, hot and inchoate that it has taken me these many years to articulate it for the first time. I was filled with a sudden, violent and all-encompassing thirst to know, my Billy. Like an innocent Adam locked out of the garden by three wilful Eves, I demanded entry – demanded to feast on the fruit of the Tree of Knowledge. The trees I saw then, however – in the silhouetting light – were the plane and oak trees of Blackheath Park.

Black – Heath. Haunt of highwayman Dick Turpin, they say – haunted by his fellows, too. The area aptly named Shooter's Hill. Yet here was this small – black – ignorant child, away from all I had known, and utterly alone in the world. Too tired – nay, too frightened – to go any further – still more terrified of the consequences if I was to return to the Greenwich Coven. I lay under an immense gorse bush, where only a curious natterjack toad kept me company. I was very cold, exhausted and, in all honesty, despairing. I crawled deeper into the dense heart of the bush, curling into myself, in a position to bring me comfort and a little warmth . . .

When I was hauled out from my hiding place by the collar of my thin waistcoat, I had been insensible for no more than thirty minutes, though I was deeply asleep already in that time. My dream had been so sweet, the sweetness of my dreamland so very intoxicating, that the terrifying contrast of what was happening to me and the reality of my situation did not take hold for several seconds. I was being slapped about the face by a man's hand, the size of a gammon. This hand belonged – unbeknownst to me – to the famous Jonathan Sill, a name all slaves and free blacks know well. And for good reason. His sharp smell of tobacco and stale alcohol was almost overwhelming. A male smell. An animal smell, and one very unlike the sweet, though ambiguous, comfort of Miss Abigail's lavender and rosewater. This man meant to do me harm, and no amount of squealing or struggling was going to affect that. I became passive – inert – useless to myself, and almost about to soil my breeches in abject terror. My name – demanded with such menace and force that, at first, I thought he had only made a grunting sound – escaped my knowledge. I would have answered to anything at that point, so complete was my dread.

Jonathan Sill: about six feet tall with shoulders that would have spanned at least three and a half – or so it seemed to my childish eyes. He wore dark clothing, in so nondescript a fashion that it is very hard for me to recall exactly what he wore, save to say that the whole ensemble fitted his bulk neatly, without causing him any loss of movement. The musk of the man was emanating from these garments, too, as if they were his hide. His North Country burr was the only clue to his origins. To describe his face, I must remember what he looked like the next time I saw him and not at this first encounter. For I could not bring myself to gaze upon his terrible countenance this night, nor meet the baleful glare that shone from eyes of the bluest blue. Eyes that might have been seen as near beautiful, if the intent within them were not so cruel and deadly. His mouth was a slit in a face darkened by the elements of a climate not our own, and spoke of an earlier life at sea, lending his features the resemblance of a knight's visor – inscrutable – immoveable. A terrifying death-mask, all humanity seemingly extinguished beneath it, marking him, to my young mind, as one of the four horsemen – a warrior without mercy.

'You Sir, what do you there? Unhand that young boy, if you will.'

Out of the near darkness came a voice of command that could not easily be ignored – in truth, demanded to be answered.

'What business is this of yours, Sir? We are apprehending a runaway nigger, is all. Let us conduct our business without molestation, so please you.'

It was only then that I noticed Jonathan Sill's young apprentice. A facsimile of the man himself, more bovine and less handsome than his master, a boy who seemed intent on violence as a first resort.

'You mistake me, Sir. I do not mean to question your action, but the legitimacy of it. By what authority are you presuming to lay hold of that young lad?'

What would this powerful man with the grip of iron do? Just then, out of the shadows of the trees along the nearby path, stepped forward the bold interrogator – a white man in his fifth decade, of very slender build, but with an upright deportment. His face was long and kindly. I guessed at once the man was a lord of some kind, for his fine periwig was fitted expertly on to his narrow head, his waistcoat of deepest blue was studded with silver buttons and he carried himself like a man used to wielding easy authority over others. The two men confronted each other for an instant with their eyes – and just as soon as it had begun, the challenge was over. The bully had undoubtedly recognised the superior man, and executing a low – but somehow sarcastic – bow, said:

'Your Grace.'

'And to whom do I have the honour of addressing myself?'

'Jonathan Sill, Your Grace' – said with not a little hint of pride.

'Ah, Slave-Catcher, they call you, do they not?'

'Ay, I have the honour of possessing the title of Thief-Taker, Your Grace.'

'A dubious honour, Jonathan Sill, dubious indeed.'

Sill plucked up his nerve and with a flash of defiance, declared: 'I own a pride in good, legal work, Your Grace. And no man can say I break one jot of any law of this land or any other that I know of in Christendom, Your Grace.'

'A little too much "Your Grace", Sir, and not enough true grace. This lad has been sought for by his master?'

To give him his due, Jonathan Sill replied with a shake of the head after a moment's hesitation, and released my collar that instant. The heat of his sudden breath made me jump, as he swiftly rasped the following promise into my ear: 'I'll have you yet, butterball.'

Nodding to His Grace with no trace of deference, Sill walked swiftly back into the darkness from whence he came, taking his shadow – the young apprentice – with him. I started to weep almost at once. Sweet relief swept my little frame and try as I did to resist tears, I was overcome with childish, racking sobs for some moments. My heaven-sent deliverer approached me and held my face in his hands. He examined me for a long time, then from his pocket produced a yellow handkerchief of silk, embroidered with a dark blue thread. I noticed this detail because he rubbed my face in several places with this cloth. It smelt of cologne – a smell that lingers on my memory to this day. It is the smell of hope and liberty to me. Then from his other pocket he produced – like a street magician – a grease-stained paper bag, offering me the contents with a gentle shake. I hesitated to guess his meaning.

'Macaroon?' he asked. Then, as I ventured to take one: 'What need you cloud so jolly a face as you possess with so grim an aspect? Rejoice rather, for you are saved, young man.'

'Sir, what use is joy to a worthless blackamoor like me? Were you I and I you, perhaps then I'd sing a different tune – I mean to say, I thank you, Your Grace . . . '

My expectations of the white world being so low, already, I braced myself for the inevitable dressing-down my tired outburst would elicit. My little life – as they say – appeared before me. I could see my days ending as they had begun, in the heart of the slave trade, on board a slave ship or toiling, ceaselessly, on a brutal sugar plantation. But my new acquaintance had no such thoughts. He laughed his gay, ringing laugh – clapped me on the shoulders – looking at me with what appeared, to my astonishment, to be admiration. He had *seen* me – he liked what he saw. He had also *heard* me – and liked what he'd heard. It would seem my cheek, a source of pain to my three guardians, was a delight to this strange man. There and then, I resolved to use this innate skill to rescue myself in future from such dangers and misfortunes as I had that night so narrowly escaped. Taking me by the hand, and without another word, my rescuer led me across the park.

We came in time to a bridle path that skirted a large property, entering its grounds through a gate that had seen better days, but was all the more secure from trespassers for its dilapidated state. On our approach, I gazed in wonder at the grand house before me. It seemed a castle to my eyes. The orange glow of the tower to our right was impressive in the dying light. No sooner had the sound of the rusty hinges faded, when a lady of great beauty – despite her age – opened the huge, black doors and waved us in.

'Where have you been all this while, John? I was quite worried. And who is this?'

'I've found a little gem here, Mary; a complete gentleman of, I'd say . . . six years old?'

'Seven!' I cried, as if in defiance, but really egged on by the mischievous twinkle in his eye when he pretended to guess my age. They both laughed and the sound of that joyful harmony has never left my heart. I felt at once special and clever and . . . happy.

We entered the hallway of this warm haven and went straight to the dining room, where a plate was laid before me. The fire in the hearth – the indulgent smiles of the man and woman – all these were almost overwhelming. I cannot now recall, I who love his food so, what they fed me. It seemed to me Ambrosia, the food of the gods, and all that I ate was of the best quality and copious. A glass of watered wine was offered, which I refused, until the man insisted. John, for so his lady called him, never left off staring at me with a mix of curiosity and a kind of pride. Yet how could he be proud of one who he had only seen that night? His wife gestured for him to leave me alone a while, and they both stepped into the entrance hallway. My years of training with the Coven had taught me well how to listen through even the thickest doors or walls. This following is what I heard as I ate:

'You cannot think to keep the lad, John; he must be returned to whoever owns him. For you can plainly see, he is a boy belonging to a gentleman's household.'

'I see he is a lad of energy and intelligence, that is all, my dear. We cannot know if he is slave or free by his demeanour nor, indeed, his dress. Now, fear not, I will have him tell me where he resides.'

'Since he was on foot in the park, he must belong nearby, at least.'

'Yes. And he has no foreign accent. Save for that sibilant trick of the tongue, he speaks like any English boy of seven.'

A *sibilant trick of the tongue* was the most pleasant way anyone had described my permanent lisp in speech. Even this man's observations of my faults were kindly done. The pair returned moments later, and I pretended to have heard nothing – sitting with my hands neatly clasped on my lap after eating – as the Sisters had been at pains to teach me to do – my head bowed. The man, John, approached me and lifted my face towards his from my chin.

'Lookee, young man, I must return you from whence you came. This you comprehend well enough, I'd hazard?'

I nodded, sadly. As if he might take me as his own. Foolish, foolish boy.

The door to the dining room opened and a young black lad – about fifteen years old – came in. He approached John and whispered something in his ear. I thought he was telling him to get rid of this waif, as there would surely only be room for one Negro boy. I was surprised, therefore, to see that John nodded to him in assent and the lad returned moments later with a coat about my size. It was made of a rough worsted and looked worn, but warm and clean. He put this coat gently around my shoulders as if I were his master, patting my head in affection. Upon which, I burst into a fit of crying. The whole ensemble laughed gently, but not mockingly, to see how easily I could be driven to tears by kindness. I suppose, till then, I had not known such civility to strangers could exist in the world, and to a sooty stranger to boot.

'I am called Rio. William Montagu Rio,' said the lad, proudly.

I blinked. I knew that he meant for me to say my name and hesitated only to think which one to give him. I knew, too, that I must inevitably be returned to the Coven, but hoped I might spend one night – one glorious night – away from them. Perhaps – if they didn't know my name – they would be forced to keep me until they discovered it. Foolish, I realise now. John lifted my chin again and asked me directly what I was called by my guardians. I duly told him.

'Charles Ignatius. A fine name. One that suits you well.'

'But my Ladies call me Sancho.'

'Ah ... Quixote's page. I see ...'

And I knew then that he *did* see – that he saw everything: my lack of choice in my naming – my status as a pet – an ornament. Rio looked down at me with the most profound sorrow; I could not think but that he pitied me. I resolved to resist pity and began to say I liked my name well enough, when John rose abruptly and declared that I must be returned at once to my home. Those who had charge over me were likely to be mightily afraid for my well-being, he said. I told him as best I could where and with whom I lived. I was placed in a carriage by John himself, and together we set off at once for the Ladies' house. I cried no more. I hoped only that Providence had not given me a glimpse of heaven, only to torture me with the knowledge that I would never again experience it.

My Billy, here I have written of being seen for the first time by John, Duke of Montagu, one of the best men ever to grace this earth. You will, I pray, never have cause to feel yourself invisible – insignificant. Being seen – when first it occurred – was a kind of revolution in my world.

Miss Abigail had clearly been presentable in her youth. Her startlingly pale blue eyes arrested one immediately. Even Duke John – when first he came to ask the Ladies' permission to educate me – was taken aback by Miss Abigail's sharp and piercing gaze.

'Learning? Oh, Lord Montagu, you appear to me to be in a state of some confusion as regards the abilities of this piccaninny . . .'

An instant coldness entered the receiving room, then. I braced myself. I was used to her preternatural ability to alter the very air by a sigh, a look, or at times with a simple, unexpected silence. Duke John, however, unused to such sorcery, was made a breathing statue by Miss Abigail's hypnotic gaze, as much as by her frosty manner.

She continued: 'He is not one of those rare and fortunate blacks who possess character. He is singularly timid and, if malleable, it is due to our rigorous harnessing of his limited abilities.'

'Timid? Limited abilities? He?'

'Quite so. Trust our judgement, Your Grace, he will not amount to other than what he was created to be: a servant, due his place only by dint of hard work and honesty.'

Miss Abigail rose abruptly at this juncture – the interview, she had decided, was at an end – and as Duke John stood, she took me by the hand: her property. Her pet. I complied.

'I thank you, however, for returning him to his rightful . . . guardians. And we will, rest assured, discipline him according to his deserts.'

Duke John, this kindly stranger, looked to me – my eyes downcast – and rallied:

'Ah, my lady, if we were all to receive our just deserts, which of us would 'scape judgement? Shakespeare . . . or the Good Book, I believe? Yes! Shakespeare . . . ahm . . .'

Though justice be thy plea, consider this –
That in the course of justice none of us
Should see salvation . . . '

He trailed off. Miss Abigail looked as if she could do him great harm for a moment – then she recovered herself and treated him to one of her *winning* smiles. ('Oh, that one may smile and smile and be a villain.') She gestured to the receiving-room door – Duke John took the hint and bowed. I reached the entrance door with Tilly beside me, who had been summoned by the ringing of a small bell on the table in the centre of the receiving room.

'Here, lad, I've a sixpence for you,' said John, in a voice so low I thought he had merely sighed. As I hesitated for a second, Tilly urged me to take the proffered coin, sneaking a quick look behind her, and shielding me slightly from Miss Abigail, who wore the oddest expression on her face: was that jealousy? In that instant, it was clear to me that Miss Abigail loved me in her way and wanted none but herself to have my affection. She must already know I loved my Tilly, who was beneath her consideration. But here, she could see that Duke John, my blessèd rescuer, had my affection voluntarily, as I embraced him in a wild burst of gratitude. On breaking my clasp, I realised that His Grace was handing me not just a naked coin but a coin clothed, roughly, in a stiff piece of card. His Grace winked at me. No man – of whatsoever origin – had ever winked at me before. I was delighted and terrified all at once, in case there was some protocol for men who wink that I had totally failed to learn in this house of women. I instinctively rammed the coin deep into my pocket as quickly as I could, hoping Miss Abigail would not see. I needn't have worried. For, as Duke John tipped his black velvet hat to Tilly and sauntered off into the night, I turned to see that Miss Abigail had vanished like a phantom; all the more disturbing that she was there one moment and simply gone the next. Supernatural. All-seeing, all-knowing Miss Abigail.

In the still of the night, I reached under my pillow and found the crumpled-up piece of card that John Montagu – the Duke of Montagu! – had given me. The guinea that it contained was a marvel, all shiny and new. I rubbed it, as if it might bring me a genie, like a story in the *One Thousand and One Nights*. I gazed on this coin for so long, my eyes began to droop with a pleasing tiredness. Though I had only briefly experienced the delights of Montagu House and had felt the warmth of a loving household for all too short a moment, I seemed to hold it in a place in my frame that even the cold room in Greenwich could not chill. I recalled every detail of the hall-way with its strange and exotic ornaments and hangings. Its ceramic vases decorated with dragons; its Chinese hangings that led to rooms hidden behind the thick drapes. Every corner of the Duke's home seemed to come from a part of the world I could not even guess at – clearly neither African nor European in origin. Had he travelled to all these places? What were these lands called? Did the people there speak in a tongue not our own? Of course they did. What did it sound like? I had seen Chinamen in Greenwich, frequently, and there was many an East Indiaman to be seen in the markets there, but I had never spoken to one or heard them speak.

In the carriage back to Greenwich, Duke John's aide,

Charles Manwell, had been silent and respectful with me. This tall, slender black man could have been from anywhere in the world. I did not know for some time that he was a Yorkshireman, as he did not address me this night. His treatment of me was always polite and I gathered fairly soon that he thought me quite the gentleman, always treating me this way, from our first encounter. I felt like a prince. I loved the feel of the soft seats inside the Duke's coach. The Duke himself sat opposite me with that same strange, familial and proud expression on his kindly face that I had noticed in the dining room. I longed to question him, to ask him why he had been so kind to me, when others treated me with immediate hostility on first acquaintance, and evermore. What had prompted him to come to my rescue? Had he rescued other young children of whatever shade? Was he like a highwayman for runaways? A type of Thomas Coram, but with a dashing air of Robin of Loxley? Shyness overwhelmed my desire to interrogate him. I loved him that instant – and always will. It was he who taught me to stand tall and say who I was, and what I was about. He taught me to see myself as he did. A lad, capable of anything.

When he left me on the doorstep, I thought I would die of a type of grief. How could God have given me a glimpse of such a life and such a person, only to snatch them from my sight so abruptly? It seemed a kind of petty cruelty by the gods.

In the safety of my bed there was a sense that the night had ended as well as it might, given the anger of my Ladies and the awful encounter with Jonathan Sill.

My thoughts were arrested of a sudden, as I looked more closely at the card by the starlight admitted through my bedroom window. It was no ordinary piece of card, but one with writing on it. I had no clues as to what it might say, but mouthed my guess of its likely wording:

'John, the Grand Old Duke of Montagu, Black Heath Castle, Heaven!'

I believe this was the first night of my short life in which I fell asleep with a smile on my lips, and a lightness in my heart.

Not even the morning – with its fear of reprimands from the Sisters Three – could dampen my mood. Tilly came into my room and held me close to her. She smelt of lye soap and sweat, a not unpleasant aroma and one I associate forevermore with cleanliness and industry. She took my face between her two pink, clammy hands – pink from scrubbing one surface or other. They were never soft, Tilly's hands, but rather like the rough hands you might expect a monkey to have, who spends its time hanging from the boughs of sharp-barked trees.

'You'll listen to ol' Tilly now, Charles, an' listen well. You must behave like a good boy or you'll find y'self on the street. Now, for a soft one such as you, that'd never do. D'you hear me, Charles?'

I nodded assent. What she had said was Solomonic in wisdom and there could be no judge in the land who could gainsay it. I must tread with my better angel, Caution, as my guide. The Coven would be sensitive, I knew. Miss Abigail, doubly so. It was she who had endured the interview with John the night before. I washed at the basin in my room – then spent time at the window, looking down on the street and its quiet bustle, subdued today, as if in recognition that something momentous had happened the night before – a type of reverent stillness. I descended the stairs a little too jauntily, perhaps, and slowed my pace down, lowering my gaze in preparation for the coming ordeal. I need not have worried. All was as it had ever been. The Ladies must have decided to pretend that nothing had changed – that all was as it had been the day before. Frankly speaking, I was mightily relieved to see it played this way. In their heavily decorated breakfast room, so pathetic to my newly-expanded – nay, exotic – tastes, I stood at my usual spot next to Miss Abigail's chair – who reached out and squeezed my hand. She held it a moment too long, gripped it a little more forcefully than was her habit. The difference would only be noted by the two of us. It was a grasp at once part forgiveness, and part warning – a proprietorial gesture. I was back in the fold once again. I felt relief. Yes, despite the fact that I knew now what kind of life I could have lived had I been in another household, I felt relieved that I had not jeopardised the safest place I truly knew. For the streets were no place for a blackamoor who stood out as an exotic pet, and whose ignorance of himself, England and Africa was as vast as the ocean he was born on.

Tilly it was who first mentioned it. I had spoken to her about Duke John's calling card, and she herself had seen the strong affection the Duke had for me. Tilly thought he meant for me to call upon him, and she vowed to devise a plan to achieve this. The risks for her in being discovered aiding me were great, and to this day I thank her for this kindness. The workhouse – the Sisters' consistent threat – was no place for one as delicate as Tilly, any more than a brutal plantation would have been for me. She had no means – no husband – and a family that relied on her to provide a basket of necessaries once a week. Having three brothers and three sisters below her age, Tilly was the only person save her father, a stablehand, to bring food to her large family's table behind the Oxford Road. Their dependence on her made the risks she was taking for me all the more astoundingly generous.

I had never visited with Tilly's people. She changed the subject instantly whenever I mentioned I would like to one day. I longed to see her clan in the flesh, instead of imagining them by her close description. So well had Tilly painted the picture of each of them, that in my mind's eye I could almost see Jemimah, Tom, Albert, George, Sarah and Baby Meg. Her mother, Barb, had taught her to cook, clean and wash clothes, she told me proudly. Her diligence she said came from her father, Herbert, who worked from five in the morning till seven o'clock at night; longer in the summer months, as the Horse Guards were required for parade on a regular basis. In times of threatened war, he did not come home at all, but slept in the stables alongside his charges, whom he knew all by name and disposition.

Once, she said, there was a fever in that quarter, some say borne of a horse-influenza, that none could be cured from. They lost two children that year, and almost hoped for more to pass away, so severe was their want. Her father's work in the Horse Guards' stables brought little revenue but might have, cruelly, brought the disease. Many families she knew had lost at least one child. In one poor family, all were carried off. I knew then that I was the most fortunate of blacks – or whites. Slavery travels hand in hand with Poverty – and they are not plagues that confine themselves to merely blighting the lives of Africans – the wicked trade in human flesh is no respecter of shade. Humankind is the cruellest of creatures, using others as beasts in a way that only the barbarians of Afric are said to use their people – said, I must note, by those who have never visited that continent in their lives. I wonder daily about this reported barbarism in the African world. Is that really the case across that enormous continent? Who is the savage and who the civilised? The enslaved, *rescued* from heathen religion – or the Christian, whose lavender-scented hands strike that man or woman with the whip in the name of Christ?

Eventually – when I had almost forgotten our dream – Tilly formed a strategy to visit Duke John at Montagu House in Blackheath. She would ask permission of the Coven to have me help with her weekly shopping tasks every Thursday. We would endeavour to call on the Duke in hopes that he may take a shine enough to me to ... And there we foundered. What exactly did we hope Duke John to do? Adopt me as his ward? Pay the Ladies to have me in his service? Besides this distinct lack of strategy, we did not even know whether the Duke desired my presence, or was merely being cautious in wrapping the guinea in a convenient calling card. Nevertheless, we both resolved that it was worth the chancing.

Tilly had made me wait a fortnight before she would enact the plan. She said it was best that we let the dust settle on the Blackheath Incident – we didn't want to arouse the suspicions of the Coven. Clever, clever Tilly. After a truly agonising fortnight of patience, Tilly ventured to directly ask if I might help her bring the provisions from market that the grocer could not supply. Asparagus being in season, though not yet stocked in our local shops, the Sisters Three were happy to have me accompany her. And so, after she had been given a long list of necessaries by Mellor, the cook, we set out one Thursday morning at eight o'clock to collect our items. We did indeed go to the grocer's first, for the blue for washing, as well as sugar, salt, tea, cocoa and bread. Then off to market for the remainder; however, before arriving there, we made our audacious move. Crossing from the market road, in front of the Naval Hospital, we made our way to the other side of the park. Soon, we came to the old gate that I had told Tilly about, proud of myself that I could find it. But how to enter? Should we, in fact, make our way around to the other side of the house, in order to approach more formally? Or was the rear entrance more fitting for those of lowly status? As we stood uselessly staring by turns at the gate, the wall of Montagu House, the park and each other, we were made to jump out of our skins by a shout from nearby.

'Sancho!'

Recovering our senses after a moment, we looked about us.

'Up here, children!'

And, sure enough, in the high boughs of an apple tree on the other side of the wall was John, Duke of Montagu. He threw two ripe apples to us and began to descend. Tilly and I looked at the fruit in our hands that had dropped from heaven, and promptly burst out laughing. A thing we had not done in a long, long time, I realised. The gate opened, and the perspiring Duke, in his shirtsleeves and rough worsted breeches, waved us both in. We looked about us like thieves entering a house to pilfer – he greeted us as honoured guests – even bowing a little – theatrically. He shut the gate behind us and hurried us up to the house. He marched us up the staircase, burst into the music room on the first floor – hardly giving us time to catch our breath – and surprised a woman of about twenty-five who was playing the harpsichord there.

'Mary! You'll never guess who I've found.'

'The famous Charles Ignatius, no doubt.'

The most beautiful woman I had ever seen rose gracefully from her stool and approached us. Not beautiful in any prosaic sense, but with a light that shone from an internal spirit that loved and was loved. I had never seen anyone look more radiant. Tilly practically prostrated herself before her.

'Well played, both. However did you manage not to be discovered?'

We neither of us could answer her, so overwhelmed were we with the welcome these extraordinary people had offered us. Tilly was the first to recover.

'If it please you, Madam, I must not stay, but must go a-market. I fear I will be tardy and miss the asparagus . . . Madam.'

This last, accompanied by a further bobbing sort of curtsy. The Duke and the young woman I assumed to be his daughter smiled indulgently, delighted with Tilly as much as Duke John had been with me. With what I know now, Mary, Countess Cardigan had every right to be offended that Tilly had used the incorrect address to a countess: Madam? Instead of Lady Cardigan? Shocking. Who were these people who found those so far beneath their consideration such an infinite source of delight? I was struck again by the sense that I had entered another world altogether.

'Well,' said Her Ladyship. 'We mustn't keep the asparaguses waiting?'

'Asparagii?' suggested Duke John.

At which they both burst out laughing. Tilly and I were
at a loss.

'Well, that will be the first thing we'll look up, my lad, will
we not? Asparaguses or asparagii, eh, what? Tilly, we must have
you swiftly to market and back. Shall we say an hour? Charles!'

Moments later the tall, black, graceful aide to the Duke,
Charles Manwell, appeared – smiled at us both – bowed
deeply – and receiving swift instructions from his master,
ushered the bewildered Tilly to a carriage below. Before
they had even disappeared, Duke John took me by the hand
and led me into an adjoining room, which was lit by candles,
despite the brightness of the day. I marvelled at this space
more than I had the dining room of a month ago, for this
room was round. I had never been in a room like it. It was
the tower that I had noticed that first night. I was within the
glowing structure and here was the source of that ethereal
light I had been so struck by: books. Wall to wall to wall to
floor to ceiling, books. *Words, words, words* indeed.

'Can you read, Charles?' asked Duke John.

I shook my head.

'You must speak, lad, no mutes allowed here.'

'No . . . Your Grace,' I managed.

'Then we must remedy this, and soonest the better. Mary!
Let's have some tea and scones brought up. We have much
work to do, much work to do,' he cried, with his customary,
delighted smile.

My first task, he told me, was to fetch a book that he would point out to me. With that, he promptly dropped to one knee with a little grunt and tapped his shoulder. I had no idea what he meant by the gesture.

'Climb aboard, Sir, climb aboard.'

And that is precisely what I did. I had rarely been this close to anyone but my Ladies – Miss Abigail in particular – and that was unpleasant and strange. I had received the odd embrace from my Tilly, yes – and Hincham, the footman, had pinched and clipped me round the head once or twice. Not to be outdone, Mellor was not averse to using the same tactics in her kitchen. The only other male I had ever been in close proximity to – apart from Mr Henry – was Jonathan Sill. So, to have a Duke act as a beast of burden! – have me climb onto his shoulders – was both exhilarating and frightening. The musty-dusty smell emanating from the books rose up at me. I felt the vertiginous lurch of my stomach at being suddenly so high in the world. I could see out of the high windows now, over the whole west side of Blackheath Park. I felt a giant. Appropriate then that the first book Duke John insisted I pull down was Swift's *Gulliver's Travels* – His Grace guiding me as a blind man might be guided to where his hat lay.

'No, too far right. Yes, just down a little. *No!* Ha, ha, ha. Now, try your left a bit. Down and . . . Yes. Got it!'

We laughed together like schoolboys then, and I could not help wondering if this was a kind of madness we had contracted. We laughed so much that morning that my first three letters learnt – *A, B, C* – were conned with not a hint of effort. I could write them before I had finished my fourth – yes, fourth! – scone. Well, they were small . . .

*

Ah, our Achilles heel, I fear, my son; our thorn in the flesh.

I started writing whole sentences about two months after we began our lessons. Every fortnight John would give me two sheets of paper – I was to fill them with observations and anecdotes. Even when he wasn't home, it happened that one or other of the staff would let me in, allowing me to read, and bringing me tea and scones. I was quite fat from these as well as from the fact that when I had completed my many cleaning chores in the Ladies' house, I now spent most of my time lying on my bed, secretly practising letters. I began to borrow books, returning them after I had devoured them two or three times. My Ladies did not seem to notice the change that had come over me when they were teaching me to recite by rote. I learnt things far more swiftly than before, due to the fact that I copied them out, at first phonetically, then I would verify the spelling with Duke John. His need for words was infectious; spoken or written. It seemed nothing short of an addiction as strong as any opiate. He had to have words.

'Words frame ideas, Sancho, as borders frame nations, eh what?'

That very first morning, in Duke John's library, the sound of Charles Manwell returning Tilly in the carriage was the most unwelcome noise I had ever heard – save the squawk of Miss Beatrice singing Handel's *Oreste*. But this morsel of paradise had to end some time, I knew – it was all I could do not to burst out crying. I restrained myself – for fear that the Duke would conclude that he should no longer be kind to me. I was about to leave His Grace with my precarious dignity intact, when Lady Cardigan came to tell us to hurry along and that I must be sure to come each Thursday to see her father, unless he be away in London or Northamptonshire. I nodded at this angel, politely, but she rushed to me and embraced me to her. I promptly broke into sobs ...

> O, that this too too solid flesh would melt
> Thaw and resolve itself into a dew!

Anne needs my aid, as a consignment of sugar has arrived, and she loathes chopping them into lumps for sale – the reasons too obvious to mention here. Not yet, son, not quite yet.

I will continue my tale of scholarly improvement and introduce you now to Francis Williams, Jamaican scholar and teacher. I see from my diary that I wrote an extensive entry on my first extraordinary encounter with him at Montagu House, Blackheath.

Chapter III

*In which we meet Sancho,
the Entertainer, and Francis
Williams, Jamaican scholar.*

1740

❧

Eleven years old

Soon, I no longer waited for Tilly to collect me, but ran to meet her at the entrance to the market at eleven-thirty. We were as punctual as clockwork and always came home with that we were sent for. 'As reliable as the tide,' Mellor would say, in her only recorded compliment to us.

My secret tutors, Duke John and his daughter Mary, Lady Cardigan, began in earnest to teach me the rudiments of music when I reached the age of eleven. I had picked up so much by ear by the time I was nine, that Duke John presumed I read music fluently. I disabused him of any illusion about my level of musical competence one day when he suggested I play for George Frideric Handel, who had come to visit him one Thursday morning. Mr Handel was not a smiling man, but he seemed pleased enough when Mary and I performed a duet on the harpsichord. It was the 'Belle Dee' from his *Giulio Cesare*. Inaccurately played by me, I might add – though well sung by Lady Cardigan – who had a lovely, if undynamic, tone. Mr Handel was still throughout, polite, but not overly enthusiastic at the end. Perhaps he was the more honest soul for that.

Fortunately, I was a quick study and soon mastered the scales on both harpsichord and mandolin. Duke John had many musicians who came to stay, or used the Blackheath residence as a lodging, if they had business or concerts in London. They all took turns being my music masters and mistresses – some knowingly. What a joy it was to hear them play in the music room as I pored over some tome or other in the library next door. I must have learnt much from eavesdropping, for within a year, I had sufficient skill in composition to perform a piece one morning for some French friends the Duke had visiting him. They clapped enthusiastically, I remember, and asked His Grace if I might entertain them that evening at his soirée. Duke John, in informing them that I could not, told them of my living conditions, adding:

'You see, my friends, how quick-witted a lad of Sancho's race might be, if given the foundation of learning?'

They all nodded and murmured their assent. I felt at once proud, at once like a specimen.

It was earlier that month that I had met Francis Williams for the first time, and he had planted an unwelcome seed of cynicism as to the Duke's motives in aiding my education. Francis was a free black man from Jamaica. He was tall – very thin – the thinnest man I think I'd ever seen – and deeply dark in complexion – with a large head on his narrow shoulders. It was as if this clever man's body could not contain the intelligence that burned within him – and since his frame could not do justice to that intelligence – his very head had enlarged to fit his brain.

Not scientific, by any means – to take such a statement as science would be foolish, indeed. Though some bright sparks, who ought to know better, begin to speak this kind of nonsense in circles of the learned. I have known the most ingenious servant with the littlest noggins out-think the largest-pated fools – be warned, my son – lettered folks are not always the better folks.

Francis Williams was sitting in the library one Thursday morning, eating *my* scones. I was irritated by him instantly. Who was this Negro man, I thought, taking up *my* place, eating my scones? His look to me as I lingered in the doorway was not a warm one neither, for his part. He did not rise, but merely nodded, took a bite of scone as he examined me, then went back to reading the volume he had before him.

I bowed, but he had already looked down and I felt foolish, as if I'd lost a game without really knowing what the rules were. I went to the seat that was usually reserved for Duke John, for he liked to look towards his library shelves and not, as I did, out to the distracting vista of Blackheath. And it was then that Francis stood. He offered me his hand and I took it. I realised then that he wasn't being unfriendly, he just saw me as a fellow scholar. He was, in fact, treating me as his equal. This world of the Montagus' was very confusing at times. It occurred to me that I had been rude and defensive. It reminded me of the night when Rio Montagu had handed me his coat – when before this kind gesture I had taken him to be my rival for the Duke's affections. I felt ashamed. I rose.

'Forgive me, Sir. I was only surprised to see another ... another here. For I am in the habit of being alone in the library.' Francis rose.

'No matter, young man. If I would be offended by every gentleman who looked at me askance, why my life would be full of conflict and miserable indeed. I am Francis Williams, and you are Charles Ignatius Sancho. Pleased to make your acquaintance.'

His accent was soft and lyrical, with a hard edge of something undefined. It was not an accent that was familiar to me at the time.

I had no friends from Africa or the West Indies, Billy, a loss I suffered until your wonderful grandfather John Clarke-Osborne brought the remedy – and more.

Francis then offered me my seat and we both sat and ate a scone in silence. That made two for him. Soon, we had settled into a reserved stillness. Francis broke this, gently.

'His Grace is mighty fond of you, I know. Please be aware that you are very fortunate to have fallen into this man's hands and not another. For, though he sees the African as a fit subject for experiments on his theories on learning – his whole heart is not that of a mere man of science. There is goodness in it, too.'

I struggled to know what he could mean. Was he suggesting that science might be the enemy of goodness, somehow? I thought he would say only good things about Duke John, but he seemed to be implying some impurity in the motivations behind his advocacy of African intelligence. Francis could see this in me, no doubt, for he added:

'Do you know the story of Job Ben Solomon?'

I shook my head. Francis then rose from his chair, and taking a small stool to one corner without the least searching, pulled out a slim tract. He walked over and laid it down before me. He sat, then, and recommenced his studies, whereof I saw that he had been reading Henry Fielding's *The Grub-Street Opera*. I had expected some work of mathematics or Latin, but he seemed to share my love of plays. I warmed to him slightly, then, but could not see what this book he had selected had to interest me. Indeed, what had it to do with the subject of our aborted conversation: the motives of John Montagu? The title of this little tract was:

Some MEMOIRS of the LIFE of JOB, the SON of SOLOMON, the HIGH PRIEST of Boonda in Africa; Who was a Slave about two Years in Maryland; and afterwards being brought to England, was set free, and sent to his native Land in the Year 1734.

A title that flows, trippingly, off the tongue, I thought, with an unworthy cynicism. It was by Thomas Bluett, a gentleman, by his own description, 'who was intimately acquainted with him in America, and came over to England with him'. The book was dedicated to 'the Right Honourable His Grace the Duke of Montagu'.

I laid this book aside and began to read another on the knights of the round table. I had an obsession at that time with these likely mythical figures. Francis looked up from his studies and examined me. There was no judgement in his eyes when I finally met them. He seemed to read me like one of His Grace's books. He rose from the table with his play in hand and walked into the music room. I breathed a sigh of relief. I had the sense that I might have disappointed Francis Williams with my wilful lack of curiosity. Just then, a skilful rendition of a song I knew well – all in England did – wafted in from the other room. Francis was a very competent player, an even better singer. It was from the play he had taken out, and went thus:

'When mighty Roast Beef was the Englishman's food
It ennobled our veins and enrichéd our blood
Our soldiers were brave and our courtiers were good
Oh! The Roast Beef of old England
And old English Roast Beef.'

He sang with a clear and strong voice. His breath he used as singers do, forcefully and with confidence. It wasn't pretty in a lyrical sense but was all the more convincingly compelling for all that.

'Our fathers of old were robust, stout, and strong,
And kept open house, with good cheer all day long,
Which made their plump tenants rejoice in this song—
Oh! The Roast Beef of old England,
And old English Roast Beef!'

Francis Williams could modulate his tone so that he seemed to be satirising these fine lyrics. It was confusing all the more for the proud bearing he had at the harpsichord while he sang this. As if he both loved and despised the words he was singing, as if he at once believed and disbelieved them, too.

'Oh, then we had stomachs to eat and to fight
And when wrongs were cooking to do ourselves right.
But now we're a bunch of – I could, but goodnight!
Oh! The Roast Beef of Old England,
And old English Roast Beef!'

He looked up when he had finished, his dark brown face
shining with sweat and his eyes glistening like a man who
had just done battle. I could see the mischievous glee with
which he had delivered this performance hovering around
his countenance. The chimes of midday sounded from the
clock on the stairs, and I rushed downstairs without saying
anything more to him. I was in a state of some confusion.
Was he friend or foe? Did he intend to tell me something
more or have me learn these mysterious things myself? He
was not like Duke John, who spoke so straightforwardly that
there never could be any mistaking his meaning. This black
man made me wonder about everything – he meant me to see
the world differently – perhaps, to see the world as he did?
Whatever his motivations, as I ran from the house, there was
no doubt in my mind: Francis Williams had frightened me as
much as Jonathan Sill had on that night so long ago.

1775

❧

Forty-six years old

Sad to relate, Billy, dear Mary, Duchess of Montagu, my first patron's daughter, was laid to eternal rest today. I mourn her life as if she were my family – which, if I am not presumptuous in saying, she was. Having returned home from the obsequies today, I saw that I had two visitors – one, your godmother Miss Lydia Leach, milliner of Bond Street and gentlest Christian Methodist of this parish – and none other than Davey Garrick – Kindest Soul in London – Greatest actor of this or any other century – and right good company. I distracted myself from cares this evening with memories of theatre and the hope this great institution once offered me. A diary entry from my twentieth year may suffice to introduce to you my enthusiasm for those things pertaining to the forerunner of all actors: Thespis . . .

Duke John took me to my first play, at Drury Lane, this last evening. Shakespeare's *Richard III* with Mr David Garrick.

A noise on the stairs – only Tilly? I will continue to compose the rest in my Other Place.

Ah – this Other Place will need demystifying – next.

. . . Safe.

Drury Lane is a seething bed of luxury and debauchery. We entered, Duke John and I, by the stage door. Not because the Duke wanted to enter discreetly but because, as he assured me with a wistful look: 'All the best parts of the theatre are hidden away from the audience, laddy. We must see beneath the marionettes' skirts to know how the strings are attached and who manipulates them. The Houses of Parliament are no different, rest assured.'

Hardly understanding his full meaning, I walked like an innocent into what can only be described as the Second Circle of Hell – or, at the very least, Lust's anteroom? I cannot say which, but I will say that I am changed for ever. I am in love with this place as one falls in love with a beautiful, dangerous and enticing woman of mature years. A woman, moreover, who is capable of great grace and crass pragmatism, at once high-born and low-living. I could no more deny my instant passion for all things theatrical, than I could deny my love for Mr Garrick, Mr Charles Macklin or Miss Peg Woffington; the stage hands and carpenters, the scene painters and the charming chorus girls . . . They all inhabited a magical land, where a boy could lose himself entirely. Added to which there were African dancers and musicians amongst this ensemble – seemingly happy and living an almost egalitarian existence alongside their European counterparts. What is more important to me, they seemed – all – to *see* me, too. To see me as Duke John had seen me. My determination is to escape the clutches of the Greenwich Coven and strike out for a career on the stage! I will do it, if heaven allows. Nay, I must!

My youthful dreams did not, however, turn in quite the way I was expecting. But – the Other Place.

1739

❧

Ten years old

In my mistresses' kitchen there is a large pantry – slightly below ground. In the whole of the kitchen, it is the only spot with a window. Darkened and hidden remained this window for years, behind a tall shelf in the pantry. I accidentally – fortuitously – found this priest-hole when I was left to my own devices one day when I was around ten years old. We had been entertaining guests that night and Miss Abigail had been so pleased with my rendition of a passage from Donne, that she had instructed me to fetch a small tart stored in the pantry. Mellor had shown me where to look with an impatient wave of her flour-covered hand. I entered the pantry with no more idea of the significance of this moment than Romeo had when he walked into the Capulets' garden. I was surprised to see a sliver of window, just above the height of the highest shelf. A faint light from the street could be seen through its opaque glass. If it had been half an hour later, it would have been night and the window would have remained unnoticed, perhaps, for ever. I stared, fascinated, at this glimpse of the outside world. It was as if a fairy-land lay beyond its mottled, greying surface, like a thin film of gossamer separating the world of witches, demons and goblins from the real, dull world that I inhabited.

Small wonder then, that this was the spot – behind the shelf and hidden from the door – I chose to use as my intermittent, impromptu and secluded study. My Other Place. I procured a tall stool from the old study that was mainly used for storing unwanted bric-a-brac, next to my tiny room at the top of the house. I carried it down one day with my heart beating like a shuttlecock on a weaver's loom: *thok-thok, thok-thok, thok-thok* . . . But carry it down I did, and managed, with a bit of luck, to get into the pantry and hide the stool so well that from that day to this, it lies undetected by any. Excepting Tilly, but only because I told her of it, eventually. It was there that I kept my writing material and a small carving board that I had requisitioned for my table. There I wrote, whenever the Sisters were distracted enough to forget my presence. The older I became, the easier it was to slip away unseen. The servants' secret weapon: Invisibility. I could spend an hour in there, regularly, and never be discovered. My ally Tilly was always willing to warn me with a song whenever she suspected I would be missed, or if one of the Coven, usually Miss Florence, had entered the kitchen to discuss some detail of the evening's repast. A safe place, then, in a very precarious household. I loved Tilly so much for being my lookout. No highwayman could have wished for a better or more fearless accomplice. And so, I wrote . . . Sometimes, simply observations as:

When parts of the Thames freeze over, it really is a glorious sight. As if Nature had commanded the waters to be still – and at her voice, all of creation took a breath and waited for her command to move again. Two skaters fell through the ice last week. I wonder if they had tested the ground – the ice – before skating out onto the frozen flood. Foolish not to be cautious when such danger lurks beneath a seeming tranquil surface.

I wrote, too, of more sinister moments:

I fulfil my duties here, without life or any sense of it. Duke John is away and Montagu House shut up for the moment. The only thing that caused my heart to race a little recently, was a moment of brief terror when I was walking back from the grocer's store and saw Hincham, the Sisters' footman, leaning out of a tavern window. He leaned back inside and when he reappeared, he had a man next to him who I recognised instantly with a jump of my heart: Jonathan Sill. So, they were friends? I felt sweat at the nape of my neck. I took a handkerchief out of my frock coat pocket and wiped my face as I passed them. They both laughed.

'I'll have you yet, butterball.'

Which brought another eruption of laughter from Hincham. Jonathan Sill's loyal apprentice – son? – was no longer a lad but, if anything, an even larger hulk than Sill. He leant against the pub doorway with a flagon in his hand, eyeing me with coldness as I passed. I felt foolish and powerless, yet again. The years since my first encounter with Sill and the slave-catcher's apprentice fell away at that moment, and I did not feel safe from them until I arrived back at my Ladies' house. I had never felt so glad to shut the door to my cage.'

I promised you diversions, Billy, and so for no other reason than a fuller understanding of the geography of my youth – the macrocosm, as it were, of my little world – I present to you a brief description of the town I was raised in.

On the hill overlooking the town of Greenwich, are houses built at the turn of the century – where the Sisters Three had their property. The façade of the house was nothing but practical and lacked any original style in my opinion; it was all rather cold and austere with pretensions to classical architecture.

The streets about were quiet in the evenings and very early mornings. During the day, the bustle of a large town – not a village – was to be seen. Oyster-sellers, ironmongers, knife-sharpeners, flower-girls, costermongers, with their cries and songs to attract customers, could be heard calling out from seven in the morning until more or less dusk in the winter, and around six o'clock in the summer. On the other side of Blackheath Park, resided my belovéd benefactors, the Montagu family – may heaven bless their souls forevermore. Duke John and I often went back to the spot where he once found me – we frequently reminisced about our first encounter. How fortuitous! – How providential! – What blessings that encounter had since provided!

All through my youth, I believed that I was fortunate – as my Ladies and many others told me, frequently – to have been brought here. It was around the time I entered my twentieth year that I began strongly to desire knowledge of how life was lived in Africa – perhaps by this to find out what native parts I might have, hidden, but naturally in me. For example, where – I wondered – in Africa were my parents from? The Gold Coast is vast by any reading of a world map. Were we from the north of this region, where contact with the European world was soonest? Or further south, in what is often described as the dark and forbidding zone? Where wild creatures live with – and devour – the men and women they find there. The people there would be wild, too, knowing nothing of European achievements in art and science – I imagined, then.

From the accounts of slave colonies that His Grace had given me, I could say with confidence that I was blessed to have escaped New Granada and the regions around the sea of the Carib. Cruelty beyond my imagining, he assured me. But, I wondered, was Africa – at least the parts that birthed my parents, and therefore, surely, formed some parts in me – was that particular Africa simply a place of wild things, or of great learning and artistry? Were the Europeans right to think of African achievements as 'naturally' inferior to European ones in these fields? For where – I asked myself – were their Newtons and Platos – their Michelangelos – their Sistine Chapels – their Christopher Wrens – their St Paul's Cathedrals? Were they to be found anywhere on that mysterious continent? Or did they not exist at all, as I feared? My ignorance was fathoms deep – my world, a minuscule nutshell – Greenwich – the River – Blackheath Park – and nothing else.

There was a moment that began to change this narrow view, however. To travel backwards into my diary for a moment, then . . .

Last week on passing through Greenwich on an errand for my

mistresses, a young man of about my age – nineteen, perhaps twenty – African in origin, I believed, from his demeanour and fearful look – gazed upon me in the street as he was being led between two fearsome-looking white men. These persons carried cudgels and held the black lad's shoulders as if they meant to arrest him – or hang him, immediately. The strangest thing about this scene was that he seemed to be quite used to this treatment, and offered no resistance. Struck by his gaze as he passed me, I resolved to follow him a little way to see what would become of him, corralled so inescapably as he was. As they turned the corner opposite the far end of the naval yard, no doubt bound for a slave-carrying vessel, the black lad looked directly at me – and that look arrested my breath in a way that no gaze had before. They then took him away, and that was the last I saw of them.

Many days later, the thought occurred to me in a sudden rush of enlightenment that this man – the African man – had looked at me as though I were . . . an Englishman. By this, I mean free. More precisely, carefree – and subsequently, from another sphere entirely to his. I, who had been born a slave, like him – had been shipped wherever my master willed, like him – was seen, by him, as one of *them*. The Freeborn. The privileged few: Black *and* Free. And the two thoughts combined at that instant and set a thing in motion in me that I could hardly articulate at the time, but began shortly afterwards to see all too clearly:

I am my African brother's keeper. I have privileges beyond the reach of many of my kind. And from him to whom much is given, much will be expected. 'It is The Cause, it is The Cause, my soul.'

No small day, then.

I have wondered every day since about that man. Where did he end his journey? Did his ship founder? Did he escape the wreck and swim ashore, to be rescued by some kindly fishermen and taken to a hut to warm his hands – given food and drink, perhaps a bed for the night, and finally a job alongside his rescuers – his fellow-mariners? Wishful thinking – in this case, not likely. Not useful for the Cause. The truth is that he would have been beaten on board his master's ship, shackled and kept in the dark of a stinking hold, then forced to relive his original horror voyage in reverse – back to the Guinea Coast, where he would be joined by hundreds of fresh captives – held in the same conditions he might have survived as a child but was much less likely to survive as a grown man – in very real danger of being unceremoniously tossed into the sea if he died or became ill. He would consider himself lucky to reach land in the West Indies, alive – only to be chained – forced to breed – worked till he was useless to all but the worms ... I think on this, even now.

It is the cause, it is the cause my soul.
O, let me not name it to you, you chaste stars,
It is the cause.

Childhood behind me, I now come to the worst of times in Greenwich. I trust that Billy, the man, will have the stomach for what follows. I will let my younger self – the closest eye-witness to what follows, after all, take up my tragi-comic tale for a few pages.

Chapter IV

In which Sancho is imprisoned.

1749

Twenty years old

A birthday should be a day for rejoicing. Mine only ever remind me – with painful regularity – that I have passed another year under the verbal yoke of these Sisters Three. The Greenwich Coven. The Weird Sisters. Today, my twentieth invented day of birth – invented by the Sisters – well, today was no exception. Miss Beatrice was endeavouring to scold me about her suspicions that I was learning – somehow – to read. Her anger was fierce today.

'Never has a blackamoor been treated with so much care, so much respect and attention as you, boy. And how do you—'

Here she had to leave off to blow her long, red, hook-like nose, hard, into a lace handkerchief. What was the purpose of such an item, I wondered, as the nasal fluid congealed and hung in globules about her fat fingers and between the strands of fine lace.

'You have too often been cautioned about your stubborn

insistence in this. His Grace is at fault for spoiling your nature. Oh, you think yourself most ingenious, no doubt, in concealing your visits. We have eyes in this town, boy, and we know your exploits only too well. Trips to the theatre, recitals at Montagu House. You fancy yourself quite the courtier, do you not? You are a sneak, Sancho, and you will come to a bad end – *atchoo!*'

So they knew ... I wondered for how long. Cutting off my rising panic, Miss Beatrice was suddenly attacked with another bout of sneezing and wheezing and simply took herself off – a martyr to mucous – to find a more robust receptacle for her nose-water. She had a strangely youthful complexion – pale as a Renaissance beauty – and one would think her beautiful indeed, until turning her physog directly to starboard you could see that the whole was not greater than the sum of its parts. Returning with renewed steam and blowing into a damp flannel, of all things, Miss Beatrice launched into a familiar refrain; in fact, I could not breathe in her presence without her reviewing my whole person and making this common inventory: 'Black as night, fat as a suckling pig – *cochon, chien* – devouring chops like no other – free board and lodging for a minimum amount of toil – you are an archetype of your kind, Sancho – greedy, indigent and ignorant. Sit up straight, thing!'

At this, Miss Abigail entered, waited a moment or two and then pronounced gently but firmly: 'Enough, sister. Truth with love is the perfect admixture. Gall it is, merely to itemise Charles's many faults. Fetch supper.'

This last to me. I think she meant this as a kindness to remove me from the deadly gaze of Miss B—.

*

The whole kerfuffle began on the afternoon preceding this day, when I accidentally dropped a pencil on the stairs. A too-grand term for the implement. A half-stub of lead, stolen from Duke John's desk on my last visit a month ago. I was interrogated about this in the day room for nigh-on half an hour. The Ladies could not accept that I had used the piece of lead to make sketches of flowers and plants in their garden. I assured them – looking at the floor as instructed from an early age – so as not to seem combative – that this was what I had indeed used it for and they, naturally, demanded I show them my drawings. I refused, on the feeble grounds that these were so appalling, only I could stomach seeing them. This time, instead of the usual retort from them that as a member of their household there should exist no secrets between us, I dared to look up, directly at Miss Abigail – and that look from me to Miss Abigail when she was about to begin this well-worn invective seemed to freeze her like a blast of Nature's icy breath upon the Thames. My look – direct and lacking servility – reminded her of our night-time routine. It seemed to shame her into silence. She made an impatient gesture with her hands, and commanded me to leave their sight – much to the bemusement of her sisters. I couldn't help but smile at my secret power to silence Miss Abigail. Oh, it delighted me so – it was all I could do not to skip out of the room humming the tune I had composed at Lord Montagu's on my last visit.

I long to use this power daily; to wield it whenever I wish to shame Miss Abigail into silence or into compliance with my wishes. But I am – rightly – afraid. The consequences would be awful if she felt herself manipulated by 'her blackamoor'.

*

Shortly after this seeming triumph over Abigail, my 'wings' were well and truly clipped. Let me place here a diary entry from my seventeenth year that might illuminate much ...

Close to midnight, a candle passes by my room, which I can see by the light of the window above my door. If the candle passes once, then Abigail has gone to bed and wishes me to remain in my room. If, however, the light reappears, my heart sinks and I must rise and go to her. Always, she is sitting up in bed, happy to see me, I know – but never showing it. I walk to the far side of the bed in her large room and feel her eyes following me, until I gently pull back the covers and climb into bed. In my younger days I used to sit up alongside her, sometimes leaning on her shoulder in the pathetic hopes of a little maternal tenderness. Often, she would push me away – occasionally, she would allow me this crumb of intimacy. That has not felt like decent behaviour these five years or so. So, I lie down immediately and turn my bulk to the window – and away from her. Whereupon she proceeds to read a book aloud, so that it is impossible for me to go to sleep, even if such a thing might be done with the tense atmosphere in the chamber. When her voice has tired, she blows out the candle on her side, then leans over my body to do the same on my side – yes, I could have blown mine out earlier, but I tried that once and was roundly rebuked for daring to darken the room 'as if we were trying to be secret'. And so, I wait to feel the weight of her heavy breasts on my shoulder – almost perspiring at the prospect of what else she might devise for my torture, if I refuse her this moment of physical proximity. We are both silently aware that this cannot continue, but I have not the power to stop her. That can only come from her. Perhaps, when she realises – as I'm almost certain she has begun to – that I am practically a fully-grown man, with desires and urges and an awareness that women are no more innocent in this than men – that they are only curtailed by conventions of decency in the expression of these feelings . . . When she eventually sees that I see . . .

The long pause in writing has been due to my confinement beneath the stairs. I have not been allowed to wander the house freely for many, many days. You must remember the stench of your own piss when you look back on these days, Older Sancho: never forget the stench of the bed linen that you soiled in your misery and fear, almost every night. The acrid smell of effluvia that awakened you, with its bite of sal ammoniac stinging your nostrils. How the Coven would not suffer you to change your linen. How Tilly smuggled a clean sheet to you one day. Food. Days that felt like a festival day compared to your quotidian life.

It all ruptured when I foolishly left a part of my notebook on my pillow as I went to make water in the garden. I had had this habit ever since coming here, as the way in the Americas was to make water outside. The Sisters had made an effort to instruct me how to use the chamber-pot, but I did not like the splash of water that accompanied my efforts to drop my stools. But persevere I did, since they beat me – well, Miss Florence beat me – if I did not comply. Despite this, if ever I was out of sight of my captors and needed to release water, I endeavoured to go to the garden at the rear of the house.

The late June day in question had been a hot one, and I had

drunk too many quenching draughts, for no sooner had I gone to bed than I felt a mighty urge to pass water. The timing was imperfect – as I knew, from long years of habit and also by the system I have already described, that Miss Abigail had not yet gone to bed. If I had been wise, I should have made water in the chamber-pot as prescribed by my Ladies. Wisdom was silenced by Imprudence, and I descended the stairs with a cautious haste, pausing for a moment on the middle landing to be sure the house was at least quiet, if not yet asleep.

Before leaving my room, I had been using various sheets from a notebook to make elaborate drawings of the letters of the alphabet. I had made three attempts at turning a capital 'G' into a giraffe; a creature I had seen in a most wonderful book in Duke John's drawing room. The legs were the basis of the bottom curve of the letter; the head, the final inward turn of the letter as it curled down from above. The whole I managed – not altogether unsuccessfully – to make look somewhat like the strange animal illustrated in the book I had only perused once. Having little skill in this area of draughtsmanship, I had needed three attempts to get this close to my ideal.

The reasons I was attempting this artistic challenge—

I will omit for now. A person whom I do not wish yet to name . . .

On returning from my ablutions, I realised immediately my mistake. I had left the pages strewn, too casually, upon my bed covers. When I came in and saw them gone, I feared the worst and my heart froze in my chest. I hoped that Tilly had come to my room for some reason, and finding the offending items, hidden them in her own chamber. But years of fear and near-constant alert to the footfalls, rustles, sighs, sniffs, coughs and aromas of the Sisters Three, had left me only too aware of what had taken place. The unmistakeable smell of lavender and rosewater was in the air. Miss Abigail had been here. Most assuredly, she now had possession of the criminal materials . . .

I collapsed on my knees by my bed and prayed to the gods of England and Africa that I was mistaken. I was wrong to pray. I should have run that instant. But it was too late and when the light of Miss Abigail's candle passed my room, I knew that I must go to her that night, even before the second signal had been given. I had never felt such terror in all my time with these ladies. I cannot say why I did not run. I had not the perspicacity to even consider it seriously. I was a blackamoor in the middle of Greenwich. I was not a London lad whose upbringing had taught him the ways of the rough streets. If I ran, I would be dead or press-ganged or enslaved before long, of that I had no doubt. My heart unfroze and leapt in my breast, then. I choked back a cry and fell on my bed as if in a swoon. I wanted to reverse the passage of time. I wanted to take back my foolish actions that day, of swallowing so much liquid. I wanted to escape. I wanted to die. I wanted to kill myself for my own stupidity in being caught in the act of writing after so many successful years of concealing my skill. But staring, wild-eyed, around that room, I knew that there was no recourse but to face my executioner. I instinctively, belatedly, hid my treasure box under my mattress. My mind a blank, no clever excuses coming to me, I left my chamber and walked the darkened corridor to Miss Abigail's room. Miss Abigail was not in her bed. Her candle had gutted. The room was lit only by the glow of the dying embers of her unnecessary fire. She sat in her nightgown by the opened window, looking down on to the garden. My first – irrational – thought was that she had also witnessed my relieving myself below. A notion that somehow chased my other fears around my head and made this night seem like my worst and last on earth. What would she say? How would the condemning sentence resound in my ears? Would I survive this night?

To my horror, I saw she held the three sheets lightly in her hand. They fluttered in the night breeze, mocking me with the trio of giraffes flicking by one after another, in an endless parade of my crime, condemning me over and over again. Abigail looked up then, and there seemed to be a look not of anger but of near sorrow in her countenance. For one fleeting instant, I fancied that her love for me would bring mercy. I was mistaken.

'You have defied me for the last time, Sancho. You will not be allowed the privileges of a ward in my home any longer. No bedtime reading. No bed with sheets like that of a civilised young man. You will sleep in the cellar, like the dog you undoubtedly are, until you learn obedience to your betters. You fancy yourself our equal, no doubt, because we have treated you as such. It is a fault in us. Papa was clear that we would be taken advantage of for our womanly weaknesses – our hearts have been too soft.'

I made no reply. What reply could have saved me, if I had spoken out? A lie? Denial was futile, since the evidence was there as plain as day. Miss Abigail rang a little bell whilst I looked down at my bare feet in fear. The door opened and Hincham, the footman, entered, and simply hit me around the head with his big hands. I cried out, but he twisted my ears.

'Cry out, again, little nigger, and I'll skin you alive.'

'Really, Hincham. No need to resort to insults and threats. Take him to his new quarters.'

As he dragged me out of the room by my ear, I couldn't help but wonder how all this had happened so swiftly. How long had I been gone from my room, that Abigail and Hincham had found the time to plot my punishment with such efficiency? It dawned on me that they had both long been aware of my literary proclivities and had just been awaiting the moment to pounce. I guessed this cruel action was Miss Abigail's way of answering my arrogance in silencing her, following my careless dropping of the pencil. I remembered the compromised look on her face, then. I had never felt so foolish. My arrogance had finally brought about my downfall. How sweet this revenge must feel to her.

Hincham, I could tell, was revelling in his power over me. He had long been a thorn in my side. As he gripped the back of my neck, fingernails digging into my soft flesh, I could almost feel him grinning to himself in the candlelight of the stairwell. We half-crashed down the stairs, so fierce was his grip and so great his speed. He was extremely nimble and I, a sweating, panicking lump. We arrived at the cellar door just before the kitchen, and opening it roughly, he threw me with such force through the doorway that I tumbled down the stairs. There were about ten of these in stone. I believe I counted every one of them, hard. At the bottom there was a mat of straw, a worn, thin sheet and a chamber-pot, nothing else. The only light was the glow of Hincham's candle in the doorway above me, then . . . darkness.

I stood for some time, every inch of my body in pain, rubbing the back of my neck, damp with my own blood – fresh from the slice of Hincham's talons. I waited in vain for my eyes to grow accustomed to the light, but there was no light to become accustomed to, so pitch black was it down here. The smell of mould and rotting earth was strong. I had never before ventured here, not once in all the years that I had lived in this gilded prison. Nothing could have possessed me to enter its dark confines since Hincham had regularly – gleefully – told anyone who would listen that the place was infested with mice and the odd rat. Tired and scared as I was, I couldn't quite bring myself to lie down, for fear one of these creatures would crawl up my leg for warmth in the damp cellar. It wasn't cold here, this night, however. Quite the opposite. There was a stifling mugginess to the air, and my face was already beaded with perspiration from the panic I had felt since seeing my papers gone from the bed. After being dragged so violently down the staircase, I was sweating profusely from every pore. Nothing could persuade me that I was safe, and I continued to sweat for minutes after I heard Hincham retreating from the cellar door. How long I stood this way, listening with every nerve in my body, I cannot tell. After some considerable time, I eventually felt brave enough to feel my path to the side of the cellar and made my way to the stone steps. Resting my head against the roughness of the wooden door, I fell into a fitful sleep.

I will say, that of the many days I lived in that awful cell, this was by far the longest night of all. Morning seemed reluctant to arrive. And yet, arrive it did, with no change to my circumstances. I was aware of the usual bustle of morning in the house. Mellor charging through the kitchen doors, making as much noise as a body could with pots and pans and slams and thumps and whisking, and the effort of kneading the dough. Six in the morning, I knew. Then Tilly, with her lighter sounds of scrubbing and polishing and the collecting and setting of the wares on the breakfast-room table. The serving bowls and ladles next, accompanied by the soft *plish* of water and milk being poured into jugs. The hunger-inducing aroma of bread and muffins in the oven, and eggs and gammon in the frying pan. Behind all this, I heard the vigorous, rhythmic, *swoosh-swoosh-swoosh* of Hincham's brush as it scrubbed and buffed the Ladies' outdoor shoes to a fine shine; accompanied – cruelly, gloatingly, to my ears – by his high-pitched whistling of a jaunty tune. I had long noted that no person ever whistled when unhappy. Not many blacks were heard to whistle. Hincham's pitch proclaimed that he was very happy indeed, this day.

As I have stated before in these pages, I had become an expert at hearing through various barriers. The following was what I could glean from the conversation which arose after a good twenty minutes. Mellor spoke first:

'Where be Sancho?'

'I do not know, ma'am, that's the truth. Not usually late down, he isn't.'

'Perhaps the blackamoor had runned away again, Tilly. Why don't you go after him at that there Montagu's house? His Grace is after keeping monkeys and all sorts of other beasts that talk and walk like human men there, so he does.'

Each continued with their tasks, though there was a question that hung in the air. Tilly wouldn't ask it – she lives in mortal fear of any confrontation that might expose her to questioning or a critique of her own life, especially as she has formed an attachment to a footman from a neighbouring house – her cherished secret, for now.

Eventually, stopping Hincham just as he was about to launch into another burst of mouth-music, Mellor spat out an order: 'Go fetch the lazy blackie, Tilly.'

'Oh, you'll not find him there. They put him downstairs.'

The silence that followed, though dulled by the door separating me and the kitchen, was sharp. Tilly rushed from the kitchen with Mellor's voice calling after her to, 'Get back to work!' I felt Tilly pause behind the cellar door and then slip back into the kitchen, where the sounds of the morning bustle recommenced. Her courage had failed her; she could not lose her place. I wept again. Without Tilly, I had no ally or friend in that house. I groped my way down the stone steps and felt for the bedding I had seen in the brief glimpse I had been afforded the night before. The straw mattress was not as rough as it could have been and there was at least the thin sheet to cover myself with, an addition that I suspected was not Hincham's idea. I lay on this mat and felt the cool of the floor immediately, which struck me as a boon. To my surprise I awoke some while later. I must have been very tired, indeed.

I cannot help but note that this was the worst incident of my time at the Coven, but I can say with all honesty and no degree of false optimism, that this nadir was the beginning of the best part of my life. Though, of course, at that time it did not feel this way at all.

Chapter V

*In which Sancho languishes
in his cellar gaol.*

1749

꧁

Twenty years old

I pissed myself for a third consecutive night. I could feel the
welcome warmth of the water as it spread over my loins and
down my leg, but felt powerless to stop it. Standing up stiffly
from my bed – ha, bed! – I felt for the steps and began to
mount them on all fours, so tired and without sustenance I
was by this point. I had been down here three days without
food or water, I guessed. Though, really, I had no sense of the
passage of time, so lacking in light was this cell. My only clues
as to the time of day were the noises of the usual running of
the house. I had tried to open the door once, but knew what I
had already suspected, that it was most assuredly bolted from
the outside. I sat, forlornly, at the top of the steps and felt the
back of my neck, now crusted-over with the dried blood that
Hincham's fingernails had drawn on that first dreadful night.
I began to wonder how long a person could survive without
water before succumbing. How long without food? It was in

the midst of one of these circular, unsolvable and terrifying ruminations, that I heard a sound I did not believe at first. The sound of the bolt sliding across the door behind me. Saved, Sancho – saved, saved, saved!

I hurried – half-falling – down the stairs and stood, politely, at the bottom – tucking the ends of my piss-soaked shirt into my breeches at the last minute. The light from above was so bright that it hurt my eyes as if someone had pushed pins into them. I cried out, so violent and unexpected was the sensation. The sound of footsteps was all I could hear, for my brain was reeling with the assault on my senses. The smell of the air above, mingled with what I guessed to be Mellor's steak pie and gravy, almost made me moan. The coolness of the outside air hit me, and I could feel the cold sensation of my wet shirt and breeches all the more sharply. I wanted to speak, but all that came was a dry groan. The footsteps came closer to me and I felt the rough hand of Hincham slap me across the head. I stumbled back and fell into a corner. The sounds that followed were obvious and filled me with self-loathing at my deluded hopefulness. Hincham was simply gathering bottles for a meal. The small wine-cellar was here, of course ... As my eyes sought to gain an image, I thought I saw another silhouette at the top of the stairs pause, then move off swiftly. Tilly? Though it could well have been any of my mistresses. Hincham's frame covered the light then, and I cowered away, anticipating another strike.

'Filthy nigger.'

A reference to my state and my soiled and stinking bedding, no doubt. I heard his mirthless laugh as he ascended the stairs. Then, after an unnecessary slam of the door, I was once again plunged into darkness. It felt like a mercy, truth be told. I noted that already I was happier alone and in the dark than exposed to the intolerable light and risk of harm at Hincham's hand. I fell to my knees then and my forehead touched the cool stone floor.

I have no idea how long I stayed in this supplicating attitude, but I gradually became aware of a noise above my head. I feared it was my first rodent visitor and scrambled away from that spot. To my utter astonishment, it was the sound of the bolt of the door slowly being pulled back. Who but Tilly would be opening the door with such caution? I bit down optimism, instinctively knowing that if I was again disappointed, I might fall into a fatal despair. This time, my eyes were not blinded as before, though I still had to squint. It *was* Tilly. Poor, broken Tilly, with her eyes swollen with tears and a look of such pity on her face for what she beheld, that it was all I could do not to wail with sorrow at what I imagined she saw. She came down the steps and observed my piss-soaked bedding and my sorry state – put her finger to her lips in a gesture of silence and from the apron she wore always, produced two small pies and a crust of bread. She lay these at the foot of the stairs together with a flask of water. Then, with one last look at my pitiable state, she scurried up the stairs as if the devil himself were after her, and shut me in once again, noiselessly sliding the bolt. I rushed to the victuals, only thinking to be cautious after I had knocked the heavy flask over, spilling some of the contents on the step. Thankfully, that left more than half of the liquid, and I drank a deep draught, telling myself not to finish it – though with every fibre of my being I desired to do just that. No liquid has ever tasted sweeter. Feeling around for the pies, I devoured one in moments and began to eat most of the crust of buttered bread, when a feeling of such great nausea arose in my stomach and up to my gorge, that I felt I would vomit the precious morsels and waste the bounty that Tilly had so bravely brought me. I wrapped the remaining pie in my sheet – using the only corner that wasn't damp – and took it to the middle of the stairs. It would be safe from the mice here, I reasoned, and I would have time to remove the sheet were someone to come into the cellar unexpectedly. I sat on the lowest step and breathed a sigh of relief. At least Tilly had recovered enough of her courage to come to me. I guessed that she could not do this every day.

I would be glad that I had restrained myself from eating both pies, though I longed to, as the next day was one where I had no visitors, kindly or otherwise. The night of that first visit, I lay on the damp straw, which warmed to my body's heat after a time, and fell into a deep, uninterrupted slumber. My first, for days.

I was awakened by an unexpected sound. Music. And lovely music it was, too. Where was it coming from? After a few moments of listening to these dulcet sounds, I realised that they were in my head. I laughed, just once, in an involuntary bark of inchoate joy. I was composing music in my head. I have never heard anything more beautiful before or since. I will never hear this sound in life, but I avow I heard it then. Indescribably beautiful singing – a woman's high voice – too high for any earthly singer, be she never so skilled – and was that the faint sounds of a choir underscoring the soaring lyricism of this heavenly soloist? Music saved me then, as surely as Tilly's little morsels and her kindness would save me in the following days.

The music of my captivity haunts me even as I read these words, many years later.

The mind is a strange beast, at times, and would not leave off retracing – in a seemingly endless circle of repetition – the mistakes of the last few weeks. As if in repeating them they would present a solution to my present predicament. Having no other companions except my memories and imagination, I tormented myself by reliving the events leading up to my incarceration – events which had truly begun many weeks before.

The Treaty of Aix-la-Chapelle having been recently signed, incited a great deal of ill-will towards King George II. As a distracted Duke John explained to me, with some force I might add, there were many great fools in England who saw this peace – or capitulation – 'as a sign that the German kings of Britain are far more exercised over keeping hold of their Hanoverian possessions, than shoring up Britain's interest in Europe'.

Duke John, as Master-General of the King's Ordnance, as well as his many other titles and duties, was frantically bustling around town, inspecting the preparations for the Royal Fireworks celebration at the Green Park. April was the chosen month, though why anyone who had experienced an English spring would contemplate an outdoor display of this kind in the middle of our *monsoon season* was beyond most to fathom. There were altogether too many frayed tempers involved in this piece of public self-congratulation; a mere distraction from the actual losses this treaty had really purchased. Chief amongst the antagonists, and the source of much of poor Duke John's distress, was the King himself – a man I had met only once, when I had spent a rare evening with the Montagus, reciting extracts from Ovid's *Metamorphoses*.

King George had been adamant – when he commissioned George Handel to compose an orchestral suite to accompany the grand fireworks display – that Handel not use any violins in the piece, for His Majesty wanted it to be martial and violins were for polite music, not for a display of violent, military might. Handel demurred – well one would, this was the King – but he could not pretend to be happy about it. Duke John was the arbiter between the volatile disputants. He never revealed the conversations he was having with His Majesty, but rumbled under his breath every now and then about the immoveable Teutonic temperament. Handel was no better tempered, which I witnessed first-hand one morning at Montagu House. A muffin was thrown, is all I'll say here. No books were damaged in the incident, though one wall will forever bear the mark of a genius's wrath – in damson . . .

In imagining the spectacle of so many fireworks being let off, to the glorious music of George Handel . . . Well, I could think of no more romantic a setting. The operation to escape the Sisters and get myself to the park was quite successfully executed. No one in the household suspected anything, as I had kept myself firmly confined to the house as much as possible in the preceding few weeks. The tensions around my last visit to Montagu House – someone had informed them, of course, as our world is small – had diminished greatly. Beatrice was less snippy, Florence found me diligent and malleable – I hardly contradicted her pronunciations of the Latin in *Faustus* at all. Bloody Marlowe. As for Abigail, she was a little distant, but nothing my age and the unspoken end of our era of *night visits* would not explain.

I determined to look my best for the grand gala and elicited the help of Tilly and Charles Manwell in the task. Charles had found his master's old blue velvet frock coat. I had my own cravat, one shirt that might serve, and a pair of not very good, but very 'the only ones you have' breeches – as Tilly pointed out, helpfully. A green waistcoat was found at Monty House. The Duke is taller than me by some inches, but my girth necessitates a larger fit. The waistcoat was skilfully let out by Tilly. Stockings I had, white, and a hat that was too small, and so I would carry it in my hands as if it might fit if I cared to put it on. Using the pretext of carrying rags to the poor, I hid my *costume* within the bundle and made my escape around the corner.

It felt grand to be out on my own in order to attend the event of the year. The long journey from Greenwich via the ferry to Westminster Stairs – where I met Duke John – only served to excite my imagination. Duchess Mary and her daughter Mary, Countess of Cardigan, together with her spouse George Brudenell, Earl of Cardigan, were there – having come from their other home in Dover Street, May Fair, in order that the whole family might travel to the Green Park together. Earl George is a little serious for Duke John's taste, but the Duke knows he is devoted to Countess Mary. I like him for his gentle and even-tempered manner. He is never anything but polite and respectful to me, though I hold no status in the family whatsoever.

Charles Manwell, consummate footman, had outdone himself with fitting out a larger carriage than usual and, in his finest livery, rode us proudly to the Green Park – about an hour's journey, due to the number of people heading to the festivities in carriages and on foot. The roads were pleasant enough, though it had rained quite a bit in the last week; the clouds, however, boded ill. Sure enough, by the time we had passed the massed crowds on Piccadilly, the rain was coming down in earnest. The pale and anxious Duke was pained to see this deluge; he kept shaking his head and muttering to himself that, 'This will never do ...' He appeared to be ageing right before our eyes. The hero of the 1745 repulsion of the Jacobite Rebels looked every inch his nearly three-score years. How is it that one can seem quite robust one month and shorn of all energy and youthful spirit the next? Life is strange and time is cruel. Once this momentous occasion was over, however, he would surely recover his vigour and, more importantly, his humour. It had been some time since we had laughed, I noted sadly.

The setting for the Royal Fireworks was every bit as spectacular as Duke John had described. A veritable Château de Versailles had been constructed and every inch was covered in either cannon or fireworks. The orchestra was placed on huge rostrums and amounted to about sixty musicians, of which twenty-four were oboes and about half as many bassoons. But, no violins! The crowd were excited before one fuse was lit and despite the downpour, which had passed for the time being, a faint light shone through the thinnest of the clouds. Charles Manwell halted the carriage almost as soon as we had entered the park, as the throng would not allow any further incursion. I helped Charles with the ladies, who alighted gracefully onto the wet grass; their shoes were soaked almost instantly. George Brudenell actually had to help Duke John alight as his limbs were stiffened by the unexpectedly long journey. A veritable picture of old age and the coming infirmity of that penultimate stage in Shakespeare's ladder towards Oblivion:

> ... the sixth age shifts
> Into the lean and slipper'd pantaloon,
> With spectacles on nose, and pouch on side,
> His youthful hose, well sav'd, a world too wide
> For his shrunk shank, and his big manly voice,
> Turning again toward childish treble, pipes
> And whistles in his sound.

Though I now see that Duke John was far from this figure. Not yet.

I left the family to get to their places beside the King and moved to join the rest of the throng. I had no status other than that of protégé to His Grace and felt no sense of being left out. On the contrary, it was the first time in my life that I truly felt free. I sauntered through the crowd, who noticed me from time to time – not with hostility, only a piqued curiosity. I appeared to be alone, with no master and yet quite well attired. People were wondering about me, I knew, and like my hero David Garrick, I began to naturally assume a rôle. I was a great Lord of Africa, I was the ruler of an exotic kingdom far superior to this I walked through. With my head held higher than perhaps was necessary, I enjoyed a good half-hour of my *performance* until passing a couple of young fashionables – dandies – I overheard one of them mutter: 'Smoke, Othello.'

At which they both giggled like ladies into their scented handkerchiefs. I did not hesitate, but turned on my heels, overtook them, and rounding on them, halted their progress. I think they were almost as surprised as I was – I *maintained my rôle* as Mr Garrick had instructed me once, and in my strongest voice said: 'Othello, eh? Ay, Sir, such Othellos you meet with but once in a century. Such Iagos as you we meet with – in every dirty passage! Proceed, Sirs!'

This last with a gesture of imperious command. They neither replied, nor dared to even question my authority, but scurried off in the direction they had been going. Several folks who had overheard the exchange applauded my performance. I was quite puffed up. One young maid, with her sister-companion, smiled at me so sweetly that I felt bold enough to approach her with as polite a courtly bow as I could manage.

'Charles Ignatius, at your service, Mesdames.'

She – the one who had smiled so sweetly at me – curtsied. Her friend, a little awkwardly, did the same. There was a moment of silence before this sweet creature said, 'Eliza. Eliza Buckhurst. And this is Maisie. Maisie Wilton.'

'Charmed to make your acquaintance, both.'

After a moment of hesitation, none of us knowing which was the right thing to do – go our ways, or remain together – Maisie saved the day.

'Oo, would you see there, Lizzie? They've ices, they have. Want one?'

'May I purchase them for you, ladies? It would bring me enormous pleasure.'

They both nodded, sweetly, and I made to get them. But Maisie, realising that this might be a missed opportunity for her companion, asked if she might fetch them, as they always serve a lady first. I thought her wisdom sound and gave her two shillings that I had in my waistcoat pocket. Eliza and I looked at each other, and then away almost as quickly. She was very lovely. Her hair was a deep chestnut brown, just as her eyes were. They sparkled like gems in a face that was a perfect oval. She had something olive in her skin that made her look aglow and healthy, though from the softness of her hands – which I took, after a short while, to lead her to a bench that had just become free near us – she worked indoors. Not as a maid, like Tilly, I guessed, for they were well manicured and tender to the touch. She spoke very softly and with a London accent that had hints of country in it. She explained that her people were originally from Cornwall but that her parents had come to London when she was only five. Her father, a tanner, had sought work in the city to feed their four children, and Eliza, their second child, was happy to be in the bustle of the metropolis. She lived in Smithfield and worked as a seamstress near the Tower of London.

'London ... I like the way it's all so big. Some would be afeared, but it makes me feel safe, somehow. It must be hard to live in a small village, where everything you do is seen by all, don't you think, Charles?'

'I'm in love with London. I cannot get enough of it, though I rarely get to visit. My ... guardians seem more afraid of it than of anything else.'

'Guardians? At your age? That's funny.'

'I suppose it is. But I do not yet have means to leave them.'

'Are you ... Are you a ... Do you belong to them?'

I was struck by this question. So struck, that I could not answer for a moment. I had never really thought about my legal status in this direct way. In the way of being owned. They had told me so often that I was fortunate not to be a common slave on a plantation, that this negative appeared a positive. Which, make no mistake, it was. But not being one thing does not confer on one the status of being another. It felt complicated to contemplate, and now did not seem the time to think about it.

'Truth be told, Lizzie ... I don't know.'

We sat in silence then and looked away from each other for the first time in a while. After a few moments, we realised that we had continued holding hands. Passers-by glanced at us, but nothing like the looks I got in Greenwich. Without a doubt, London was a freer place, just as Lizzie had described it. We turned to each other at the same instant and smiled. Maisie brought the ices, breaking our reverie, and we three sat, as old acquaintances do, in a deep and peaceful silence, eating our frozen treats. Delicious. All of it.

Then it began. The first martial strains of the 'Ouverture'. We rose from our bench and turned to the palace that had been constructed at great expense and trouble by Duke John and his team. I glanced over to the Royal Pavilion, where Duke John was taking his place not far from our sovereign. King George was not smiling. His eyes were not on the palace about to be lit up, but on the dark clouds hovering overhead. Once the 'Bourrée' commenced, some dancers were seen cavorting expertly, and the firework display began. It began in twilight, which was not altogether wise, and things took an immediate turn for the worse when the heavens fulfilled their promise and opened. Several of the firelighters were seen in a corner extinguishing a blaze that had taken hold of one of the pavilions, and a man had clearly burnt himself in the process. But that all paled into insignificance when a loud bang incited an even louder cry, and a soldier was carried away from the commotion with his hand, or what remained of it, wrapped up in a makeshift oilcloth bandage. King George had a face like thunder, which matched the sound of the one hundred and one cannons that went off, seemingly of their own volition. The sky duly responded with its own timpani, whereupon the whole shook the earth and atmosphere like the very war it was there to commemorate.

The downpour would have been comic in any other context, but this was not only a disaster for King George, but more importantly to me, a tragic failure for Duke John. While it was not his fault the heavens had opened, he might have foreseen it, forcing a postponement until the weather became more clement in June. But King George had insisted the event happen as shortly after the treaty had been signed as possible. This literal damp squib was the result. When I looked over to Duke John, he seemed slumped, diminished. Duchess Mary took his hand, but he remained resolutely looking outward, glumly, like a child who has had a toy taken from him when the punishment wasn't merited. The music of the 'Bourrée' felt incongruously jolly then, though it was mercifully brief. It must be said that it was only the interested parties in the Royal Pavilion who were put out; everyone else, especially my two companions, was having a wonderful time. The rockets and wheels lit up the sky and it was a marvel to behold the way things were timed to coincide with the mood and rhythm of the music. George H looked diligent, yet as though he were deriving no pleasure from the occasion. This was graft, this was toil to him, and whilst he would execute his part with aplomb, he was not going to enjoy it one bit if he could help it. Ah, the vicissitudes of genius.

The regal crescendo to this piece brought a spontaneous round of applause from the thousands present. When a rocket shot across the green during the stirring 'Le Réjouissance', having drooped on its stick and pointed into the crowd, a woman cried out as she was hit in the small of the back by this fusillade. She caught alight in an instant, and only two brave soldiers ripping her clothing clean off her saved her from serious injury – though her pride would never recover, and I heard she had moved to our colony in America to avoid this unmerited notoriety. The incident only lasted a few moments but that near disaster signalled the end of the festivities. As the musicians played the final movements of the minuets, the crowds began to disperse. The royal party left first, in something akin to indignation. I knew that I would have to return to Greenwich under my own steam.

I took my companions by the hands then, and we made our way to the Mall side of the Green Park. We managed, by some miracle, to gain a carriage, and I offered to take the ladies home to Smithfield. They graciously and gratefully accepted as the crowd was intolerably pressing. Those long three hours were the happiest of my short life. I had never felt so manly, so capable, so independent. I gazed at Eliza as if it were she who had bestowed this gift of freedom on me. And, foolish as it may sound now, I resolved to ask for her hand in marriage once we had a quiet moment to ourselves. The opportunity presented itself in this whirlwind of an evening, after we had let Maisie down in Covent Garden, for she had decided to stay with her fellow-worker who lived nearby, rather than go all the way home. Lizzie would inform Maisie's parents of her whereabouts when she got back to Smithfield, to avoid them fretting over their child.

We sat together, then, on one side of the carriage, looking out over London as we travelled east along the Strand. Ironically, it had transformed into a beautifully clear night. The stars were out, and an unseasonably warm breeze was gently swaying the oak and poplar trees all along that thoroughfare. I turned to Eliza Buckhurst and kissed her. She did not resist – on the contrary, she returned my kiss ardently and warmly. I was in a kind of heaven for another hour then and though we did not kiss again, I knew that this was my wife as surely as Romeo knew that Juliet was his. As I helped Lizzie down from the carriage, I asked if I might court her. She blushed. Her eyes filled with tears and then she nodded, smiling up at me with such sweetness it was all I could do not to sweep her up in my arms again and plant a million kisses on those pink, full lips.

'We mustn't say anything as yet, though, Charles. Let me talk to Mother and Father. And you'll have to talk to your people, too, of course.'

My heart sank at this, and she saw.

'We must do it right, if we are to be together, Charles. Or we'll be seen as too hasty. Do you see?'

She touched my face so tenderly then that all arguments to the contrary dissolved. I would speak to the Coven soon and visit with her on Sunday, if she'd allow it. We parted, reluctantly, the music of the Royal Fireworks and the thumping of my heart accompanying me all the way to Greenwich.

Oh, to think of that sweet evening from my dank cell. A night where I had enjoyed the full freedoms of a Londoner and dared to hope of a future filled with love and liberty. My pitiful surroundings mocked the foolish aspirations of the preceding weeks, but I clung to my daydreams.

Brave Tilly had left a key for me behind a plant pot in the front garden, meaning that I slipped into my chamber undetected. In the morning, after a fitful night of dreams and excitement about my future life with Lizzie, I went downstairs and pretended to a feebleness that I was far from truly feeling. What an actor, Mr Garrick, what an actor! The look of melancholy, the drooping eyes, the sighs, not too many or too heavy, but enough to have my Ladies look up each time I did. Tilly's face was unmistakably disapproving. She felt it was one thing to lie to the Ladies every Thursday for over a decade, but this was a line crossed. I hadn't done it for my education, nor to learn a trade of some kind, but to have a frivolous adventure and rub shoulders with the hoi polloi. She had a point.

I met Eliza six times in three weeks. I did not tell a soul. I wanted to keep to myself the joy of finding this angel who let me hold her hand in the street, in defiance of the looks we sometimes received. Only once or twice did the usual shouts of contempt reach our ears. We were quite oblivious to it, most of the time. We largely kept to the embankment around London Bridge, as it was the easiest place to meet for both of us; or the parks, when we had more time to ourselves. On Sundays, I was able to pretend to the Coven to be going with Tilly to the Oxford Road to see her family, and to pretend to Tilly that I was off to see Duke John. One afternoon, I seized my moment to tell Tilly where I had spent most Sundays lately. She brightened considerably.

'You wee devil. What's her name?'

'Eliza Buckhurst. Lizzie. She's a seamstress, and has the most delicate hands, Tills. Soft and gentle with—'

'English? She's an Englishwoman, Charles?'

Our conversation ended there. She saw my look and I saw hers. We saw each other, then. For the first time. Until then she had been just Tilly, and I, Charles. But that moment changed us for ever. I could feel, rather than see, her shaking her head. I stormed into the house in a rage. Rage – a constant companion all my life; it only needed air to catch alight and flare. I marched into the drawing room, and startled the Ladies, who were all buried in some task or other. They all looked up as if I had shot a pistol in the air. I could have robbed them at that point and not heard a squeak out of them.

'My Ladies, I have met and intend to marry a girl. Her name is Eliza Buckhurst, and she is the daughter of a tanner of Smithfield. We intend to be married and she will be a seamstress, as she is now, and I will . . . I will find . . . a trade. I am a competent worker and will do something in the line of manual work until I can gain a proper apprenticeship. And that is all.'

Abigail recovered first, giving a small signal of patience to her sisters who were watching me as if I were a wild animal in their midst. She spoke slowly at first, gathering her wits.

'So, you mean to depart from us, without our leave? I see that you are determined to do so. It is not for us to keep you prisoner; you have always been free to leave as you wished. Your ... your master was always quite clear on that point. Now, is this girl ...?'

They were all so obsessed with this.

'Yes, yes,' I spat out. 'She is English. A white. But what of that? She loves me as truly as if I were her equal – which I am, am I not?'

The childish conclusion of my outburst heated my blood. I'd felt I'd had the upper hand until then, but this last made me seem a boy. I composed myself during the following. Miss Florence, now:

'No one can deny you are quite the young dandy, Sancho. With fine friends, like Mr Garrick, we hear, and His Grace as your patron – but mark us, you are not of her race, nor of her low social standing, and that will show in time. Tell us, have you sought her father's permission for this ... course of action? I should have thought you must, before you put yourself out of home. For what if he refused you?'

I hesitated then – what she had said rang true. I saw now that I had been too hasty in confronting my Ladies before I was sure of Eliza's hand. But I was determined to press home my waning advantage.

'Eliza is a woman of independent means, Miss Florence, and may support herself if it came to that. Therefore, her father's consent will matter less than if she had been dependent on him entirely.'

'Not everyone is as kindly as you have found in polite society, Sancho,' added Miss Abigail, in her infuriatingly reasonable tone. 'You may find a certain reluctance among the lower orders to mix with Negroes as family members. They are not all as *enlightened* as *His Grace*.'

This she said with the usual snipe at Duke John, pronouncing the words *enlightened* and *His Grace* with a kind of sarcastic sneer. I would not wait for Miss Beatrice to pipe up in her turn.

'I shall ask his consent this very day, and then we'll see, will we not?'

A long silence, where only the sound of the clock on the mantel could be heard. There was nothing more to be said. I had spoken my mind. I had defied them without somehow committing any real crime. Yet I was a criminal in their eyes, suddenly – a stranger, at least. It was the oddest sensation; at once liberating, at once exposing. As though I had stepped into the icy Thames without knowing it was even winter, I had stumbled blindly into adulthood before I had noticed I was no longer a child. All in the space of a conversation.

I left my Ladies silenced. I did not slam the door, nor did I rush out to the street; I did not run to the Thames, nor did I even walk to Blackheath and the Montagus. Instead, I calmly collected some coins from my box under my bed and walked to the ferry. I arrived in a daydream at Eliza's house, a small cottage on a dark and dusty street in Smithfield. The smells of London almost overwhelmed me – redolent of tanners, brewers and horse dung. I rapped on the door that I had seen Eliza go into on the days when she allowed me to walk her to her street corner, and was met with the grubby faces of two children who stared at me with eyes as wide as saucers, and as chocolate-brown as Eliza's. These – perforce – were her siblings. Behind them came a tired-looking woman of about forty and upwards, but seeming older due to life's toils. She wasn't unhappy or unfriendly looking, just exhausted. She smiled easily at me.

'Hello, dear. What can I—' she started, and catching her breath, quickly changed her tone and manner. She shooed the children into the house and said with an air of some trepidation but not hostility: 'Why, you're Charles, aren't you, lovey? Eliza's . . . friend?'

I nodded, grateful not to have to explain my presence. Mrs Buckhurst opened her door a little wider, and stealing a look down both ends of her street, ushered me in.

The corridor was dark, but once I'd entered the main living room, where the whole family lived in relative order and cleanliness, I could see that this was a house of light and love. It was not decorated with any sense of style but it had a charm about it, although the thick walls and lack of sunlight rendered the space chilly. The children played at the hearth, tossing little pieces of coal in to watch them sparkle and blaze. I turned to Mrs Buckhurst, who offered me tea, and I braved the subject we both knew I'd come for.

'We haven't known each other long, Mrs Buckhurst. But, I do believe – we have an understanding, Lizzie and I.'

'She says as much, Charles, she's told her father and me all. But Lizzie's a soft-hearted thing, I'm sure you've seen, and we were afraid she was being foolish.'

'I am very sure you are right to worry for her, Mrs Buckhurst. A lovely girl like your Lizzie, must be the Portia of the Smithfield strond. "And many Jasons come in quest of her . . ."'

Mrs Buckhurst wore a blank look. It was one of the reasons I had trouble talking to people of small education – I made allusions that no one understood. I knew from bitter experience that it was best not to explain in detail, as this only tended to make any distance that much wider.

'She will be quite the catch for any man worth his salt, I mean to say, Mrs Buckhurst.'

She nodded, then, relieved to understand. We sipped our tea awhile; it was very good. I raised my cup in approval and she smiled. I could see where Lizzie got her smile from, though her mother's face was slenderer than her own. The door burst open and a man-mountain entered, making the boy at the hearth suddenly come to life with a 'Paps!' He ran to greet his father, who had the oval face of his daughters. Mr Buckhurst hoisted the boy onto his left hip and, glancing at me with a quizzical but, again, far from hostile look, gathered up his daughter onto his right. He looked the picture of Vulcan, the Smith to the gods. I had learnt my lesson well and refrained from commenting on this. I rose and gave a polite bow, trying not to appear too flouncy. He put his children down and, while they clung to his leg, he wiped his palms offhandedly on his leather apron and offered me a manly shake. The couple looked at each other, and Mrs Buckhurst, understanding her husband's ways, took charge of bathing the children. The sounds of the kettle and pots warming the water and the children squealing to be put in the metal tub accompanied our conference.

'Smoke?'

'Thank you, no, I don't, Mr Buckhurst.'

'Ay,' was all he offered, lighting his pipe, and taking a long draw before exhaling the curling, blue-grey smoke. I sat on the edge of the small armchair as he stood by the mantel, poking the fire in a vague sort of way.

'You mayn't marry Lizzie.'

I was taken aback. Not so much by his words, though they pierced me deeply enough, but by the gentle, matter-of-fact way in which they were pronounced.

'It ain't nothing to do with your colour, mind. I don't hold for that nonsense, man's a man for all that. But you have a way about you that won't suit Lizzie in the end, d'you see?'

'How so?' I said, knowing already what he meant.

'You'll pardon me for saying this, Sir, but you're not of her rank, is you? You know a bunch of learning, I'd reckon. That might be all right in Greenwich, but won't serve a man on these streets, here. No offence, but – look at you. You're a man of another world to Lizzie's, Charles, if you don't mind. And that won't serve either of you.'

He was direct, I'll give him that. Not in the least hostile – just sure of what he was saying. In truth, I should have listened to him – but I felt myself thwarted on every side, now.

'But I love her, Mr Buckhurst. And, I'd hazard my life, she loves me.'

'And love will conquer all, is that it?'

I could see the foolishness of making any statement in support of what now, in this dingy room, with the picture of my patron's patron on the mantel, seemed like the most childish of aphorisms. I also saw how hard this was for this tough man who had a family to keep together. Here I was, offering all the practical help of a man waving a powdered wig at a drowning sailor. Try as I might, I could think of no solution.

I rose, then, and shaking his hand once more, vowed to try again very soon to persuade him that I would love his daughter no matter what the obstacles from without. He nodded, respectfully, not in the least convinced. I went to the yard and thanked Mrs Buckhurst for the tea and the welcome. I left the house and walked back to Greenwich – which took hours. I hovered around Thames Street at the foot of the north side of London Bridge for a time, in hopes that I might see Lizzie, but she took several routes home and today was not a London Bridge one, evidently.

On arriving back at Greenwich, I went straight to the plant pot. Dear Tilly had shown foresight in leaving the key once more. I felt benumbed by the day's events. It confirmed everything I should have known; that the opening of my heart to others would lead to the stealing of my joy. I vowed to never let another soul see my happiness, if such a thing were ever again granted me in the future.

Chapter VI

In which our Hero finally attempts his escape.

1749

❦

Twenty years old

One morning, about . . . I don't know how many days living in Purgatory . . . the Angel Matilda appeared to me through my crusted-over eyes, which over the course of my incarceration had become blighted by infection. She lifted my head from the floor of the cellar and poured Nectar, the drink of the gods, into my mouth – much of it ran down my chin and onto my filthy shirt. I tried to laugh at how sweet it tasted. Nothing but a croak came from me.

'Oh, my poor, dear child,' whispered the Angel Matilda. And I wept. The tears sharply stung my eyes for they had nowhere to go. My eyes had been encrusted for so long that I was no longer able to open them when someone came in. I knew that Hincham had been, because he never left without a word – usually some insult or other. Even Tilly's visits brought me no real joy these last days, though I was grateful for them. I felt for the food and liquid she brought, rather than saw them. They tasted like so much sawdust to me, for the most part – except for one magical day, when she brought some syllabub. It was so unexpected that I grinned for fully an hour – like an hysterical Bedlam inmate – at the incongruity of such a silly dish to serve to a prisoner.

A warm sensation bathed my eyes. The Angel Matilda was rubbing them gently with a cloth soaked in warm water. It stung a little, but I was glad to feel something other than cold. And, as if by magic, my eyes snapped open, and there she was. My Tilly. We held each other a while. Poor Till – I must have smelt appallingly awful. But hold me she did. She cradled my head for a time, stroking my hair and my face, singing softly to me – some air I cannot now recall – but it was as lovely as any my mind had composed in that period. At last, she held me by the shoulders and made me look at her.

'There now, you look a sight better than you did just now. How do you? If you can speak.'

I croaked and gestured for more of the heavenly liquid, and Tilly duly obliged by giving me another sip of the milk she had brought down. I felt ready to speak then – but suddenly my strength left me, and I merely lolled in her arms again, so safe I felt within them. She lifted me off her and said with an insistence she had not shown before: 'Speak now, Charles. You must speak.'

'Yes. Yes. I am well. I am well, Tilly – how do you?'

'Foolish boy. We must get you clear of here before they do for you. I will come down tonight and let you go. But you must promise me to never come back. They are done with you, your ladies, and mean to send for Sill.'

At the mention of his name, my mind became agitated

with a kind of panic. Not one that would leave me confused, however, but the kind of panic that concentrates the mind and communicates that focus to the sinews. I sat bolt upright, then.

'That's right, boy. We've no time . . .'

Tilly laid out her plan of escape. After she had given me the rest of the milk and a lump of soft bread with the most delicious hard cheese encased within, and handed me a pair of my shoes that she'd had the foresight to retrieve from my room, she nodded at me once and swiftly mounted the stairs – but not before placing her stub of a candle in my hands. The clang of the bolt made me momentarily lose faith that what had taken place in the last while had truly occurred, so accustomed was I to my prison routine. The light afforded by the candle almost made the place seem festive. It was also the first time that I was able to look at the conditions I had endured for so long. I paced the cell to wake up my limbs and saw the pools of damp that gathered at the bottom of the walls on all sides of this place. The wine shelf was not very full, but I took a bottle and, pushing the cork with some difficulty into the neck of it, drank near a quarter of its contents in one long swig. It felt good to steal from my captors, even if it made me retch for twenty minutes or so afterwards. The stupefying effect of alcohol should have rendered me a little dull, but on the contrary, I felt a lucidity that had been absent from me these many days. I sat back on the middle steps, stretching out my little-used limbs.

I suppose to strengthen my resolve to survive this ordeal, my mind vividly conjured that night that I had thought to send a letter to

Lizzie, declaring myself ready to defy the world and be married to her as soon as she would agree to it. To further embellish the note, I had decided to decorate each page with a letter that I would draw into an animal shape. I composed a silly poem in my room entitled 'Ode to Gretna Green' – now, thankfully, lost. I would use the letter 'G' of both 'Gretna' and 'Green' to form giraffes in a romantic intertwining. Ambitious for a non-draughtsman, but 'love can conquer all' – even a lack of skill. Surely.

Night must surely have come, I thought, as the effects of the Burgundy wore off. How long had I been in a half-dream land? The hunger that I had become used to crept back to let me know that it had been hours since that heavenly cheese and bread. I paced for a moment in the dark, the candle having gone out hours before. However, the schematic of my home of many days was firmly embedded in my brain, and it was as I moved past the wine shelf on my left and touched the crumbling brickwork of the wall for the fifth time, that I heard the bolts of the door slide back. Why a feeling of utter panic and fear swept over me at that point, after all that I had been through, I will never know. But I felt that my escape was doomed to fail, as I had failed in so much that I had imagined possible in my life. I could not move. And whoever had slid the bolt hadn't opened the door to help me with my sudden and overwhelming indecision. Had that been the plan all along? I could not now recall if Tilly and I had decided that I would wait till she had gone back to bed, or rush out the minute the door was unlocked. Was she going to leave me my necessaries outside the front door, or was I to wait for her to come down to the cellar to give me what I'd need to survive the next few nights? I could not, foolish as this sounds, think which it was. And so, I waited. Longer than any person wishing to be free from a prison, and seeing the cell door open, ought to wait. What on earth was wrong with me? The phrase, 'better the devil you know than the devil you don't' came to mind then. I was afraid. Not that I would not escape – but that I would. What would I find in the world that the Coven had protected me from? Was I even ready for what was to come?

I waited, indecisive, at the most important moment of my life, until, eventually, I shook off my stupor and began to climb the stairs. I halted and returned below to fetch the flask from the cellar which I thought might come in handy, and then mounted in earnest, pushing the door to the cellar open with caution. The hallway was dark, save for the moonlight that bathed it from the window above the entrance. I could see my carpetbag was opposite the cellar door, and a swell of gratitude for the risks that my friend Tilly had taken for me drew water to my eyes. Wiping these useless tears away and taking a mighty gulp of the freshest air I had tasted in weeks, I marched down the hallway and made my escape.

Opening the door with a confidence that surprised me, I was immediately confronted with a sight so horrifying it almost made me run back to my prison below. Hincham had his palms out to receive a sum of money from a man whose back was half to me, but there could be no mistaking who it was: Jonathan Sill. Seeing Hincham look over his shoulder, his eyes widening in shock, caused Sill to spin around. I had a moment to choose my course, but it seemed my body was ahead of my brain for once and, swinging my arm with all its might, I smashed the heavy flask across Jonathan Sill's brow as he turned to me, shattering it, blood springing directly from the wound which opened instantly. Sill covered his face – turned ghostly white by the remaining milk from the flask – and cried out. I launched myself at Hincham, who, coward that he was, stepped back in fright. Where I found the strength, to this day I will never know. Fear, mixed with a desire to flee, gave me the wherewithal to kick Hincham – hard – between his legs, eliciting from him an inhuman squeal. I ran before either man could recover and, looking back only once before turning the corner into the main thoroughfare, I saw that both men were too busy tending to their wounds to give chase.

I did not suppose that state to be a permanent one and, hugging my carpetbag to me, I ran until I had no more breath to run. I was in Blackheath once more, and this time knew exactly where I must go. Opening the rusty – painfully noisy – gate to Montagu House, I ran for the door and rapped the knocker in a panic – turning to the pathway all the while – expecting to see Sill and Hincham approaching in revengeful haste. All that greeted me was a silence so profound that I thought the house deserted. The Duke only kept three staff on when he was not in residence, as he evidently was not this night. No doubt the staff had all gone to bed ...

I leant against the door then and caught my breath as best I could. I would need every ounce of stamina, for I would have to run now in earnest. I left by the main entrance and began running along Shooter's Hill. The place held less fear of robbery for me than the situation I had left behind. I was quite sure that I would be a match for any who might try their luck with me that night. As it turned out, there was not a soul on the road, and I slowed to a fast walk. A beautiful night it was – for all the fear that it held. The few clouds there were merely added to the spectacle of a clear and starry night. The fullest moon shone so brightly that I could see the path to London very clearly and determined that I would make my way there. I would head west for London Bridge and wait till morning to make my crossing into the city. What I would do then was a decision for later. The first and most vital thing to do was to get myself out of Greenwich.

The walk did not exhaust me, but rather I gained more and more energy and hope the further I travelled. The sound of a carriage coming towards me was the first time that I really considered my situation beyond the urgency of the chase – I was a Negro with no fixed abode, on the road at night with a bag full of – what had Tilly given me, I wondered for the first time? I ducked into the scrubby bushes along the side of the road and watched a mail coach ride by in haste. I opened the sack and inspected its contents: two shirts, the blue frock coat from the fireworks event, a lump of bread and cheese, a half-full bottle of wine, and wrapped in a large handkerchief, my treasure box. I opened this – and saw that all was as I had left it. Three guineas and a few shillings – quite the fortune; the beautiful shell, the ring from New Granada with the green stone; Duke John's calling card from all those years ago; and my notebooks. I was very happy that Tilly had thought to bring them, and surprised that she even remembered their existence or where to find them. Clever, green-eyed girl, who saw everything, always. Most pleasing of all was a folded scrap of paper where Tilly had, in her childlike handwriting, written the address of her family on the Oxford Road. This was the real treasure: somewhere to go, someone to stay with while I found work. I'm not ashamed to say that I wept for love of that kind soul.

When I looked over the metropolis from the south bank of the river near the dark silhouette of the Tower of London, I guessed it to be near four in the morning by the moon's position in the sky, which was already beginning to lighten towards the Isle of Dogs in the east. I thought of Lizzie, then, and wondered if I should try to see her now. I resisted the idea, as it was imperative that I establish myself in London before I sought her hand in marriage once more. I only truly felt safe from my would-be kidnappers when I viewed the dome of St Paul's in the growing light. Workers, heading to the docks, began to move along the streets now as four o'clock struck in a nearby church – possibly the twelve bells of St Saviour's, so deep and heavy sounded their peal. Dawn came up in earnest then, and the city was slowly bathed in a pinkish glow that seemed to come from a thousand hidden lanterns, for I could not see the sun as yet. With the ever-growing light, my night-fears dissipated. Finding an alleyway just opposite London Bridge, I changed my filthy prison garb, which was attracting unwanted looks. Bad enough to be a rare black man on this side of the river, let alone to look like a vagabond. The last thing I wanted was for some diligent beadle to ask me about my business. I had thought to change only my shirt, but I could see that all needed to be removed, for my breeches were smeared with dirt of the most disgusting kind. The thought of the filthy conditions my Ladies would find in that cell made me shudder more from shame than the cold morning air. But the shame should be theirs, for leaving me in that sorry state for so long.

By the time I had crossed the already busy bridge, London

was fully awake and about its bustle. The walk to the Fleet was fascinating for the souls I saw along the way. A plethora of professions and hawkers, men and women of all classes and from every trade known to the city and the country. I even saw a man driving four oxen along the road at the crossing of the Charing River. St Martin's Lane held countless delights, too, I could tell, and I noted that many an artist's apprentice was to be seen sipping chocolate along that thoroughfare. At the corner of the Tottenham Road, I turned westward on to the Oxford Road, the road to Tyburn and the executioner's scaffold. London had never seemed more real to me than this day, and I resolved never to leave this place as long as there was breath in my body.

The kind of welcome I'd receive at the home of Tilly's family, the Grants, was a mystery to me. Shy of inviting me to spend the day with them in all the time I'd known her, I believe that it was more the idea that I would look down upon them for their lack of means that had prevented Tilly from inviting me to her home before now, rather than any snobbery on her part. Truth to tell, she was not altogether wrong. I own a sense of pride in dress and deportment, a feeling that I know what it is to live in style, and have tasted luxury far more than many, be they white or black of skin. But that was not of as much import to me as it had been – for the idea that one could have nothing and yet be more generous than a prince, struck me then and has never left me. All that I have seen of life these twenty years has led to this conclusion: Kindness is the greatest richness a life – any life – can afford. Kindness – the notion of kinship – should be a universal religion.

*

*How simple the philosophy of my youth seems to me now, Billy –
and yet how many times have I been forced to learn these lessons
over and over again . . .*

Following Tilly's written instructions, I found myself in an
alleyway off the Oxford Road that gave on to a small courtyard. The houses here were wooden and so close together
that they seemed to be holding each other up. There were
several small children milling about and at the sight of me
they gathered around, without a hostile word, merely –
unashamedly – staring at this alien who had appeared in
their midst. To their great credit, none of these – frankly
filthy – urchins thought to be rude in any way, but merely
watched me as I gazed by turns at the paper in my hands and
the hovels around me, trying to guess which dwelling 'in the
alleyway to the left' Tilly meant. A large, pink-faced woman
came out of one of these with a tin basin full of clothes, and
set it down on her small stoop. She entered her home again,
and emerged with a boiling cauldron of water which she
proceeded to pour over the linen in her tub. She sprinkled a
blue powder over the whole and with a clean wooden stick
began to stir the contents, all the while humming a tuneless
ditty. I approached her and she looked up at me, registering
me with mild surprise but, I was pleased to see, no hostility.

'Hello, laddy,' she called out. 'Lost your way from the
palace, have ya?'

She cackled at her own good-natured jest, and I could
see she had lost all but five of her front teeth. I smiled back,
tightly, and bowed, a little theatrically, playing up my rôle. She
smiled back and continued stirring her cauldron of washing.

'I seek a Mr and Mrs Grant. Are they to be found here?'

'The Grants? That's Barb you want. Down that alley there, Sir.'

I bowed again.

'Away out of it, you lot!' This she directed to the urchins, who scattered at the voice of command, like so many pigeons when a dog is chasing them. Whoever she was, she was the Authority here, and no mistake. I envied those children then, and ever do, for they were as free as any child ought to be. The only pity is their childhood is so short-lived, not just through disease and early death, but because they will have to work from the age of seven or so to earn the money to feed their little stomachs. Even on my first morning in London, I could see the privilege with which my life had been blessed up till now. I determined to be grateful for everything that followed in my journey; I had spent too long complaining about my condition without giving true consideration to those whose life was far below mine in comfort and luxury. The Cause may need to be expanded, I saw.

The alley narrowed towards the back of this courtyard and became darker the deeper one ventured into it. Despite the heat that was already beginning to be felt at seven o'clock, the air was cold and damp here. One suspected that it was nearly always so, as so little light penetrated this constricted space. Four doors confronted me. I took a chance on knocking on one of these, only to be met with silence. My luck with gaining entry to places was holding true to last night, and my aborted attempt to gain access to Montagu House in Blackheath. I was wondering whether I shouldn't try knocking on this door again, when the second door on my left opened and another woman with a large tub of washing came out of her home. This had to be Barb. Tilly had described her as tough, and she really looked the part. Huge arms, a short, stocky frame, and hair pulled back off her kindly – strong – features. She held the tub as if it weighed no more than an empty box, though it was piled high with clothes, and swung her free hand behind her to close the door with a slam so hard it shook the other three doors in this narrow passageway. She pulled up short when she saw me, and nearly dropped her tub in her haste to rush towards me. I don't think I have ever before or since been embraced with such vigour, or enveloped in such unconditional affection. She took my head in her hands and kissed my forehead, looking me directly in the eyes as if to instil the lesson she was about to give:

'For however long you need it, Charles, this is your home as much as any of my brats. More so, for you never knew your kin. But we're your family now. Do you hear me?'

I nodded. It was all I could do not to weep. But I had vowed that I would be grateful, and this unconditional welcome was not a cause for weeping.

I would do anything for this woman and this family. I always will be grateful to them for their ready acceptance of me.

Barb made a bed up before the feeble fire in their one room, and I slept soundly – dreaming of a life with Lizzie – until around three o'clock. When I awoke, Barb gave me a lump of bread and some warm stew. It was delicious and hearty. In turn, I shared the contents of my carpetbag with her. She refused to take any of my coins, however, and sweetly broke my heart anew with her generosity.

I met the rest of the family later that day. Herbert was a gentle man, quite short but powerfully built. He had rosy cheeks and a twinkle in his eye. He loved a drink, but was never rough or ill-disciplined. He had absorbed much of the Horse Guards' attitudes and bearing. If he had been of another class, I dare say he could have made a fine Guardsman. Meg was the only child who still lived here with her mother and father – now twelve, she had recently commenced an apprenticeship to a seamstress in Covent Garden.

I spent my time confined to the little alley; I had little stamina for much else. I felt safe and welcomed by the Grants, and I looked forward to the day when I could thank Tilly in person for her kindness and reckless generosity.

After a week, I felt I had spent enough time recovering my strength from the ordeal in the cellar and wanted to see London in all its glory – and my Lizzie.

Both Barb and Herbert were immoveable on my need to stay and recover my strength completely. London was no joke, they said, and my soft, provincial ways would be tested if I went out there half-starved and feeble. I couldn't fight them both. At last, following another whole week spent moping about the courtyard, I was allowed to accompany Herbert to work. Unfortunately, the head of the stables would not have a blackamoor 'spook the horses', as he said. Never mind, I thought, I had no love for the smell of manure all the livelong day. I rather enjoyed my walk that morning, back through the park along the long lane that separated Tyburn from May Fair.

I felt like a Londoner for the first time. Since I could not work with Herbert, I was confined to the courtyard once more, and the group of mothers became my social circle. However, helping the ladies with the washing proved bothersome, more for them than for me, as my hands were not used to working with such scalding hot water and I waited too long, they rightly observed, before I scrubbed the sheets with the wire brushes.

'That there water's colder than me Jack's feet of a winter's night, Milord!'

The ladies loved to cackle over that one on a regular basis. I felt a little foolish – but never cruelly used. They were right, too. I was not made for this kind of work. *Milord* was an apt pet name for me. I imagined that I might have better luck nearer the city, as an apprentice clerk, or working for a bookseller in Covent Garden. Now, that would be a dream come true. And so, after making myself look presentable in the Royal Fireworks costume, I walked out of the courtyard and on to the Oxford Road, turning east toward the City of London. Along the way, I caught glimpses of a capital that I was never told about by any who knew it well. It was the admixture of abject poverty and great riches, which coexisted in the most surprising ways, that astonished me most. As I reached the top of St Martin's Lane, I recalled that Lizzie's friend Maisie had said she worked at Maison Montmorency in Long Acre, Covent Garden. I made my way there, asking directions as I went. Most folks were friendly and directed me as requested, others merely ignored my enquiry, as if they had no truck with addressing Negroes, however well-spoken they may be. From these early encounters, I knew that I would have to make a vow to treat each man and woman with equanimity and not expect too much from any encounter. I hoped by this philosophy to be pleasantly surprised by a kind word or a helpful action. In this way, with varying degrees of success, I made my way to the French quarter of Covent Garden and stood outside the shop front of Maison Montmorency.

The only clientele seemed to be ladies of high class, and so I immediately felt intimidated. I resolved to wait until I spotted Maisie coming out of – or going into – the store. As luck would have it, opposite was a coffee house and, purchasing a small pot, I sat on a stool and waited for Maisie to appear. I must have sat for two hours before the wary looks of the serving-men forced me to rethink my strategy. The last thing I wanted was to be questioned about my motivations in sitting for so long and watching a shopfront like a hawk, looking up whenever a fine lady either entered or exited. I duly paid my three pennies for the two pots I had drunk and walked the streets for a while; never going far, for fear that Maisie would leave the shop when my eyes were removed from the entrance. I had never drunk coffee before. It was very . . . stimulating.

I was passing the suspicious serving-men for the fourth time when Maisie came out of the shop, securing her bonnet with a pin. I walked across the road briskly and caught her on the corner of Long Acre and St Martin's Lane. She jumped a little when I touched her arm, but recovered immediately, recognising me with a smile.

'Sancho. How are you? I haven't long before I need to be back. Stingy cow only gives me ten minutes to eat and take a breather. Come on.'

And, so saying, Maisie led me by the arm to Old Slaughter's Coffee House on St Martin's Lane. She was a regular, it seems, and not the sole young lady there. The ale we were served was for special clients, exclusively. There were painter's apprentices, clerks and the odd wagoner, here. Although, most of these, Maisie informed me, preferred to drink in the Seven Dials, because the Irish served the best small beer, if you could stand the stench of a nearby abattoir. She was a mine of information in one way or another, was Maisie, and so I pressed home the question which had been on my heart since I'd arrived in London.

'Oh, don't you know already, Charles? Lizzie's been married this fortnight or more, she has. Did she not ...? Oh, poor lad.'

She saw my look of sudden, stabbing grief and kindly poured the rest of her ale into my now empty glass. I looked about me at the London I had so loved just this morning, and felt a complete fool. I had thought that our love was true and I had convinced myself that Lizzie had, too. But how could it have been, if she could not only forget me in a month, but find another and marry him, too? Rage rose like a tiger in my breast, and it was all I could do not to roar and curse and dash my glass to the floor. Maisie, seeing my look, took my hands in hers.

'Now, you listen to me, Sancho. A girl like Lizzie has many a young man smiling and a-charming her all the livelong day. What was she to do when you disappeared for weeks without so much as a by-your-leave? And then there's her father, wanting her married with her kind. Not English, you see, just ... someone like her. She's a good girl, as I know you know. She'd never have disobeyed her father, Sancho, not in a month of Sundays. But you knows that, I'd bet. Don't ya, love?'

'I suppose I hoped that what we had was … true,' was all I could think to say. Maisie sat back in her chair and smiled sympathetically at me.

'True or not, she's a girl with mouths to help to feed. Now, what trade do you have? What were you to do with a wife, then a child, with no money and no apprenticeship? A lad of twenty? She had to make her way in life, Sancho. You see that, don't ya?'

And, in that moment, I truly did. I took a deep draught of the pungently ripe London air. It wasn't that I hated Lizzie; I understood her. She was no freer than I had been in Greenwich – than I was now, come to that. For, what prospects did I have? Maisie rose then, and giving me a soft kiss on the cheek, wished me luck and hurried back to her job, late already on my account. I sat there for a good thirty minutes before I had the energy to move again.

In my fug of disappointment and depression, I found myself wandering the streets surrounding nearby Drury Lane. Bad tidings kept me unwelcome company all that day, and in the subsequent weeks. Negroes were not permitted to work in the City by order of the Mayor. I was left with less hope than I had started with when I had run from Greenwich many weeks ago. This city was truly exhausting. I had few prospects and fewer friends who could help me.

One obvious avenue remained – and only pride and a sense that they would not have approved my running away from 'home' had prevented me seeking this way from the beginning of my life in the capital … The Montagus.

Book Two

1749–1752

*In which death comes to Sancho's world –
the Author's quest for freedom continues.*

For many reasons a man writes
much better than he lives.

DOCTOR SAMUEL JOHNSON
1709-1784

Chapter I

In which our Author seeks employment in London.

1775

Forty-six years old

Son ... I am, in truth, in no mood for writing and have not been these three weeks past. Your poor sister Lydia struggles on with her joint pains which echo her poor father's gouty extremities – though her whole frame seems to be wracked with that we cannot discern by enquiry to our medical friends – nor by any quackery known to this corner of the capital. It renders me most melancholy – added to which my best half – my Anne – your darling mother – suffers from fatigue and a lowness of spirit induced by fear for Lydia's welfare. This, the reason she weeps so ...

But to the task in hand:

'Know thy father.'

Looking over my past correspondence, I see the consciousness of my race has caused me at times in my life to lay aside a certain manly dignity in favour of smooth relations with my English brethren and sisters. By this, I mean I tend toward the self-deprecating – though Dame Sancho rightly accused me just

*yesterday of too often carrying this to the borders of self-loathing.
I defended myself – unworthily – and left her now a little more
exhausted than I found her – Foolish Sancho! Unkind friend!*

*I would have done better to have acknowledged her honest and
not unkindly appraisal – that I am a man too ready to be the
first to step aside into the gutter to allow one who thinks themselves my superior to pass upon the street – I am not the man to
barge unworthy office aside. I strive to maintain a sanguinity of
spirit. Like Francis Williams, I seek to live my life and not spend
it all in offence at the notions and actions of unthinking fools.
Were I to acknowledge each insult an ignorant, cruel and hateful
populace might care to throw my way, or the way of my darling
Sanchonettas, I would be as exhausted as Sisyphus – pushing the
boulder of Self-Defence – endlessly – up the steep hill of Human
Ignorance. I am a product of my upbringing it seems. Those
influences have rendered me . . . what? A man who does not
respect his shade? Is this so? I fear Anne has the measure of me.
I have frequently stated that more is to be gained by carrot than
stick – perhaps I have not the balance quite right. I stood before
her – at first repentant and apologetic – as she read over my rough
copy to dear Mr Browne. She took offence at my use of the word
'Blacky' – a name Mr Lincoln, a friend I sought employment
for from Mr Browne, himself finds amusing – to describe said
Lincoln. I wanted to advertise his suitability for a valet – and
one who knows his way around our equine creatures – as well
as his skill in hairdressing and his general deportment. I wrote:*

> *. . . a merry, chirping, white-toothed, clean, tight, and light,
> little fellow! – with a woolly pate – and face as dark as your
> humble; – Guinea-born, and French-bred – the sulky gloom of*

Africa dispelled by Gallic vivacity – and that softened again with English sedateness – a rare fellow!

She saw my use of the ironic in the epistolary art as unworthy of the dignity of my people. I then lost some patience with her and defended my choice of wording as appropriate, since I know Mr Browne to be a generous soul who knows all too well my proclivity for the humble phrase, but when Anne read the letter – sent some time ago, I might add – aloud – in the presence of your eldest sister, Mary Ann – well, I could see – of course, I could see what she meant to say. I will endeavour to mend my ways in this, and seek to avoid insulting any – least of all my African brothers and sisters . . . I should have known better, but old habits have a – habit – of sticking.

If time allows – and while I have my final pipe of the night – yes, another habit that has stuck since becoming a seller of tobacco – I will collate more of my diaries for you. For the grown man, Billy – or will you be William?

Poor, dear Lydia coughs and coughs, poor darling. I must go to her, for my Hen needs rest, too.

Lydia lies next to your mother and both sleep soundly. I will continue my task of setting out my life for you to peruse in my absence. The following – my final interview with John, Duke of Montagu – is taken from my diaries written shortly after the time the events took place. I will trust my younger voice to tell the story more accurately than I may at this remove.

1749

❖

Twenty years old

It should have come as no surprise to me to find that the two souls who deigned to give me directions knew – without hesitation – the precise location of the White Hall home of the Montagus, and were familiar with the name and person of Duke John himself, famed for his kindness. A man who had played such a crucial role in my early life and who was now my only hope of salvation in a city that had devoured much of my monies, and nearly all of my optimism. But before I even knew of the existence of the house on White Hall, I was to learn that finding Duke John would not be a straightforward affair. I could not ask every sundry soul where the Duke might be found. This city was not one in which to signal one's ignorance, for many would take advantage of one thought to be an outsider. Superadded to which, a black skin, a round paunch and clothes that bore the marks of infrequent laundering ... These were not the adornments of a man likely to be received with glee by any in London. Taverns – I found – were a good source of gossip. Though I found too that I could drink the night away without having discovered anything but the safest doorway in which to sleep off the intoxicating liquor for the night. Drury Lane was as far as I dared venture south, as I feared the Sisters might be in town for a brief visit, and they hardly ever ventured further north than Pall Mall.

A greater deterrent still was that a mere stone's throw from the taverns and inns lay the Strand and east of that, Fleet Street. Folks informed me that Fleet Street was home to at least one tavern frequented in the main by blacks, Indiamen, Arabs and all other earthly races. I felt my foreignness to these unmet people in a way I hardly ever felt with English folk. Europeans peopled my world, and I knew them. Knew what to expect of them in many given circumstances. Knew what they thought of me the moment I opened my mouth – and even before – as they regarded the colour of my skin and adjusted their behaviour accordingly. But my fear of those who looked like me – a fear that they would judge me – for not suffering? – had kept me from making any deep friendships with the black servants I had known since Duke John had rescued me in Blackheath Park. Rio Montagu was home in St Kitt's – sent back on his request, to be reunited with his people. Bonds of family are strong, it would appear, and I felt Rio fortunate to have such sentiments to drive his actions; I knew nothing of these ties in my life. Even Francis Williams was an alien to me, a black scholar now teaching children how to read and write in his school in Jamaica. Happy children! But all our conversations ended with disappointment for one or other of us on every occasion that I could recall. The Cause would have to wait until I knew for whom I fought, perhaps.

I longed at times to be invisible. For, even in a city as well-stocked with blacks from all points of the barbaric Atlantic slave routes as is London, I stood out for many reasons. My clothes were no better than those of the next black servant or mariner, but my deportment stood out as ... different. Dainty, somehow, despite my bulk. My frame had been unchanged by the limited fare served by dear Barb, but I became very lithe with all the walking I was doing.

My sojourn with Tilly's family had proved to be intolerable to me after a time, alas. I had not seen Tilly from the moment I escaped my mistresses. She stayed away, for fear the Sisters might ask her whether I had made any overtures of communication to her, and poor, honest Tilly was afraid that she might not play her part as convincingly as the skilful Peg Woffington at Drury Lane. So, she reasoned, if she did not return home, she would not have to lie. A state of affairs that was evidentially not designed to be sustained over any length of time. I will only say here that I could no longer bear to be the one who robbed the food from the mouths of Tilly's family. I hold Tilly's family in the dearest regard. They were simply not in a position to feed a man who could find no employment remunerative enough to repay them for the food he consumed. We all agreed, despite my initial protests to the contrary, that I needed to keep what monies I had for my uncertain future. We shed tears when I departed, but I comforted myself with the thought that they would soon be cheered by the extra lump of meat they might each get in their stew that night.

I had left there many days ago, intending to seek Duke John's aid in securing my future, and was now embarked on this quest across the dizzying assault on the senses that is our Capital. Doorways were my bed for many a night, if one of the lads I ran with had no floor to offer me, due to the strictures of their landlords. I strode through London, being increasingly noted for my incongruous tone of voice and my outlandish – to the natives – vocabulary. I began to detect in myself a kind of pride of difference, of exceptionality. A dangerous and intoxicating brew of aggression and flamboyance. I made friends for my wit and seeming sophistication, which was naught but shyness and ignorance thinly disguised as nonchalance. These friends were gamblers, prostitutes, thieves and vagrants, many of whom had been tars or gentlefolk's pets. When they reached the age of twelve or thirteen, many told me, their mistresses in particular suddenly took against their presence in the house – and out they were sent. Some of these were young Negro girls, who became easy prey for unscrupulous and lustful men. A girl could make a living in these streets – but her avenues of opportunity were narrow in the extreme. A wealthy patron was the holy grail: a man or woman who would guard them from the workhouse, and from the beds of men whose smell could never be washed away. A cheerier group – despite their lot – I have never had the pleasure to encounter before or since. I laughed my way through much of my remaining monies before a full moon had passed, however, and only thanks to a drunken carpenter who had temporarily attached himself to our little band of rogues and slatterns, did I learn that there was building work afoot at Montagu House in Bloomsbury. I thought

I might seek the Duke there, or enquire in what place he may be found.

Waking up that morning in the doorway of the very same inn where my knowledgeable woodsman had given me this crumb of information, illustrated all too viscerally the measure of how much alcohol had had to be imbibed to squeeze this nugget from the seam. I vomited. Then, wiping my spittle on the remaining clean portion of my once-fashionable frock coat – a costume that had degenerated from the image of Grace to being a suitable garment for the tragic protagonist in a later scene of Mr Hogarth's *A Rake's Progress* – I made my stumbling and bleary way to Montagu House, Bloomsbury.

The front doors weren't even secured and a mere leaning of my hand upon the pane permitted entry. If I could gain access to the Duke's home with such unmitigated ease, then who may not? These thoughts were swept away immediately when I gazed on the ruin before me – startled – at nothing as much as at the certain image of what this house had once been. The vast entrance hall was shrouded in a dusty darkness; the once-sumptuous velvet drapes now threadbare and moth-devoured, great gashes of light pouring through their tattered splendour. The sweep of the double staircase was all that remained of the grandeur of this place. The rope-thick cobwebs, dust, dead birds and the pervasive smell of decay were rendered all the more tragic for the contrast in my mind's eye. I would have had no idea of the geography of it or what this place was called – I remembered being here – I might have been eight – perhaps nine years old. A ball? Music, lighted tapers and candelabra glistening, the swirl of perfumed silk taffeta, the rustle of gowns, powdered wigs, ladies with their delicate shoulder-coverings fluffed into gossamer, gentlemen looking like so many Adonises – Adonii? – worship-worthy in their perfect features, deportment and youthful promise. Such as these I had longed to imitate – nay, more – to be. And I had become them in my heart that night.

When the mind's eye had left off dominating my other five senses, I realised that the dismal scene had some rather ominous musical accompaniment: viz., one hammer, one nail. It sounded like nothing short of a nail being driven into a coffin. At any other time, I might have thrilled at the atmosphere of this eerie place, but this ruin seemed to me to embody the state of Duke John himself in ways I could not articulate. What I imagined, or intuited, had me hurtling up the dusty staircase and hurrying around the corner to light upon the source of this macabre sound. I encountered a man in labouring garb, attempting to place slats of wood over one of the hallway windows. He glanced up, and through his bushy brows I detected a quizzical look. When he suddenly smiled, the admixture of his scraggy grey beard and brown – not entirely absent – teeth caused me to jump a little, though his intent had been to be polite. Recovering, I began:

'Good day, Sir. May I ask the whereabouts of His Grace, the Duke of Montagu?'

Naturally, this was not the question he was expecting to be asked by anyone, let alone a black whose look suggested anything but 'a Friend of the Duke's'. 'What?' was all he would offer; though the sound he made could well have been a mere involuntary groan of incomprehension.

I clarified: 'John, Duke of Montagu. My patron. My friend.

I've something of a need, you see, of help from His Grace. So, if you would do me the favour of telling me where he may be found?'

The look of incomprehension deepened, if anything.

I tried another tack: 'Are you alone here?'

'Ah,' he assented, I intuited, by the vertical inclination of his head.

'Good. So. The Duke?'

'Oh, His Grace? Ah. He ain't here. The other 'ouse. The one on White Hall. That's where you'll find the poor devil.'

I nodded my thanks as I backed away and, turning, fled the house. The square before me was silent, although it was now seven o'clock in the morning. It was as if the world were holding its breath, waiting for me to decide what to do next. Turning into High Holborn – and asking the first passer-by the way to White Hall – two words echoed through my mind. *Poor devil* . . . Why had he said that? Why had I run from there as though pursued by robbers?

A day of contrasts.

If it was meant to intimidate the casual visitor, the main hall of Montagu House, White Hall, was effective to the point of worship. A veritable cathedral, not to any deity, but to Style itself. Nerves were getting the better of me and I was irritated by everything, from the reluctance of the gatekeeper to let me pass, to the faces of strangers, who were servants that I had never met and who knew nothing of me. Like a poor, vain actor wanting fame and adulation despite having never performed for his audience, I looked for the bright light of recognition and found it nowhere. Then I saw that, standing very still at the top of the staircase, beside the habitually friendly, jolly and round chaplain, Mr Cutts Barton, Charles Manwell had appeared. The chaplain's unsmiling face expressed much – and I knew, more than any words could articulate, what I was facing. I looked down, mute. In order to gather my courage for a moment, I focused on my surroundings for the first time since entering the house. It wasn't that I had not noticed certain works or objects, it wasn't even that I was too ignorant to know what masterpieces I beheld – no – it was the fact that a man I had known for more than half my twenty years was not just capable of such breadth of taste, knowledge and style but was willing to amass such a vast and eclectic collection – monumental beyond belief. Silks, damasks, picture frames of gold leaf, chinoiserie, pots and urns, drop-glass chandeliers, and paintings by the great masters of this century and many others. He was a gourmand for life, and wanted not just to visit other worlds, but to live in the world of the *other*. Perhaps, I was one of many experiments in living life with the *other*. Francis Williams had certainly intimated something along those lines. What I had thought was love was in fact . . . a collector's curiosity, not much more than science. This instantly seemed a childish supposition, unworthy of the man I wanted to become: open, forgiving, fair and honest. I loved John. He loved me.

At last, I looked up.

The ever respectfully patient Charles gestured for me to ascend the staircase. Before I could reach the landing, however, Mr Barton stepped down towards me, embracing me like an uncle, and asked to be remembered to my *godfather*, as he put it. That there was still time to deliver the chaplain's message made me jump with an inappropriate jolt of joy, as if the greatest indulgence in the world had been offered to me. Charles – always so understanding – nodded his approval of my sudden haste and gestured to a door behind me, just ajar enough for me to see the sunlight streaming onto the coverlets of a large bed. I nodded my gratitude to the stalwart aide and swiftly crossed the hallway, after a cursory nod of appreciative thanks to Reverend Barton and, entering the room as quietly as I could, shut the door behind me.

Duke John lay so still in his bed that I was afraid I had misunderstood and that he was in fact deceased. A gentle exhalation of air from my former patron allowed me to breathe in turn. The early morning sunlight, streaming so lavishly through the window onto Duke John's face and coverlet, rendered everything in a silhouetted light that was hard to penetrate. I moved, softly, to the other side of the bed, regarding him all the way round. His skin had developed a translucence that reminded me of a new-born baby's flesh. The dark circles that had been so evident in the few months leading up to the frenzied – fraught – Royal Fireworks event – the event that had aged him more than any military campaign ever had – were absent – and the skin around his eyes had a freshness to it that was remarkably youthful. I decided there and then that I would like to die like this. With the sun in my face and on my body, the breath-freeing smell of lavender in the air, being visited by the ones who loved you the most. And then I was weeping into his neck; great, choking sobs heaved out of me, as my soul seemed to vomit up all hope and prospect of future life. Selfishly, I thought then most potently of the aid that Duke John's patronage would no longer afford me. I thought of how easy it would have been to have asked one of his publisher's circle to hire me as an apprentice. Where would I now source the shirts that he had given me, some hardly worn twice, or the breeches that his shrinking frame could no longer fill?

And then I stopped. Stopped crying – stopped breathing. I thought of how self-interested I had become. Despite my own admonition to value my life more and to see the suffering of others more, I had thought only of myself in these last few moments, with the dearest man in my life – the only *father* I had or would ever know – dying before me. I pulled away from him and found that his eyes were open and saw me very clearly, or so I thought. I sat on the edge of the bed and we gazed at each other in that way for some moments. Then Duke John smoothed out his coverlets, as he used to do to his waistcoat before greeting the first guests. I choked back a sob of loss, and gripping my hands together, attempted to be controlled. Duke John regarded me with the gentlest of looks, full of tenderness and understanding, as if everything I had thought since I came into this house – every anxiety I had at this coming separation – was known to him. He reached out his smooth hand, cool as he touched mine, and squeezed. It was at once tender and a little desperate. I looked to him enquiringly and he spoke in a tone so quiet that I found myself leaning my head towards him by the time he had finished talking.

'Neddy? My son, Neddy? You have returned. Older now, of course, for you were only two when we parted, dear Neddy. Dearest child ... Wait. No. That's not quite right, is it? Sancho. My dear Sancho. I feel I am in one of Mr Garrick's old comedies, when the doors are forever opening, and everyone seems to enter or exit, one after the other ... I hardly know who I am addressing ... But I would know you, my boy, in the dark and with no candlelight ... You are my flesh. Do you hear? My boy. My dear Edward ... And then a few years to the day, you came into my world. Like an angel. I'm proud of what you have become, Charles. Now ... I must needs rest.'

So saying, he leant back against his pillows and closed his eyes in the peaceful way that one who has completed their tasks for the day might lie back in their favourite armchair, satisfied with a good job done. He appeared to be smiling, and another choke of loss escaped my throat.

'Dear Charles, you came, at last.'

Duchess Mary sat in an incongruously lovely blue gown, in the only corner of the room where the shadows could hide her. It seemed she had fallen asleep as she kept vigil and had no doubt been awakened by my strange groan.

'Come kiss me, my dear ... and then you must leave us.'

Wiping my grubby sleeve over my damp eyes, I crossed to Her Grace, and kneeling before her, buried myself in her lap. I took in a deep draught of her faded perfume – lavender, but of a quality of freshness unknown to the awful Miss Abigail – emanating from the skirts of her deep-blue dress. She had never been motherly with me, but had always treated me as a young man. She had respected my right not to be coddled and babied from the very beginning, and would admonish Duke John if he ever presumed that I could not do a thing for reasons of age or education. Once, when Duchess Mary had asked me to fetch a turtle from Mr Brownlow the grocer, Duke John had tried to insist on accompanying me or at the least sending me with his aide, Charles Manwell. Duchess Mary would have none of it, and sent me out at nine years old to complete her commission. My sense of pride in carrying the creature – heavy as it was – safe to the door of Montagu House – had been immense. I had felt my competence was a skill; that I could organise my monies and the conversation with Mr Brownlow, that I could be given a task and execute it. This had been her gift to me in my youth. She had resisted treating me as a child from the very beginning.

Though I knew with a certainty that I could never return here and live the life of my dreams, self-preservation, I avow to my shame, rose afresh in my breast and I now pleaded my desperate cause with Duchess Mary. She remained silent throughout my litany of miseries and heartache; my story of incarceration and escape brought only a raising of her brows and a near-imperceptible widening of her eyes, but naught else. She appeared unmoved, truth be told. Gazing over at her love, peacefully asleep in the sun, she lost my presence for some time. It was with a slight jolt that she remembered I was kneeling, still, before her. The shawl around her still-pretty shoulders fell open a little at her sudden movement and the rarely exposed wrinkly skin of her neck could be seen just below her sharp but elegant chin. She had never seemed old to me until this moment, and I wondered if we lost half our life-force when our belovéd loses all of theirs.

'You must not tarry, Charles. His Grace would not want you to see him pass from this world. He charged me to instruct you – for he thought on you, kind soul, he did – even in his agony . . . We thank our Lord the draughts given by the doctor have soothed his pain and he sleeps more than wakes.

But soon, Charles, no medicine will help him. He did not want you to remember him that way. Depart this place and do as he required, hoped of you: live life to the full.'

'But I am not free to "live life to the full", Your Grace. I have not a paper about me that grants me freedom. Am I slave or free? I cannot say. To abandon me now, Your Grace, who is all goodness to me – to abandon me now, would see me doubtless pressed into service on the sea. I would not survive that, Your Grace; I am not built to toil in this way.'

'Desist, Sancho! You have an ingrate's air when you speak of your delicacy, when your fellow African brothers and sisters languish in a living hell in our West Indies.'

Shame came to sit upon my heart for the second time that day. How miserable I was, that in this hour of the Duchess's greatest grief, I would choose to petition for my own life – placing as secondary the fast-ebbing life of her husband – choosing to favour my speculative future fortunes for her present, agonising, imminent loss – this woman, who had loved me with a muted passion since I was seven years old. What of my fellow Africans, what of the Cause? Selfish, Sancho. Foolish, Sancho. I wept, anew, begging her forgiveness for my unworthy self-regard. After a few moments:

'Time, Sancho. It is time.'

I nodded in agreement. There was no succour to be found here. Not because the Duchess Mary was without sympathy, but because she needed me to do my utmost to succeed on my own, of my own volition. My heart, at once, expanded and contracted and desiccated at that moment. I had nothing to hope for here, and nothing to look for abroad. I had my freedom, but a freedom to do naught but starve, it seemed to me then. I wanted with every atom of my being to stay – safe, known, admired and loved in this house. However, I rose and simply bowed to Duchess Mary, who was already gazing over at His Grace, who in turn received my final bow to him with his eyes gently closed, and a faint smile on his lips. I left the room, glancing back at the scene in silhouette. It is the final image I have of my great patron-father, and I will never erase it from my mind's eye.

As I wandered, motiveless, into the main hall, my eyes lighted upon two beautifully rendered, full length statues: one of Minerva and the other of Leda and the Swan. These were set in alcoves opposite the entrance door – and more interestingly, above and between the two protagonists, an owl, stuffed so generously that it seemed well-content still with its last meal. Above me, Duke John was breathing his last and soon he would be as this owl, once full of blood and motion and now simply an object – rendered inert for the lack of that Promethean spark that must be in all living creatures if we are to breathe and move and have being. How flimsy a thing is life? How insubstantial the thread that holds us here? How easily are the moorings loosened of who we are – at least, who we thought ourselves to be? For Duke John had been breathing and seeing and speaking to me, but he had not been present. His lucidity had been temporary, his grip on temporal concerns so very weak, that he had hardly known who was stood before him.

How strange, to die in a state of such fracture of the soul that you no longer felt attached to life, when merely weeks ago you could think of nothing else but the dreadful robbery that was imminently to take place. We make no bargain with Death; it simply demands its due and offers neither discount on the cost nor refund for the good you have done. The bargain is all Death's, and there are no returns.

> ... but once put out thy light ...
> I know not where is that Promethean heat
> That can thy light relume ...

Cutts Barton had been by my side for some time, I believe, before I became aware of his presence adding to that of Leda and Minerva before me. His beady blue eyes were red with tears shed – it was over – and I felt for him so much gratitude for merely standing with me – facing the mythological beauties and that extraordinarily content owl – resisting the urge to placate my nascent grief with platitudes of a religious nature: *He's at peace, now. He's gone to a better abode. The Lord has taken an angel to himself.* The litany of empty words that accompany our fear of death have lost any power – if ever they possessed it – to soothe or comfort the grieving. It is simply a childish way of skirting the truth: we are born alone, and we die alone, trapped in our own version of purgatory or hell, before the heavenly release from pain. None can travel with the pilgrim there, and if we choose to follow, voluntarily giving up our gift of life, we are condemned, our theologians tell us, to an afterlife of naught but agonies. We ought to figure to ourselves the injustice of such a punishment, on top of the already straitened circumstances that doubtless led to this deadly course: *felo de se*; self-slaughter. Divine justice? Or cruelty heaped on cruelty? *Qui sais, sauf Dieu?*

'Sancho. If ever you need a friend to talk to or a place of shelter, please—'

'Oh, Your Grace – your solicitousness is a boon to me – an undeserved boon – but all is well. I am not without prospects or employment – fear not – I will make His Grace proud of me – you will soon see . . .'

'But if ever you need shelter . . .'

I did not appreciate Reverend Barton's look of sympathy, then, for it felt to me that he lacked faith in my ability to fulfil this promise made. My irritation rose, again, in my breast, and bowing abruptly to the chaplain, I left Montagu House with an attempted air of stoic resolve. A resolve that melted the moment I had closed the door behind me and leant back against it, suddenly exhausted. Where would I begin? Who could I turn to now?

A large, tall white gentleman and a skinny black boy were making their way down the path towards Montagu House. The man seemed agitated and physically eccentric – his arms flailing arrhythmically at random angles – talking – softly barking – incessantly to the lad, who appeared a sullen, handsome boy of ten or so years, and who kept trying to break away from the man – who had to leap onto him and push him forward when he did grasp him – which was by no means a given success as the lively lad attempted his escapes at irregular intervals. The man's scarred face added to the macabre and darkly comic effect of the pair. It was quite the show. They took a fair few minutes to get within hearing distance and so I waited and watched, glad of the temporary respite from the gloomy limbo I had entered. The odd couple were far enough away for me to observe without being observed. The most striking thing about them was how like a father and son they looked, despite the difference in their hues. The boy was not under any duress, it appeared, and the man was not violent, just a little out of control of his limbs, and – though he barked short, incomprehensible phrases – he did not appear angry, no matter the torrent of words that poured from him in a series of twitches and tics.

It was as the man shot up a random hand to the sky and bobbed his head numerous times while doing it – loosening further his already precariously balanced wig – that I guessed at last who this must be. I had had Dr Samuel Johnson described to me, and judging by this man's deportment, his food-stained – frankly soiled – clothes askew – the shaking of his head – I deduced it was he. Eyeing him now, I fancied that the good doctor lived in a world where words swam around his body, drenching him – his very eyes blinded by a storm of clauses, codas, information, definitions and classical allusions – he must never be alone. How wonderful. How terrifying?

Dr Johnson pulled up short on seeing me. 'Ah. Ah. You. You must be the . . . The lad. Ah. Ignatio? Ignatius!'

I nodded. He was pleased with himself for one moment, I could see; pleased that his memory was so reliable. An involuntary bark of a laugh burst from him and I jumped a little. Pushing his young charge forward, clumsily, Dr Johnson proudly presented: 'This. This. Boy!'

This last was not addressed to anyone in particular, I believe, it was merely what he was thinking. The child stepped forward shyly and offered me a bow. It was executed to perfection, but when he looked up, he merely glanced at me then seemed to lose all interest, instantly, and gazed across the gardens as if he were no longer with us. They made a very unusual family indeed, for this was no servant, I could tell – no – this lad behaved as if he were the true-born son of the doctor. I felt a pang of jealousy at his nonchalant privilege. The luxury of being sullen is not a safe indulgence for any black, but seeing this boy – whose name Johnson had completely failed to tell me – disregarding his luck stirred up that self-pitying spirit that had plagued me in Duke John's room an hour before. I looked upon this child as I suppose Duchess Mary had looked on me when I pronounced my unsuitability for a life of toil on board a ship. Did this lad reflect back to me the attitudes others saw in me? Was this why I had no black friends to speak of, in fact? Was I as complacent of my position as this boy? I was irritated with everything, most of all myself.

'You are seven years of age, Frank, it's time you did more than bow, is it not?'

Seven, I thought, raising my eyebrows a little. Tall lad, this Frank. Seeing my look, the tightly smiling doctor nodded, profusely. I immediately lowered my expectations of the lad. He was probably hungry; I knew I always was at that age. I nodded my encouragement to the boy, who stepped forward, and with the accent of the blacks in our West Indies, began: 'Good day, Sir.' Then, looking me up and down and with hardly a hesitation: 'You are very fat!'

'Young scoundrel—'

Dr Johnson pronounced this with a futile leap after the fleeing youth, who scampered, nimbly, around the corner of the house. The doctor began racing after him, calling over his shoulders to me, thoughtfully: 'Your patron has great affection for you, lad. He has charged me to see you settled ...' This, with a look about him so lost and full of worry that I almost laughed. Days gone by with Duke John ... Laughing with John ... A man who seemed so revered and important outside of his home, but so childish and playfully energetic inside – as if the world kept him buttoned up for use, but home was where he really slipped the fetters and let fly his imagination.

Johnson stopped to catch his breath halfway around the corner of the house; for a moment pausing his pursuit of the boy, Frank; his only movement as he gazed up at the Duke's bedroom window, a gentle, absentminded scratching of his posterior. I smiled, then. Duke John would have smiled, too, but, alas ...

For a moment, Johnson was still, reading me ... the story was clear. Duke John had gone and he had missed his last interview. A powerful look of grief passed so swiftly across Dr Johnson's countenance that I caught my breath. Recovering, but with a face reddened with the effort, Dr Johnson smiled for what seemed like an age. Then:

'Come to the Ivy Lane Club, tonight? Ask your way, 'tis known – nay, notorious ...' This last said shamefacedly. 'You must be helped if we may.'

On enquiring – politely – who he meant by *we*, fearing he meant to engage the nonchalant Frank in my service, I was relieved and intrigued to hear him say – bark:

'Ah, yes. Confusion. Frank Barber! He's not mine, you see. The Colonel's, that is to say, the Doctor's, his son – left the boy in my charge – busy today, so – I was left in care – charge! – though forgot this one – sad – errand stood in my way – day ... '

He looked lost for a few moments. I started, when he suddenly and multi-tonally stated the following: 'No! Ivy Lane! Yes! Friends. A club! Actors, writers of all stamps, a dauber or two, toilers and wastrels in turn, all. The odd Whig may be found lurking in a snug. Frank's guardian, Dr Bathurst ... Do come – Boy!'

He had turned and run away before I had time to recover from jumping, yet again, at his sudden ejaculation – *Boy!* – directed, scattergun, toward his vanished charge. I took one last look at the house and, on walking away, was aware that I was likely being watched by Cutts Barton. Duke John lay dead and I would never see him again. The sky, previously a whitewashed blue but brightly sunny, had filled now with high clouds whose density promised showers later that day. The wheel of my life had come full circle, yet again, and I found myself without a mode of escape. An anger rose that threatened venting – the injustice of Death – taking a saint like John Montagu and leaving the earth peopled with so many devils like Sill and his ilk. Choking back the cry of rage that boiled so fiercely in my breast that it hurt my throat, I resolved to think of myself alone, for who else would save me? Dr Johnson? Even now, as I glanced back over my shoulder, he was disappearing once again into a hedge on the far side of the Montagu property, calling on the boy all the while.

Still ... When one's hopes are in people one has never met, one develops a kind of blind faith. Dr Johnson's unknown benefactors appeared in my mind's eye like so many angels, rallying to the cause of the *godson* of a dead duke. I strode away from Montagu House, from the grieving Duchess and the late Duke ... I walked away with such purpose that any who may have seen this young man striding this path would have thought him confident of success in his fortunes – as if all life lay before him.

But to observe what befell your father next, dear Billy, is to witness the fall of man in miniature.

Chapter II

*In which our Author visits the Ivy
Lane Club – Our hero purchases a
pistol – The unwelcome return of
Jonathan Sill, slave-catcher.*

1749

Twenty years old

The Ivy Lane Club – I soon discovered – was a tavern, the King's Head, where the city's leading luminaries would gather on a Tuesday night to discuss matters of an intellectual, political and artistic nature. The tavern was off Paternoster Row in the City – a stone's throw from Cheapside, which, even at eight o'clock in the evening, was full of bustle and commerce. Turning west off Cheapside and on to Paternoster Row itself, I saw many servants of the gentry laden with goods for their masters and mistresses. In the corner of every alleyway, beggars and thieves lurked, hoping to find a generous shopper or an inattentive one. Ivy Lane, though close to so much activity, was a much quieter street that rose slightly to the south and west. St Paul's dome could be seen from here, its presence comforting and solid. Outside the King's Head tavern many men, some in their labourer's smocks, were drinking on various benches. The intermingling of working man, merchant and man-of-letters was reassuring to me, as I would not stand out in a crowd of so many differing sorts.

Entering the establishment, I saw that far from a chaotic scene of raucous men released from their marital or paternal duties, it was a picture of calm. Men gathered in small groups, talking quietly – some conducting business while sending the post-boys out to fetch information and deliver messages. I surveyed the room in earnest to seek out the doctor and his companions. A dense fog of tobacco smoke curled and twisted gracefully around the figures of the men as their pipes sent clouds of blue-grey billowing over each other's heads. I felt a sudden sense of dullness and lethargy overcome me; I was almost nauseous with hunger. It was then that I noticed the aroma of roasting meat and baking potatoes, and I longed to sit – as one couple were doing in the window alcove – and devour several large slabs of seasoned flesh – I fancied I might not stop until I had exploded with feasting. Passing further into the tavern, I noticed curtained booths running the length of the building. Not wishing to disturb a party of strangers, I hesitated before the first of these snugs and strained to listen. I could hear no noise emanating from behind the curtain, so I pulled it aside, gently, revealing a gentleman fast asleep with a pint of ale resting on his corpulent belly as it rose and fell in a regular rhythm. I almost reached out to adjust the tottering vessel so as to prevent its almost certain spillage, when I was tugged out of the snug – not roughly, but with haste – by my arm. Standing before me was one of the jolliest men I had ever seen. The landlord, no doubt. He seemed a creature from the pen of Jonathan Swift. Just under five feet tall, with a round body that seemed to have no need for a neck; he appeared to be all of a piece. His face was a riot of red; his mottled skin bearing the deep scars of a childhood pox. Despite this, his was an amiable aspect, as much friend as host, and he seemed to have no hesitation in treating me with a fair amount of equanimity. He gave the impression of being a friend to all who frequented his establishment.

'Young man, what may I assist you in? Seek you food or a room for the night? What's your pleasure?'

'If it please you, Sir, I seek a Dr Samuel Johnson.'

'Ah, the good Dr Dictionary, is it? Doctor of Words. I tell you, lad, I'll not be calling on him for so much as a splinter in me arse.'

And leading me deeper into the tavern, he greeted all we passed, unceremoniously drawing back the curtain of the last booth from the end. I stood before five men, only one of whom was familiar to me: the good doctor. To my shame, I hardly registered the other members of Johnson's circle, as my eyes, indeed all my senses, were locked on to the objects of desire laid out so generously on the table before this group. There was a still-steaming pot of what looked very much like mutton stew, something depleted, sitting – tantalisingly – in the centre. Four baked potatoes lay in another pewter dish, beside the leftovers of a large bowl of cabbages and onion. Flagons of ale and the remnants of a jug of lemonade cluttered the table still further, as the whole ensemble fought for space with newspapers, pamphlets, books and other writings strewn over the table's surface. I marvelled at how close these papers were to being soiled by the supper that the five men had devastated before I arrived.

'*Pauca verba*, gentleman, "use few words", for we can see

where this young man's needs may be met – easily and immediately – he barely acknowledges our presence, so desperately
he hankers after sustenance. Come, Ignatius, come.'

So saying, Dr Johnson rose, and taking me by the shoulders,
drew me down to the bench and sat beside me. 'Brave Host,
we would have more ale for the gentlemen, and my young
companion here will need a pot, too. Go, brave Horseman,
use thy shanks!' The expression of which sentiment caused
the assembled company to roar a loud – encouraging –
'Huzzah!' at the little man, who grinned like a child and
seemed to almost scamper away with a glee that many a
servant in a great house could do well to note and imitate.

Bowing politely, I settled in beside the good doctor – he
thrust an empty plate before me and smilingly offered me a
ladle for the steaming pot of mutton broth that I had gazed
at so longingly the moment these club-men had been revealed
by Mr Horseman, the landlord. In truth, I was simply grateful
to be in this company and would gladly have been ignored by
them in order that I might partake of their wisdom while I—

And now comes my confession.

After the first flagon of ale, my memory becomes ...
fragmentary. I awoke in a doorway of a Smithfield baker's to
the torturous smell of freshly risen dough. My mouth had
all the flavours I had ever tasted dancing within it – I knew
my breath to be a lethal admixture of unpleasant odours. I
wanted to vomit, but my stomach seemed solid, as compact as
a full barrel. I thought for a moment that I had near doubled
in girth overnight, but then began to doubt that the events at
the tavern had been a mere few hours ago. Moments came to
me ... I remembered David Garrick had been there, but I had

no picture of him in my mind's eye. Like a familiar-unfamiliar face in a dream, nothing of the detail of the man would stick. I remembered a similar thing being said by the man who had come from his nap in the next booth – Mr William Hogarth, a large bear of a man, with a thick Smithfield's accent and almost as brusque a manner as Dr Johnson. His waistcoat of toughest worsted – though the weather was muggy – had been stained with the ale that had doubtless cascaded down him as he rose from his sleep in the snug. He had claimed that both he and Thomas (Gainsborough?) were finding it deuced hard to *capture* Davey, as his face never stood still for a moment's respite from its fidgets ...

There had been the moment when we had all marched like a troupe of drunken elephants down the Strand and into Fleet Street, where we visited Dr Johnson's home. I do not recall how we got there, just that I found myself there and surmised that I had not been transported there like some figure from the Old Testament. The boy, Frank Barber, was there, and a Mrs Williams, who was blind, poor thing. Mr Samuel Foote, the playwright, and other figures whose names I cannot now recall ... Garrick – without a face – sat with one leg over the armchair, while Hogarth leant precariously out of the window to smoke his pipe. Later, I recall being taken in a bearlike grip around the shoulders by Mr Hogarth and marched to his old haunts in Smithfield – my negligent benefactors, long forgetting Duke John's admonition and charge to look after my welfare. Though I could have tried to resist Mr Hogarth, I had not the wherewithal to know where I was or what was my very purpose in life. I was therefore content to be led wherever I was led. In this case, to a gambling den near the

Fleet Prison. They were playing Ombre, a fiendishly tricky card-counting game, similar but possibly more convoluted in its rules to our English Whist. How I followed the game, I cannot tell, but I achieved the three hands I played with nine trump-hands won, before passing out once again, only to regain consciousness as I disgorged the contents of my hastily consumed supper into the Fleet ditch. My next recollections are, if anything, even more vague. A girl. Flesh. More ale, a flash of thigh . . . Darkness . . .

And then, there I was, sitting upon the pavement outside a baker's store near Poultry – wondering how I happened there. I rose with all the control of a leaf in a steady breeze: swaying, subject to every gust of wind. I steadied myself on the building's façade and tried to collect myself. The early morning activities of London had begun, and I took myself into a nearby alleyway off the main street and, after passing water, found a corner with a few rags bundled in a heap. Several empty barrels were beside this bundle and I crawled behind them and lay down, believing myself well hidden by doing so. It was as I began to drift into my second sleep of the day that a shadow loomed over me. It was the smell of this figure that struck my senses first. An animal smell, a musk that was unmistakeably male and familiar, it elicited in me an instant sense of danger, and, just as the first time that I had caught this scent, fear froze my limbs and my blood ran cold and thick. Jonathan Sill. With my body half buried behind the barrels and the rest of me half hidden in the bundle of rags – warm rags, I now noticed, breathing rags – I imitated the opossum – lying as still as a dead thing in hopes that I would be considered carrion and not fresh meat, if I was noticed at all.

Sill kicked gently, at first, at the rags beside me. They stirred – to my amazed horror – and out of this bundle rose the bald, dark brown head of a man whose life was etched on his face. I could not tell his original shade, but he struck me as an Indiaman – a man of the east, at least – who may have been as young as forty or as old as sixty. His watery eyes were crusted with sleep and some sort of liquid had oozed out of the one ear that I could see. Sill's boot kicked harder still against the rags, but the man simply gave a half-hearted groan then rolled over and slept anew. Sill walked on after some moments, not noticing me. As he walked down the alleyway, I dared to raise my head to follow his progress.

Jonathan Sill, powerful as ever, the years since our first encounter making no mark on either his stature or his aura of immense, dangerous energy. The only new addition I could include in his description was a deep, still-livid scar across his forehead – a scar made by the flask I had cracked against it weeks – or was it months? – before. He and his trusty accomplice walked purposefully down this row of sleeping figures, and one poor white soul – groaning his complaints all the way to the bottom of the alleyway – was taken by the pair of thief-takers-cum-slave-catchers. Men who ply this trade care not if their prey be white or black, as long as there be payment for their carcasses at the end of the chase.

Fear sobered me rapidly and I determined to get away from this spot as soon as I felt the coast was clear. The fact that I had come so close to my Nemesis, and he to me – and that he hadn't seen me – seemed miraculous. I had had a lucky escape. How long would my luck last on these streets? More urgently, where were my friends? What had happened after the game of Ombre? Had Hogarth abandoned me – or had I lost him in my drunken stupor? Thoughts swirled, but none were helpful. Leaving the relative safety of the alleyway, I set off with my carpetbag – amazingly I still had it! – set off for who knows where – just far from the river and the possibility of meeting Jonathan Sill and his Giant Boy. I walked all that day as far north as my tired legs would carry me, some way beyond the Mary le Bone area. The city was not safe for me. I had lost the protection of Johnson and Hogarth; I did not know where Garrick – or any of the other men at the strange wake held for Duke John – lived. I could not petition them for aid a second time, in any case, naturally. I had let slip the only chance I had at safety, and a secure future.

I found a spot along the road north to Hampstead Village and slept in a small grove of woods, far enough away from the road to lie undetected while I tried to recover my senses and plan my next move. The lonely hoot of an owl awakened me. I stretched my stiffened frame and felt a kind of damp sluggishness wash over me. Hunger, my constant companion lately, began to knock at the door of my stomach, and I felt the emptiness of having not eaten for some time. I could not leave London, for what use would it be to flee the metropolis? Would I not stand out more sharply in the villages above Camden Fields with my black skin and my – until now – overfed body? My girth would not make it easy for me to beg, and I had never tried to. The intimation that I was *remarkably well-fed for an African* was never far from most people's lips. I did not present a figure of destitution, but one of gross indulgence. Besides which, how could I work without my papers or a decent set of clothes to impress by? I sat at the side of the road, incautious with despair and lethargy. Looking through the remaining contents of my carpetbag, I found that my monies were not all gone. A guinea remained and – in the pocket of my filthy waistcoat – a few coins that I did not recall seeing before – my winnings from the game of Ombre, no doubt, that the honest Mr Hogarth must have placed about my person. I thought of Sill and how precarious my situation was. Sill wasn't the only bounty-hunter that operated in London. He may have known me from personal encounters, but the others would hunt me for my skin and the fact that I clearly belonged to no one who might protect me from re-enslavement or the press.

Walking back into London, I noticed for the first time the numerous advertisements on buildings and on every corner, it appeared to me. Two such struck me, reading:

Run away from his Master on Monday last,
   A Negro Black, squat Fellow, about seventeen Years old, and five-Foot-high, can shave, and dress a Wig very well, and answers to the Name of London.

The next read:

These are to give Notice, that on the 4th of April, run away a lusty young Black, about 20 Years of Age. He is bandy legged, having a full Lip. If any one can give Notice of him at the Carolina Coffee-House, in Burchin-Lane, or bring him on board the Charles Galley, lying against the Hermitage-stairs shall have a Guinea Reward and Charges.

This man could well have been me, by his description. A Guinea reward ...

Another read:

A BLACK SLAVE run away.

On the eleventh current there run away from the house of Colonel Munro of Novar, in Ross-shire, A BLACK SLAVE, a native of the East Indies, called CAESAR. He is about 25 or 26 years of age, about five feet four or five inches high, has long black hair, and was bred a Cook. Whoever secures the said Slave, within any of his Majesty's gaols in Great Britain, upon notice given to Colonel Munro, by Dingwall; or to John Fraser, Writer to the Signet at Edinburgh, shall receive FIVE GUINEAS REWARD. It is hoped Masters of ships, and others will be careful not to secrete or carry off the said Slave ...

It appeared from these ungrammatical advertisements that the owners themselves knew how easily a black – any black – might be sold into slavery in London. My eyes had been opened in the last few months to the abject defencelessness of all blacks. I knew myself to be no better protected than the young man I had seen long ago, when I had encountered him in Greenwich. I walked with purpose back to the city, but I would not walk back in without protection. I would arm myself and seek to take charge of my own destiny. If Jonathan Sill should attempt my abduction again, I would have an answer – either for his life – or my own. I had heard tell that pistols could be bought for a few shillings in Seven Dials near Covent Garden. I duly turned in that direction, feeling for the first time in many a day that I might have a hand in my own destiny, at last.

Pierre Blanchard had a mop of sleek black hair falling sluggishly over his face, with the remainder tied back loosely with a greasy ribbon. His eyes were hard to discern beneath his beetle-brows, which shielded the world from his gaze and might have rendered him inscrutable, if not for the expressiveness of his speech. It was as if he had swallowed a small handful of pebbles and lodged them at the back of his throat. They seemed to rattle and jostle musically in the back of his mouth and put me in mind of a carrion crow, if one such had the gift of speech.

'You give me what you have, I give you what you can afford, fair?' he rattled.

It seemed so to me, and I nodded. I calculated how much I could spare for this arm while Mr Blanchard disappeared behind the curtain behind him. I stood gazing about me in his shop, though that term is to be applied very loosely. It was, in fact, the kitchen to a small hovel on the outskirts of Seven Dials, beside the little-sought corner of the street where the abattoir stood, its aroma the only scent for many yards around. Pierre Blanchard reappeared, carrying four pistols on a wooden tray as I might have once served sherry to my Ladies in their drawing room after supper.

'Five. Three an' a 'alf. Four, that one. This, one pound.'

Much of my money would be gone if I spent as much as a pound on the instrument, but what choice did I truly have?

'You'll be needin' a few shots to go into that, *mon ami*.'

I was caught in his trap, as the lead shots for this gun were almost as costly as the arm itself. I purchased two, with powder, asking him to load it for me with a single shot. His look of affable, self-satisfied charm was altered in an instant, as he carefully loaded the pistol, ramming the shot to the back of the short barrel with the rod attached to the instrument's side. As he slid the ramrod back into place, I could sense that he knew the hierarchy of our relationship would change the moment he handed me the pistol. I held the power of life and death from that moment, and he had probably been robbed before at this very point in the transaction. I turned the pistol in my hand, more calmly than I felt. He offered me an oilcloth to wrap it in, and paying him, I placed the powder and the second shot in my carpetbag, hoping I would never need to use it either in anger or in the defence of my life.

A full two weeks I wandered the streets of London. My garments, getting cleaned every once-in-a-never, began to smell even to my accustomed nose. Sleeping in doorways was painful enough, but the privation of one meal a day was almost too much. If I could somehow multiply my remaining twelve shillings – like Jack in the fairy-tale and his magic beans – I should be able to buy the garments I needed to present myself before a prospective employer. The streets were becoming less safe for me as my figure became customary to the locals. I was known in a way that did not suit my dignity. A wanderer – a shilling-a-day man on a market stall, if he can get such a job – otherwise, simply a wanderer. How far had I still to fall, I wondered? Time passed without meeting with any fortune in my search for regular employment. I was venturing further south and east by the day, and towards the end of a fortnight, found myself casting stones into the Thames, just below the London Bridge. The setting sun played on the discharge of factories in the east, belching their noxious effluvia over the dwellings nearby, giving an impression of a great, sulphurous fire in the midst of smoke. I was reminded of Hamlet's lament to Horatio –

> And my imaginations are as foul
> As Vulcan's stithy . . .

– evoking the image of the god of fire's reeking forge. I thought of Mr Buckhurst . . . Lizzie . . . wondering what she would make of my sorry state, now. I found a penny as I walked back, lethargically, to the embankment; signalling a change of fortune, conceivably.

My inattention would have had me in hot water once again, if I had not heard the cry of a boatman on the water to his companions on shore to 'Hold fast!' – doubtless fearing his barge might be carried downstream on the strong evening tide. It was as I turned to see this roarer that my eyes were drawn to the figures of two men who strode along the embankment with great purpose. Jonathan Sill and his boy would need no introduction to any of the men who worked along this stretch of London's liquid artery. The pair greeted every other man, it seemed, and appeared respected in this part of town. Perhaps the work of clearing these areas of unwanted aliens and shipping them for use in the colonies or on board one of His Majesty's merchant vessels was seen as an act of public service by these hard-working men – fearful too, mayhap, that one of these aliens might take the work that their own hands were keen to perform. Whatever his fame, Sill's notoriety was a helpful distraction for me as I walked away from the river and headed north across London Bridge, glancing nervously down all the while to see that Sill was still engaged in conversation with his shore-men acquaintances. As I looked down for the tenth time or so, the boy looked my way. I turned away – too swiftly – hoping that he might not have spotted his old prey. But, as I turned again, looking over my shoulder and now quickening my already brisk pace, I saw the giant boy pull at Sill's sleeve and point in my direction. They did not move. Not even when I began – instantly – to set off at a waddling trot. They merely stared at me, as if no matter how far I ran, I should come full circle to them again, and this time, I would have no peer of the realm to save me from the slave ship and the iron shackles.

I felt as though I were choking with the smells of London, the weight of my multiplying concerns and the fact that I had now seen Jonathan Sill twice – within a fortnight. The trail was warm indeed and I could sense the Beast, Sill, in every alleyway and on every corner of every bend of every street.

Easy money was my only true option when all was said and done. Gambling was the easiest monies that I knew how to obtain, and I had been informed that in Seven Dials there was an establishment that catered for the tastes of those wishing to stake all on one roll of the dice. I stopped – momentarily – knowing that I was without a choice, lamenting – as a gentle rain gathered momentum with an urgency that had me pulling forward my already sweat-dampened collar – that my life had come to this . . . I reached the darkened door and knocked

in the prescribed sequence. A bolt – a creak – a waft of thick
tobacco smoke and something else – opium? – no, more pungently sweet – and the rise of voices within. A figure in the
shadows held out a hand and I pressed a penny into it, whereupon the door was opened fully. I stepped inside and found
my gatekeeper gone and myself alone in a dingy corridor that
forced even one as diminutive as me to stoop. I ventured
further down the black tunnel until I could discern the faint
glow of a light beneath a door towards the end of this unfeasibly long corridor. The warm, stuffy room beyond was nothing
to wax lyrical about. It held no allure of the strange and illicit,
even. It was as a barn in an old country setting might look –
clearly a horses' stables, from the time when this hostelry had
stood in fields above the Fleet Ditch – and smelt precisely of
all the odours of all the men in this room and every horse
who had ever been given their provender in its long history.
Every one of the fifteen or so men were of around the same
age – fifty and upward – and each held a bottle of some sort
of liquor in their hands. Some smoked pipes – most smoked
what looked like leaves of tobacco, simply rolled into small
faggots which they lit and drew in the smoke from at regular
intervals. The smell was not unpleasant – in fact, may have
been the most pleasant thing about the atmosphere of a room
that held its breath in concentration on the main event: the
game. The gamblers were a mixed bag of nationalities. The
Irishmen – by far the largest contingent, from their whispered
accents – were covered in dirt, soot and splotches of redness
from working exposed to the sun all day; big men – men who
hoiked and hoofed things – large things. Three Arabs, who
looked like brothers, stood to one side of the room – bottles

in hand – from which they never drank, as far as I noticed. An African or West Indian black of lighter shade than most I had seen, gave all his attention – even while puffing on his long, ivory pipe – to the action before us. In the centre of this room, four men sat on wooden chairs that creaked every now and then as each man played his hand. Two of these appeared to be Jewish men from the eastern portion of Europe, perhaps even as far as Russia, since they spoke no English – or any European language known to any there. A serving lad was having the devil of a time trying to ascertain their desired beverage. In the end, the boy simply plonked two bottles of the mysterious liquid before them both – they sniffed its contents – took a tentative sip – and pronounced, '*Da,*' as they drank their fill and handed the lad some coins.

As the game commenced, I saw that it was no game of card-counting or suit-following, and was not in the least complex – though – granted – it would surely test where one's favour stood with the Gods of Chance – and this was my last chance, too.

When one is forlorn and wrapped in troubles, one hardly knows what image one is projecting to the world – one hardly cares. While we feel our inner sadness most profoundly, others may notice melancholy, but cannot know the depth of suffering. So it is with the public image, Billy. We can harbour a wretchedness that is not mirrored in how the world perceives us. To imagine my effect as I stood there, pathetically, staring like a mad dog at a bone – or as I had at Dr Johnson's feast – the last good feeding I had had – well, I must have presented a most forlorn figure to my gambling rivals – of this I have no doubt – and I needs must attempt to supply you with an inventory of your father as he sees himself from this vantage point. My whole frame appeared stooped and gravely malnourished. The folds of fat that were beginning to wrinkle on my cheeks bespoke the rapidity with which the stock of ballast I had carried since birth was leaving me. I no longer felt hungry, as hunger was a permanent state. Suffice to say, my condition at that time would have been quite shocking to any who had known me in my days with the Greenwich Coven – and it would have taken a blind man without a sense of smell to miss the blatant fact that I had been drinking heavily for several days. My only possessions now were the remaining contents of my treasure box and – in my frock coat pocket – the pistol wrapped in oilcloth.

A stocky, dark-skinned black man of about forty approached me with a friendly smile. In contrast to Mr Horseman, this smile was fixed to a face whose eyes had not agreed to find anything amusing. Eyes that had seen much, I would hazard. The man held out a bottle to me and patted me on my shoulder as he did so. His accent was a husky Cockney – clearly born and bred within shouting distance of this very establishment. My reputation and indeed my intent had clearly gone before me, judging by his opening gambit:

'Ere y'are at last, my good friend Sancho! Wondered when you'd turn up. You been everywhere this fortnight, the word goes, and not visited me. I take it much amiss, Sir, much amiss. Come, join us.'

And so saying, he drew me to the central table; mine Host signalled roughly with his head for two of the players to sit out, and he and I took their places. The Jewish men around the table watched cautiously as one of them shuffled the cards skilfully and dealt with a rapidity that had me hypnotised. A strange sensation washed over me then, that I took to be hunger re-awakening in me. I felt drained of vigour, as if I had run my course and this was as far as my legs could carry me. For one moment, I even forgot the reason I had come here; but I was helped by the constantly smiling Host, who took the purse that had suddenly appeared in my hand and laid it on the table with a kind of reverence. Even I was surprised to see it heavier than expected. I touched the purse, and felt the ring that Henry had given me when I was a lad. I tipped the contents onto the table – as fascinated as the spectators were to see what I had remaining. About seven or eight shillings fell out – followed, at last, by the ring, its green stone the brightest and most beautiful thing in the room. As it caught the candle's reflection in its prism, it shot rainbows of dull reds and yellows over the plain wooden walls. The three Arab brothers stared as if I had revealed a magic trick – following the light as it shone first on the walls and then darted over the ceiling. One of the Jewish men reached forward a tentative hand and took the ring from me, to examine it more nearly in the glow of the candle. He bit it and then handed it to his countryman, who followed the same action. I was transfixed, as if this were not my property at all, but rather a ring put up for auction by a great family and I was merely awaiting the valuation of the precious heirloom. Satisfied, and with a nod of approval to me, then to my Host, the Jewish man who had taken the ring from me returned the item, and the dealing of the cards was completed. The Host looked around at us all – with a proprietorial hand on my shoulder – and like a ringmaster in a circus he addressed the table:

'My good friend Sancho comes well-armed, Gentlemen, as I told you he would. Stake up, stake up and ride the wheel of fortune! Shall we begin, Gentlemen? The game, once again, is Fives.'

Fragments, only, remain. The thirteen cards in my hand swim frantically to my vision. I'm handed a bottle and I drink. Is it my first drink? Second? Third? The men around the table never cease from examining me. I throw the dice and receive two fours. I look at my hand and wait till the symbols stop dancing and cavorting with one another, for the marks to arrange themselves and settle. I'm puffing on one of those burning, rolled leaves and a relaxation sweeps my body. I smile, despite the fact that I have lost, again. A blank . . . Now I'm winning – my Host slapping me violently on the back in congratulations. It hurts. Another swig. Another blank period . . . I laugh as I stand and remove my coat, throwing it into the middle. High up on the wall opposite my rickety chair, a tall, grimy window shows the rain has not abated, but is now falling in sheets of water. Thirteen cards are dealt, again. I drop mine and pass – briefly – in and out of consciousness as I rise from retrieving them. Another bottle is given me to steady myself. It does not aid me but renders me sanguine – accepting of my fate – or is that the effect of the tobacco leaf?

Fragments: I'm rising and shouting. In my confusion, I see that I've already staked my breeches. I am cold – cold in my legs – my arse – my back. I raise the purse in the air and slam it onto the table directly centre, challenging my fellows to one last throw of the dice, staking everything I have. My Host rises and empties my purse onto the table. The ring glistens in the glow of the lanterns and candles. A hand that holds some promise. The next three tours drift by without my discarding one card ... I look up to the tiny opening and think back to the small window in my Other Place – think of how much I have lost since those days of relative safety. That I can think of life with the Coven in this fond way is what breaks me, finally. Tears sting my eyes as I see the victors poring over the jewel I will never see again. Perhaps it is a miracle that I kept it this long. I have nothing, now, save my oilcloth bundle. I leave the room without a word. My Host tries to pull me back to offer me my clothes, but I push them away and break free into the street.

Staggering, near naked, from one doorway to another, terrified of the beadle and his watchmen, and at the same instant indifferent to my fate, I made my way without eyes; dulled in faculty by the moonshine I'd imbibed. My vision was not helped, either, by the driving wind and rain – which covered my face in a constant stream of warm water. Where I travelled, I could only tell by the location I found myself in when my legs finally gave out and caused me to stop – to rest – to sleep for a while. Let befall me what will – I had to sleep. Leaning against St Paul's Cathedral – nothing on my back but a thin shirt and the skin I was born in – the shadow of that great monument to the mercy and grace of Our Lord looming over me, I slept; awaking only to gaze at the sky as it shed more tears than I had left to weep. My only comfort was knowing that I had the means within my oilcloth to alleviate this agony of impotence and despair. The words of

Shakespeare's Gaius Cassius on his birth and death day came
to me in Garrick's voice, then:

> This day I breathéd first: time is come round,
> And where I did begin, there shall I end;
> My life is run his compass.

In the alcove in which I had found shelter, the wind could
not reach my flesh. I would not have felt it, in any case, as
my whole frame was exposed to the elements, and I could
not perceive the slightest breeze. I had become benumbed.
Looking up, I noticed the stone of St Paul's Cathedral had
been so darkened by moisture, it had become the same colour
as the skin of the broken man who lay against its buttresses.
Having escaped my Greenwich prison, London had stripped
me of every comfort and security I had ever known – left me
destitute and despairing of aid. How naïve that boy seemed to
me, now, who had left in the dark of night. I hugged myself for
comfort and was thankful that I had at least kept my undershirt. Left with nothing else that might cover my dignity, I
pulled the shirt over my bottom to alleviate the rough feel
of the stone under my seat. Now the rain came in earnest. 'A
fitting end for a man birthed on the ocean,' I mumbled. The
oilcloth bundle by my side was hidden from the rain, and its
contents bone dry. The pistol was not pretty or ornate, it was
simply practical. I marvelled at the ingenuity of man, to have
constructed such a small weapon of destruction – so small
and yet containing so much potential to damage the human
body and annihilate the human soul. The idea of using it to
rob some poor soul had occurred to me the moment I had

bought it, naturally. Why not save myself – by employing it in the highwayman's way? That violent solution had shrivelled like seed on a stony path as soon as it had landed. Robbery was not something I could ever have the cruelty or enterprise to attempt. Besides, I could think of no soul in Christendom less worthy of life than I at this moment.

Without thinking, I held the pistol and placed the end of the barrel against my heart. Was that the best place to shoot oneself? Would it be a quick death or simply an agonising one? I shifted the pistol in my hand and placed the barrel, gently, against my temple. Now, regardless of whether the bullet did its job instantaneously or not, I would at least be oblivious, I hoped. It was as I was squeezing the trigger – so stiff I wondered if it was rusted – that Dryden's words came to mind and lent a kind of despairing resolve to the action that followed my stumbling remembrance. I spoke aloud:

'"What fate a wretched fugitive attends,
Scorned by my enemies, abandoned by my friends . . ."'
I squeezed more firmly . . .

Chapter III

In which a son imitates his father in suicide.

1775

❧

Forty-six years old

I was grateful that a customer interrupted my last entry. I could barely see by the light of the candle and my gouty hands were stiffening by the second. Also, for reasons that are too obvious to state, I was in need of more than solely physical relief. My nadir is not nearly reached in my descent, son, yet I begin to doubt my intention. Why burden a child with his father's sins? Perhaps these papers are best hidden – discarded?

No – I must maintain the resolve I began this enterprise with. It will be for you to decide, my dear child, what becomes of these papers. For now, I am compelled, I fear, to tell all – now that I have come so far.

'Know thy father . . .'

1749

Twenty years old

The trigger seemed too stiff to budge. A bitter laugh escaped me at my ridiculous lack of fortune; even death wouldn't be co-opted in my cause. Was it too much to ask that I be allowed the relief of a bullet to the brain? Surely, if there is indeed One Who Sees Us All, He would not leave me to languish in my despair rather than grant me the gift of choice in the matter? Who would care if I died? Who would be bereft, who would weep, who would do aught but express a few regrets at my failings?

I tried to loosen the trigger by tugging it this way and that. When I think now how close I came to firing upon my own limbs in error, threatening to add the lot of a cripple to my current litany of challenges . . . Would I had been aware then of a mote, a speck, a spark of some Promethean fire, that might just have been enough to rekindle *Esperance*. Hope – that springs – Eternal! But, alas, I was oblivious to all signs.

I had not been habitually sober of mind since meeting with Doctor Johnson et al, at the Ivy Lane Club. I thought of the way I wanted to die, with loved ones around me, the sun shining on my face and on the rich coverings of my bed, and laughed at my own relentless vanity. Even now, at my nadir, I still harboured dreams of a grand life, ending in an even grander death? When I thought of the people that might be present at this final scene, I found it hard to conjure any person known to me. It was a tricky ensemble to cast, since no soul had auditioned for the part of friend for life. Who would be there, then? Tilly? I had not seen her since we had parted in the cellar-gaol at Greenwich. Her family were unaware of my whereabouts, as shame and pride had me avoiding the Oxford Road, for fear I would encounter Mr and Mrs Grant.

The unwelcome, taunting, thought that I would have been better off waiting for Jonathan Sill to fetch me from that cellar-gaol and make use of me on a slave ship, darkened my mood still further. Was my life worse than that of a shackled, toiling slave? Would I at least have had a bed and some sustenance, if only just enough – as many a soul I met had assured me – just enough to keep one working for the master? Was I really better off? When I observed the blacks on London's streets – begging or merely walking aimlessly – trying to avoid the beadle and his patrols – finding shelter where they would not be robbed, beaten, or most commonly, pressed into service at sea – I felt myself closer to these powerless blacks than ever I had before. I had lived a privileged and safe life as a pet – but now, like a stray cat whose history of being once admired and coddled is invisible to any who see the scraggy animal cowering in a filthy alleyway, I looked as they did: lost, forlorn and without means to escape my condition. The black tars I met, those who had fought in His Majesty's wars at sea, were not as bitter as I was. Despite the fact that many of them were not given the pension that their white fellow-mariners received in retirement, they held England in the highest esteem, and reckoned their shipmasters the best of all masters. Naturally, I could not relate my early circumstances to these; how could I, in all conscience? To tell these poor souls that my sternest duty had been to lie abed with a fine lady and suffer three meals a day and an education laid out by a duke, well . . . The Sancho of a few months ago may have been insensible to others' pain and his own fortunate position, but not the Sancho of today.

'This pistol must work', I cried out, staggering to my feet with difficulty since my entire frame had become stiffened with cold and lack of use. I leant heavily against a pillar of St Paul's and drew a cold breath into my chest. My head began to spin and what I knew next was a dull, dawn sky dropping rain onto my grubby, tear-stained face. I shut my eyes to a closed heaven and wished for life to let me go. Raising the gun to my temple for the last time, I finally managed to squeeze the trigger of the deadly weapon.

The sound of the explosion and the impact on my cranium will never – never – be forgotten.

Thunder continued to roar in my head and the lightning strikes were so frequent that I was blinking constantly against them. I could not focus my vision, and the sounds I heard were indistinguishable from the rushing swoosh of a mighty waterfall. The damp cold of my body rendered it rigid with tension and I began to shiver. It was as my body shook involuntarily that I began to fear the worst. I had not killed myself as I so dearly desired, but had inflicted a much more painful wound on my person: I had rendered myself an invalid, perhaps blinded myself, too. Tears stung my eyes and a burning sensation on my temple followed. I reached up to touch my head, but a firm hand held it away. I could not tell who owned the hand, for my eyes refused to open for more than an instant. Through a fog of sounds, I thought I heard someone shout my name and that they had 'got him, at last!' – a rumble of wheels on cobbled stones, and someone lifted my body as if it were a ragdoll. From the movement of this person – the fact that I could smell a strong body odour – the feel of their garments on my skin – I guessed that they were powerfully built and wore a rough, thick woollen coat even in the warmth of a humid morning. It could only be one person, surely. I had fallen into the hands of the only man in the whole of London who wished to do me harm: Jonathan Sill. The Gods of Chance had truly abandoned me. I closed my eyes, giving in to my fate and the darkness that shrouded my consciousness a few moments later.

I was drifting into another bout of oblivion when hands, not gently, began manipulating my body in order to put some clothes on me. I allowed myself to be moved as the one dressing me desired – I had no strength to resist, no hope of any good outcome if I did. I could not see, and the sounds of the waterfall were no quieter than they had been hours – days? – before. Water was poured into my dry mouth, causing me to cough and splutter. I felt that someone was sitting full on my chest, and only if I shifted a little could I pull air into my lungs without experiencing pain. This agony kept me distracted with every breath I took when I was awake – and disrupted my dreams when I was asleep. In one of these dreams, I was being carried onto a ship. Incongruously, I was placed in a soft bed and my naked body covered. The warm water that whoever had brought me here was using to wash my body was not unpleasant, until I considered that this might be Sill or his boy, cleaning me up for a good sale. My body shuddered with the change of temperature the warm water produced. Perhaps whoever bought me might see that I was educated; would allow me to work in their house, and not in the fields I feared so much. If I could ingratiate myself with them, perhaps this was the Lord's way for me to escape the worst of fates for a Negro man. I would happily lock myself into a gilded cage, now, if those bars might prevent me being abused by an over-zealous overseer … I tried to rise to go to the sugar cane fields, but found myself unable to move. I lay there, my eyelids seemingly sealed shut, and listened. I could hear the sounds of conversation emanating from my right side. Turning, painfully, in that direction, I thought I saw drapes billowing in a gentle breeze. This could not be a ship's window, I knew, as it was opened, and the sounds I could hear were familiar to my ear. The noise of carriages was the last thing I was aware of before I returned to the safety of unconsciousness. If I was in London, it may be that I could yet escape. Sleep cut off any further thoughts and I dreamt once more.

My vision was steady but I could make out nothing in the otherwise dark room, save that it was, indeed, a bedchamber.

I could hear voices speaking in hushed, urgent tones. Then silence. I strained with all my attention, but my childhood skill of listening through walls failed me. I drifted off again, and had the strangest of all visions ... Duchess Mary, still in the blue gown in which I had last seen her, holding a sprig of rosemary, which she laid down on the small table next to my bed. Her look was all kindness and concern and I smiled up at her. As I did so, my head swam, and a searing pain shot across my right temple. I raised my hand there, instinctively, and could feel the tight bandage that had been wrapped around my forehead. It felt damp to the touch, and when I brought my hand near to my eyes to see if the moisture was blood, I could smell cologne on my fingers and saw that whatever the liquid, it was clear.

I drifted in and out of sleep. Waking after many hours or a few minutes – I could not tell – I found myself alone. My comforting angel had departed and left behind her sprig of rosemary, the smell of which, incomprehensibly, brought tears to my eyes. I slept.

I somehow knew that this day was going to decide my fate from the moment the sun hit my eyes. The ringing sound had abated to a low hum and the thunder had stopped entirely. Opening my eyes, once they had grown accustomed to the blazing light, I noticed that the room I was in was not on ground level, for treetops were all I could see through the window. Birdsong drifted in, and the gentle breeze that accompanied it was cool but far from cold. I took a deep breath, finding the pain in my chest had eased and that I could lift my head a little from the soft pillow. The feel of the linen on the bed was luxurious, and I could not equate any of the – albeit simple – décor of this chamber to a Jonathan Sill. It seemed to be a lady's dressing room. Did Sill have a wife? A female accomplice in his body-stealing trade? Now might be the time to attempt my escape, surely, I thought suddenly. If my captors presumed I was still half dead, I might be able to take advantage of their complacency and quit this comfortable cell. That thought had no sooner entered my mind than I began to turn my body towards the window and tried to stand. My head swam – instantly and violently – my body swayed, and I sat down heavily on the edge of the bed, my feet sinking into the pile of the thick rug that lay at my feet. After a few moments, I rose tentatively, and cautiously approached the window to spy if I might escape that way. The first thought that struck my mind was that I was still in a dream, for the view out of the window was not to be believed, to be sure. Several large houses flanked the building I was in, and a deep garden stretched out below. But it was the sight of what I could see beyond the treetops before me, that had me convinced that I was dreaming – though I was as lucid as I had been for some time. A wide, dark river, and most incongruously, the spires and turrets of the Houses of Parliament; and by contemplating the orientation of the façade that was presented to my view, I knew that I was on the north bank of the Thames. Had I been sold already? If so, it seemed that my new owner was a man of means, given the location of his home. Or was the life of a slave-catcher more lucrative than I had imagined? It might be that every item in this room had been bought with the price of a black life that had been robbed of its liberty and was now toiling on a brutal sugar plantation.

Reaching the door to the room, I heard the terrifying sounds of someone mounting the staircase outside. The steps approached and I braced myself for the violence that was to come. I had backed away to the window, now, quickly calculating that I might destroy myself below if I had no means to escape by the way I would have preferred. The door opened, softly. Frank Barber entered, his eyes as wide as saucers at the sight of his patient standing at the window. We both stared at each other for some time before he shouted – in like manner to his patron-father, Dr Johnson – 'Sancho! He's awake! It's Sancho!' I could do nothing but affirm that 'Yes,' it was I.

He laid aside the tray that was in his hands with my breakfast set out beautifully on it. A bowl of fruit, cut into segments for easy consumption, with an elegant little silver fork on the side. A lump of fresh, buttered bread. A large cup of steaming tea and a scone with some sort of dark fruit compote inside. I rushed to devour the first full meal I had had in many a week. Frank simply watched me. I picked up the silver fork to shovel the fruit into my grateful mouth – ignoring the sharp pains my shrunken stomach was experiencing – and noticed the handle was replete with the family motto of my hosts: *Equitas actionum regula* – 'Let equity be the rule of our actions' . . . I gazed at the familiar words for some time.

Frank approached me, worried and wary:

'Are you quite well, Sancho?'

For answer, I rose to embrace the lad – whose body stiffened with the intimacy – doubtless he did not receive such physical affection from the ever-active doctor. His discomfort was alleviated by the entrance of several people at a rush. Duchess Mary, her eyes red with weeping, came first and

embraced me with a sigh of relief, saying, simply, 'Charles . . .'
I wept with her. Charles Manwell, her aide, all sympathy, followed with Reverend Barton, still red-eyed from yet another
bout of intercessionary prayer and crying, no doubt. Then
came another black man, tall and with the air of a serious
fellow. I could hardly believe my eyes: it was Francis Williams,
returned from Jamaica. He did not speak for some time while
the Duchess questioned me about the state in which I had
been found, and my life since I had left her on the worst
day of both our lives. We wept a little at the memory of our
last encounter – she being sweetly penitent for not heeding
my pleas for help. I, in turn, asked her forgiveness for being
self-absorbed to the detriment of my character and to the
utter shame of my heart. Frank, who was clearly bursting
with impatience to hear more of my story, urged me to tell
them how I came to possess the pistol. I did not mention Mr
Blanchard, for fear he might have been placed in a precarious
position where the laws of the land were concerned. I simply
said I had found it. No one in that room believed me – but
they were all too discreet to press their enquiries further.
Duchess Mary gestured to Francis Williams to come forward.
I noticed that he wore a thick worsted coat, though the day
was fine. He it was, of course, who had carried me to the
carriage. He was much stronger than his slender frame would
suggest. He bowed to me, politely, and related the following:

'It is right good to see you so well, Charles. We was all
concerned you had lost your life in the attempt of it. It is not
uncommon for our people to seek the ultimate relief, though
it is not sanctioned by scripture or the law of men. I thank my
saviour that his angels prevented you from completing your

desperate desire. Life is precious, Ignatius, and yours more so than most. You have much to do, Sir, and we cannot afford to lose one such as you to despair. I humbly beseech you to make no attempt again like this on your life.'

I nodded at this articulate and gracious man, thanking him for his kind words and promising that I had had my fill of testing the hand of God.

'I am gratified to hear this news from your own lips, Sir, and I am certain your friends will join with me in rejoicing, too.'

Friends? Who did he mean, exactly? Seeing my quizzical look, he continued:

'Some of us are keeping ourselves abreast of your progress in this world, Charles, and one such was present at the house of cards you visited a week ago.'

So, I had been a whole week in a state between life and death. I had had a very narrow escape, I saw. A *house of cards*, indeed.

'My countryman Cole had been a spectator to your losses that night – and could tell that you were in a desperate state. He knew that Her Grace had asked me to make urgent enquiries as to your whereabouts. Dr Johnson was only help-ful up to a point due to his somewhat . . . foggy recollection of events that night, or the subsequent five. But my man Cole, I say . . . He it was who tried to follow you, to aid you and clothe you in your own garments which the repentant gamesters had given to him for you. Cole lost the trail of you after a time and was about to give up the chase when he heard a report that sounded very much as it was: your pistol. When he found your body, he thought you deceased, as the copious amounts of blood attested. But you had merely grazed your cranium with the bullet and did no harm to the interior, from which injury none but Jesus would have been able to rescue you, be assured, my stout fellow. Brave Cole then ran to me at my lodgings nearby and we took you to the only place we knew you would be safe: Montagu House. I alerted many of your friends and the good Dr Johnson sent us his boy, Francis, to aid your recovery.'

His presence, his kindness and his story stunned me into silence, and I gazed at the rug for many minutes. In the swirls of flowers and lozenges in its scheme, I saw the repetition of patterns and noted that it gave a symmetry to the design that a less regular layout might not have managed. There was a harmony in that regularity that was comforting. I desired a quiet life, here – where else would I want to be? I wanted to crawl beneath these luxurious covers and sleep like a hibernating bear, only emerging from my long slumber when every ounce of exhaustion had left my body. I wished with all my heart to cease running – I wanted to be safe – I wanted to know a home – I wanted more than anything to sleep.

Even as I thought this, I fell upon the bed in a swoon.

1751

❦

Twenty-two years old

The ground swallowed up much of the rain that had fallen that morning; the gravediggers grateful for a little softening of the turf to ease their back-straining task. The mound was piled high above the deep rectangle of the grave. Such a little space we take up in the vastness of the world. A dark rectangle in the ground is enough to contain all we were and all we ever would be, till worms turn us to dust. The sun, poking valiantly through the thick mist, did nothing to brighten the mood of the gathered mourners. About forty in all, this was, to any observer, the interment of someone of note. The funeral cortège – carriages, liveried footmen, ladies' maids in black to match their mistresses, plumed horses, as well as the bishop in full regalia. Guardsmen and retired officers stood in solemn order, whether active soldier or veteran. The servants all had the air of true – and not simply dutiful – grief. This person was loved, you would say, as one who had treated every soul who came into their purview with equanimity and grace. Mary, Duchess of Montagu was laid to rest to the sounds of a lone cellist – an instrument dear to her heart.

Two years as butler in service to the Great Dame, and now I am without gainful employment, once again. Not destitute, though. Not ever, again. Thanks to the generosity of my late mistress, I have an annuity to nurture. Thirty pounds will be my stake and this time I will not squander all on one throw of the bones.

1775

Forty-six years old

Unfortunately, in the absence of another entry until my temporary employment by George Brudenell Montagu, Earl of Cardigan and husband to my dear patron's daughter, the Countess of Cardigan, I must briefly fill in the gaps of my life story, here. However, there is no pride in detailing what largely can be described as an erratic existence – respectability lasting a week and debauchery lasting a fortnight or more at a time . . . Suffice to say, that though I did not avoid the gambling table entirely, I never returned to that state which – near fatally – ended my first sojourn amongst the shadow-crowd. It was in one of my more sober periods that I had the good fortune that follows – which turned a life without purpose to the very opposite.

I wrote very little by way of a diary during that period. I was clearly too wrapped up in my duties as butler to the late Duchess of Montagu to do so. Time management is the hallmark of the best domestic servants, and I did little else than manage the household of dear Duchess Mary. A butler is the lynchpin of any household, as the cook is in command of the kitchen. His task is to oversee the purchase of all victuals and domestic necessaries – he is in charge of the footmen, grooms and valets, also. His skills must lie in the ability to remain unflustered – even in the face of impending domestic crises. I cannot speak for other opinions, but I believe the evidence of a well-run house is sufficient to confirm that I fulfilled this task with exemplary diligence. I have this to blame for the lack of any details concerning my years as butler for the Duchess.

Only two entries were thought by me at the time to be worth noting. They are the incidents leading to my first – momentous – encounter with John Clarke-Osborne – and my immersion in the world of theatre. I will obey my rule so far and leave these two passages as I set them out. I hope by this to have assuaged your natural frustration – a frustration that I share with you – that so much of my life will never be known to you. Still, I'd hazard many a son would not know – or desire to know? – half that which I have already told you of your father's life. I will say this in further prècis of those intervening years, that I began to write music in earnest at this time – having ready access to a pianoforte at Montagu House, and at Deene Park in Northamptonshire when I was hired from time to time by His Lordship, the Earl of Cardigan.

Here, in these more private pages I will introduce you to the people – My People – the working poor of every nation and my own black brothers and sisters … and you will also hear more from the learnéd Francis Williams, Jamaican and Cambridge scholar.

1752

Twenty-three years old

'Hear ye! Hear Ye! His Royal Highness King George the Second of England, Scotland, Wales and Ireland.'

None who have been excluded from gatherings such as these could imagine the tedium of such occasions. Assuredly, the colourful and eye-catching great and the good – and the downright evil – were there, according to George Brudenell, Earl of Cardigan. In his ceremonial uniform as Governor of Windsor Castle, he cuts a fine figure, if one ignores his obvious discomfort, for he does not possess my penchant for the dressing-up box. A new decree had urged all officers in the British Army to wear epaulettes with their ceremonial uniform. I had the very devil of a time reminding His Lordship that it was not my 'eye for the theatrical' that was 'foisting' this addition on him, but a Royal Decree that he was obeying, in adding his wings to the already heavily ornamented blue tunic of a general.

'I am no soldier, I. I am not likely to see action in any theatre of war at Windsor, Sancho. Nor would it be prudent in any
battle, methinks, to signal your importance to the watchful
enemy by the wearing of a pair of brass door-knockers on
one's shoulders.'

He huffed in that resigned way that made it tacitly clear
that I was to ignore him and place the items on his person.
And now, here we stood. Though I was not the earl's valet –
that poor fellow had been taken ill just the night before – I
relished the opportunity to understudy for such a prestigious
rôle. A room at Windsor Castle would be the prize for whoever fulfilled that position permanently in His Lordship's
entourage. I hoped, one day . . .

The Master of Ceremonies had just announced His Majesty,
and we all awaited his appearance with studied patience. I
noticed a young boy of about nine in the corner of the great
hall at St James' Palace. He had a keen look to him; a round,
brown face below a fine woollen wig, a footman's livery of
bright yellow breeches and a silver waistcoat with a dark navy
frock coat. The little silver buckles on his shoes completed
his look of a fine young footman to a great house. He was not
a footman, of course, but – like the myriad of young boys
dressed as sailors and soldiers – it seemed to amuse some to
have children dressed as grown folks – like seeing a chimpan-
zee in a man's attire. I myself see nothing amusing in the fact
that a dignity is not bestowed on the wearer for imitating a
great personage – rather they are roundly ridiculed for not
being the thing you have made them imitate. I bit down the
bile that rose from a memory of my childhood – standing in
my Ladies' drawing room and having nothing to do but look

expensive – holding a tray as if I were nothing more than the card table. And so I was . . .

The little lad focused all his attention on me. I tried to smile at him – he resembled me at that age. Then he was obscured to me by the press of bodies, as His Majesty . . .

Though the sumptuously decorated ballroom was packed with courtiers, they parted – defied the platonic laws of physics, somehow – to allow an alleyway through the centre of the great hall for His Majesty to pass – the King stopping intermittently to talk in hushed, polite tones to certain courtiers.

Duke John had always thought George II capable and serious when he was merely a prince. The latter descriptor was certainly true, judging by the po-faced looks of the few courtiers he had already addressed. In truth, he cut an awkward figure – at nearly seventy years old, he still had a sheen of boyish freshness about him. He spoke very few words all the way down this Avenue of the Fawning – choosing to nod his acknowledgements to the waiting courtiers *en passant* – till he came to our small party. The Earl and Countess of Cardigan stood slightly to my left, and were mildly surprised in their modest way when the King turned to them with an easy smile on his face. I thought him ready to move on without a word – after all, he had graced us enormously already – when His Majesty approached still nearer. Their Worships both bowed and curtsied, once more – thrown off guard by the King's intimate, unexpected attention. I dare report that the look on His Royal Highness's face was one of respite in a storm. These occasions were clearly painful for him. The King put out his hand for His Lordship to take and followed this with a hand to Lady Cardigan.

'George. Dear Mary. Radiant as ever.'

'Your Majesty flatters,' Lady Cardigan replied. Then, conspiratorially: 'My father frequently cautioned Mama to be wary of your father in that regard, you should know, Your Majesty.'

The King threw an indulgent smile on her, declaring in his strong German accent: 'Mere jealousy. Duke John knew well enough my father would have taken your late mother to wife himself, had he not been somewhat ... encumbered with one of his own.'

'Mother? Queen? As she was so fond of remarking, Your Majesty, she'd've sooner had a good cup of strong tea.'

The Sovereign squeezed Countess Mary's hand affectionately, gratefully, and seemed to be about to move on – but, to our further amazement, he then stopped before me and gestured for me to step forward, which I did not hesitate to do. I attempted a bow but had to halt its progress halfway to the prescribed angle, as a sharp, gouty knife sliced into my hip joint just at that moment.

'Sancho!' declared His Majesty.

I quickly masked my physical pain and it seemed to disappear as soon and as swiftly as it had arrived. 'Theatre: the great physician', as Davey would say.

'Your Royal Highness.'

'I wonder, Sancho, if you recall when we first met?'

'Montagu House, Your Majesty – Blackheath. I read Ovid's *Metamorphoses*, if I remember rightly?'

'Read? *Nein* ...' I may as well have dropped my breeches for all to see, from the sound of the corporate intake of breath that swept through those close enough to overhear the exchange. Until: 'Not read ... I believe you recited – from memory. Well, has age diminished your powers of recall?'

Relieved, I did not hesitate to take up the gauntlet:

'The World, formed out of Chaos.
Man is made.
The Ages change.
The Giants Heaven invade.
Earth turns their blood ... to men.'

One of those Garrickian silences followed.

'"Earth turns their blood to men" ... Grandfather's favourite passage – a timely image of our warring natures, if ever there was one. Well done, Sancho, well done. Our friend Mr Garrick is not safe yet!'

There was a smattering of laughter and gentle applause from those who heard the exchange; a nod to our small party, and the royal progress continued. As the King moved forward, silent looks of congratulation were thrown like so many roses on the stage at the Earl and Countess, who – in their natural generosity of spirit – threw their own looks of affection and gratitude my way.

Outside, in the grounds of St James's Palace, guests were beginning to leave, as they often did once the royal progress had been made through the room, and if the guest of honour was not staying, as was the case tonight. The warm July breeze was a welcome balm to my suddenly inflamed joints – the other leg had joined the first one, in sympathy, no doubt – and I sat on a bench beneath the trees. This gout had come and gone since I had entered my twentieth year. I wondered if my life on the streets and in all those taverns, before I had steadied myself a little, had been the catalyst for this recurring weakness. The grounds around the palace were black with trees and only a small spill of late dusk light reached even as close as the bench I sat on, waiting to accompany the Earl and Countess when they chose to leave. From here, I could observe a little of the activities of the closing of a royal ball. Carriages were lined up in sharp formation; valets and lady's maids were bustling to and from the hall, and the whole resembled the chaotic order of an ant's nest; not one encounter leading to a collision in the many minutes I observed this endless stream of fetchers and carriers. Retrieving a hipflask of fine malt whisky which I had had the foresight to fill from the Earl's decanter before leaving that afternoon, I looked at these servants with envy, for – unless a servant be unwell at Montagu House and I remembered as a substitute – I was without employment, and had been ever since the Duchess of Montagu had passed from the world. I did not want to admit to this generous family that I had not been frugal in my husbandry of their investment in me. Looking for work to supplement my indulgent lifestyle needed to be handled with circumspection, too, lest the Brudenell-Montagus learn of my need and rather than take pity, cast me off for ever, as a prodigal son. And so, I greeted all enquiries they made as to my financial stability with the lie that I had always an elegant sufficiency – an unoriginal line suiting an unworthy lie.

I had no papers – and could not have become apprenticed by dint of my charming speech alone, due to the unjust laws concerning apprenticeships in the City of London, which denied blacks employment of this sort. London was vast, I reasoned, and opportunities numerous, if short-lived. Odd jobs – and the occasional performance for friends with hostelries that needed a musician for a few shillings a night – plus the rare, evening's courier work I obtained from the Inns of Court, were an erratic and unreliable source of ready money. Being a kind of itinerant musician was not unpleasant work, though I never performed in the city, lest I be seen by an agent of the Brudenell-Montagus. I continued to harbour dreams of obtaining permanent work either with a publisher or with my belovéd saviours. I swiftly squandered much of my thirty-pound annuity – half given biannually – and I was still unfitted for any manual labour that I might turn my hand to.

Let us leave it at this: I made many very unwise financial investments. The constant threat of a beadle's enquiry as to my status kept me in the shadow world for much of the time – only rising in the early dusk to seek the pleasures of my habitual – and omitted largely from these pages – salacious predilections. Affection came at four shillings a night with bed and no board, is all I will say. No glory would accrue to me, no useful or uplifting knowledge to you, to recite the misadventures of my wayward, youthful heart and flesh.

I spotted – some distance from me – a group of black grooms and footmen. I longed to be a part of them. I wondered if I would always be the outside man, looking in – I feared then that this would be my fate. I must have been staring absent-mindedly at the black footmen, for they gave notice that they had seen me watching them. I raised a tentative hand in greeting. They nodded politely back at me, then moved off to be further away from the spot where I had chosen to sit. That old disappointment of my younger days, recalling my frustrated desire to engage Francis Williams as an ally, came back to me. So it was to my delighted amazement that one tall and slender black man broke off from the group and approached me. This man, of middling age, walked with a calm pace, as if he had all the time in the world – his still features giving nothing away as to his intent. He was smooth-featured with a brown skin free of mark or blemish. His hair – while woolly – had been groomed neatly and I envied him the avoidance of the unguents, hot iron combs and oils that I used to tame my head-mop. His livery denoted that he was a footman in a great house. I stood up and bowed – surprised. Expectant.

'Good evening, Sir.'

'Good evening. Won't you ...?' I said, gesturing to the bench. The man sat and after a moment of silence, I thought to offer him a swig from my hipflask.

'Charles. Charles Ignatius.'

'John. John Clarke-Osborne.'

We nodded at each other. It was all very formal. Mr Clarke-Osborne's accent was curious to my ears. Crisp, deep and formal, with a definite flavour of the Islands.

'Of course, you need no introduction, Mr Sancho.'

'Ah. Notorious, am I? The reason your fellows scattered when I greeted them, no doubt.'

Mr Clarke-Osborne handed me back the flask – observing me the while – reading me expertly.

'No, Sir. Famed, would be the correct word. They are ... somewhat daunted by your reputation.'

I liked 'daunted'. Although I wasn't altogether sure I knew how to take this interpretation of their reaction to me and I hoped this comfortingly confident man would explain more. Disorientingly, like Francis Williams, he posed a question, instead:

'Surely you realise how known you are amongst your black brethren?'

And, just like that, I was back in Duke John's library at Blackheath and Francis Williams, who had returned to complete another Cambridge certificate, was eating the last scone on the plate. Francis had asked me if I did not notice the effect I had on others. I replied with short phrases: 'Hardly. Oftentimes, my fellows – blacks – well, they absent themselves when I approach. Most strange . . . '

Francis had looked at me then with the same look Mr Clarke-Osborne now threw my way. Pity, and an incomprehension that I could not see what they clearly saw. My embarrassment was clear for Mr Clarke-Osborne to see, and he took pity on me.

'They are somewhat intimidated by your great stature.'

'My great girth, mean you?'

Thankfully, Mr Clarke-Osborne either did not hear or, graciously, did not want to comment on my feeble joke. Whatever the reason, he would not be distracted – and launching into his meditations, he explained: 'I do not mean to cause offence, Sir – merely to point out that we do not have the privilege to address His Majesty . . . as you did today.'

Drinking this in, I developed an immediate thirst to hear more from this wise new acquaintance. I glanced towards the black footmen who had now taken up a position a little further off still – as if afraid to be drawn into the vortex of our conversation. They surreptitiously glanced over to us as Mr Clarke-Osborne launched another one of his thought-inducing queries: 'May I ask, what it was you told His Majesty? He was quite taken by it, I heard.'

'Oh. How did you ...?'

He nodded then, towards the observant black page, who at that moment had just scampered round the side of the house to join the other black footmen and grooms.

'Pompey informed us. Pompey sees all, though is observed by none.'

Across the dark park, the sounds of the black footmen laughing with Pompey as he imitated the dances he had seen that night, drifted over to us. He was a good performer, this wee fellow. Memories flooded back – not all of them good – as I watched Pompey perform for his fellows, hoping to have their approval and – good lad – getting it.

'It was nothing really – I did what I always do, Mr Clarke-Osborne – what I've done since I was even younger than Pompey, there – I simply entertained.'

In the long silence that followed, many insights came to me. Why I had felt so elated when I was given the approbation of strangers – how my need to perform was inextricably connected to my need to belong. I glanced at Mr Clarke-Osborne and thought how good it would be to make a friend of him. We sat silently for a few moments, waves of melancholy washing over me. I felt terribly lonely. I had always been so, but this night brought my loneliness into poignant focus. A bell rang out from within the palace, and the rush of activity, which had calmed for a few moments, returned in earnest as carriages were hastily summoned and brought to the front entrance of the great house. We watched little Pompey race back to the main house to fulfil his ornamental duties and Clarke-Osborne, shaking himself out of his own reveries, rose with energy.

'Come with me one day soon, friend. Let me show you how the African entertains himself in London. What say you?'

Chapter IV

*In which Sancho encounters Black
London, at last – Sancho in love.*

1775

Forty-six years old

At the time I am about to recount, I resided in a small set of rooms just off St Martin's Lane with Luke Sullivan, an Irish artist and Mr Hogarth's most brilliant – if wayward – assistant. Let me relate now the night I first encountered my people, as it were – the people of the Cause. Though I no more knew this when I entered the Black Tar Tavern for the first time than an ant knows the moon is in the sky . . .

Your sister Lydia is not well, my son. I pray day and night that you will know her before she passes, if that is God's will. For she is an angel from heaven, Billy, as is your mother – who still feels the strain of birth and worries so for her little chicks. But a stronger woman I have never known in my life – she will rally, I am assured.

These reminiscences are a haven from my life at present. Thank you, son, for listening to your poor father's ramblings. Learn from his mistakes – and his triumphs.

1752

Twenty-three years old

Black London

The Black Tar Tavern in Fleet Street – my rendezvous with Mr Clarke-Osborne – was an inauspicious venue for my first encounter with Black London at leisure. I stood watching the comings and goings from across the street – afraid – suddenly – that I would be lost in this world of foreigners and working men who sweated for their shillings. All the people that entered while I stood, hesitant, across the street, were black – certainly, brown. It would appear that no whites entered this tavern and I wondered if the proprietor was happy with that state of affairs or no. Whatever the financial cost to him of having such an exclusive clientele, his hostelry was well-frequented this night. I braved the tavern, which required no special knock and offered entry without cost or hindrance. Pushing the doors fully open, I gazed at the lively scene before me. I had been wrong. There were many white faces here, scrubbed clean – as was the whole ensemble – and dressed in the finest their pennies could buy.

The tavern was large and had a tall ceiling, unusually, for an establishment on this street. It was not brightly lit, but the lamps around the room lent the space a warm feel. No fire was needed in the large hearth on one wall of the room. Benches, chairs and a few small tables were placed around the edge of the room and the centre was given over to dancers – couples – white and black and all shades besides. They danced close – without jackets or coats but in shirtsleeves, including the women in their light chemises – some dancers, I noticed, even brought their faces together cheek by jowl, holding each other in a way that left no doubt that their bodies knew one another well. It was at once thrilling and shocking. I had been a week with the Montagus performing odd tasks, being blessed by the incapacitation of Duke George's valet. I had had social intercourse with those who *knew how to behave*. But these men and women struck me, immediately, as the least encumbered of all societies in our eclectic city – Free.

The music that struck my ears was at first difficult to assess. Percussive sounds that moved in a time signature I was unfamiliar with – there seemed to be more than eight beats in each bar and the bars were not clear to my unaccustomed sensibility. It was as if one of Handel's liveliest dance pieces were subject to an urgency that rendered the melody secondary to the rhythm – constant – imperative – wild. But there was something else to the music – something other than just the beat – the richness and detail of the harmonic layers created a sense of abandon.

Five musicians – with a sixth joining from the crowd while I watched – sat or stood to one side at the rear of this space – and without sheet music to guide them – played as if they were one instrument. A tabor about the size of a large serving platter was being worked with a small stick that resembled a bone in wood – the edge of the drum resting on the knees of a man – an Irishman, I believe – who made the round instrument vibrate and boom by placing his hands behind the drum on impact with the stick. A martial sound was delivered in this way, guiding the dancers and fellow instruments in the required tempo. A curious side effect of his skilful playing was the clicks and bends from the wooden rim and the centre of the skin, respectively – the latter spot on the drum eliciting a kind of conversation with itself. That the bending of a simple percussive note could be so expressive, astonished me. The Irish maestro was not the only percussionist in this merry band to keep the crowd jumping – and they were jumping! – with a metronomic pulse. Another drum was being worked by a painfully thin and terribly old-looking, jet-black African man who sat and played with a vigour that belied his physicality and seniority. The drum was barrel-shaped and tall enough to be angled towards him, while still being largely upright as he used his gnarled yet dexterous hands to beat out the complex rhythm. The skin still had the animal's fur tenaciously attached in many places – and these the ancient drummer used to dampen certain notes as required. This drum, too, performed a kind of conversation – echoing the first drum – this element alone was worthy of many minutes' study. The body of the tune was being carried by the player, an Arab, of an instrument that resembled a mandolin – though he seemed

to only be plucking three strings of this – adequate for the
simple but alluring rhythm that these players were creating –
seemingly from thin air. An Indian fiddler – a woman! – and
an Irishman with a tin whistle, were going away at it with
vigour and the stamping of feet. The rhythm was, at base, a
jig played in Irish style and after a time one's ear attuned to
both the southern percussion and the lilting simplicity of the
Irish dance. I was held by this juxtaposition of styles for several minutes . . . These men – and that woman! – were playing
for themselves – an act of liberty – not judged or caring to be
judged by any outside critic and relying solely on each other
to guide their work.

I was mesmerised by the music – the atmosphere of raucous
but somehow decorous abandon – the laughter and smiling
faces of the Africans and Indians, Arabians and Irish – faces
smiling now when I had rarely seen them smile before – and
at what would they smile? People oppressed in their lives by
day – free to live as unmolested citizens by night. I was in
a kind of musical state of bliss – as if heaven had opened its
curtain for an instant and shown me a choir of angels – and
the gods would not have been more grateful than I, for the
chance to see this spectacle – hear these *new sounds*.

I turned my attention to the dancers, again, cavorting
restlessly in the centre of this room – for the musicians had
all uttered a manner of battle cry – prompting the crowd
to clap and begin the next rhythm themselves in so doing.
The Irish were the first to catch the rhythm around the
room – the African drummer being not too far behind. Next,
came the fiddler – and that was when all hell broke loose in the
place. The floor was invaded with dancers bending forwards

and backwards in strict time to the bass drums and in strict rows of about four – but so loosely performed that one thought a back might break – or two heads might crash together – violently – so far they bent to touch the ground before and behind them. I caught a couple hoist one another in the air by turns – yes, the stout black lady lifted her partner momentarily – but his was the greater feat as he managed to carry the plump maid a full circle before setting her gently down, only to swirl, madly, once again with his dizzy partner. I was captivated and began to jump up and down myself – making a most uncouth spectacle in the doing of it, no doubt.

Sweating profusely, I became abandoned for many minutes – the drumming took over all other instruments – the simple music that twisted and turned in an endless combination of regular and irregular rhythms and sequences began to have an hypnotic effect on my senses . . . I imagined myself by a river camp in Africa – my tribe celebrating a great victory over our nearest rivals – unlike many tribes in that coastal area, we had always refused to trade in slaves – we were proud of our name – we knew who we were – and so – we danced. Lost to locale and all temporal concerns, I danced like this until a certain gouty knocking on both knees reminded me that I was no longer seven years old. Sitting – elated and exhausted – on a long bench at the side of this large room, I spotted Mr Clarke-Osborne being greeted warmly by all who noticed his entrance. He scanned the room for a moment and my throbbing knees were grateful that he waved his hand to signal I need not rise – another signal meant he would return with liquid refreshment. I revelled in the rest my joints were receiving and gazed at these celebrants. Many of the white ladies there had black beaux and even a few of the black women were with Indians, Chinamen or whites. The Arabs alone seemed to be content to watch and drink rather than partake of any cavorting or the pressing of flesh on flesh. In the dimly lit tavern, I lost sight of individual faces or colours of skin – the mass of humanity and the twist and whirl of bodies hypnotically soothed me. Not one soul was performing for their supper, here, nor were they aware that they were observed at all – as if they were at home – and danced with an abandon that I envied.

Any would. I had never seen anything like this in my life, was the first thing I told Mr Clarke-Osborne, shouting above the bustle. Deafened somewhat by my voluble enthusiasm, he rose and lifted me up as he did so. I tried to disguise my discomfort as I limped – slightly – after him.

Sitting in a hidden snug were two black ladies. The first – older than her companion – held herself very stiffly, as if this gathering was offending her sensibilities in some way. But it was the girl seated in the middle of the table – between John, when he sat down, and this lady – who instantly caught my attention . . . I could not utter a word when I first saw *her* until Mr Clarke-Osborne clapped me on the shoulders and told me to speak up if I wanted them to know what I thought of the gathering that night.

'Exhilarating . . . ' was all I could muster.

On the right of the lady who had caught my breath was John's wife, Mary. Younger by a few years than her husband, Mrs Clarke-Osborne was thin with dark brown skin and eyes that seemed half closed and heavy lidded. This is what had lent her look a sardonic turn, where in fact she was quite the sweetest innocent, loving her moment *on the town*. I supposed that this was a rare outing for her. Her accent was not easily placed – it contained hints of Cornwall and the Caribbean region – most pleasing to the ear. The young maid who had arrested my attention wore a white, fitted bodice, embroidered in burgundy stitching, and a full skirt of the same burgundy in a light cotton. Gracing her garments with great elegance and originality, she sat upright and seemed unfazed by the noise and swirl, unlike Mrs Clarke-Osborne, who now gazed around the room with a look of childish glee on her sweet features. I had greeted them in turn as I was introduced to them, and after exchanging some pleasantries and the offer of more refreshments – politely declined – my eyes and my full attention rested once again on John's daughter ...

I had not met many black women in my lifetime. Those I had met had the advantage of greater freedom in matches than I. My Ladies would not have approved my matching with a black scullery maid, for example, of that I am assured. And not only their opinion, but mine, would have been that finding a woman of some little education would render us more compatible, as I had learned from my first taste of love. For, how would I convey my *sentiments amoureux* to one who has never read, say, *Venus and Adonis*? My means being so very small, I would require her to come into the marriage with some way of supplementing our household expenses – not very romantic, I see now, but like women, poor black men must needs conjoin with one eye on the future, leaving love – at best – a tertiary concern. The black women I had met so far were hardened by a life of being preyed upon by every man that had ever had power over them, and there were many who did, from slave to master. None of the black women I met talked at length about these incidences – why on earth would anyone want to relive details of the horrors of having their chastity breached, at will, on a nightly basis – and this from the age of eight or so? It is unendurable to think of in the light of day, but my dreams fuel the Cause – for my nights are filled with these stories of woe.

Anne Osborne – so she was introduced to me – and my life changed for ever. She hardly spoke, so I could not perform my usual trick of guessing a person's life story largely from their accent. Her simple, 'Pleased to make your acquaintance, Charles. I have heard much from my father of your exploits,' was the first thing I can recall her uttering that night. She spoke 'exploits' with a sense of mischief that I found challenging, alluring and intriguing.

To describe the angel, then . . .

ANNE OSBORNE

If I could write the beauty of
    your eyes,
And in fresh numbers number all
    your graces,
The age to come would say 'This
    poet lies;
Such heavenly touches ne'er
    touched earthly faces.'

At the risk of being accused – as Shakespeare's sonneteer would have it – of lying to future generations (you, Billy) about the beauties of my love, I fortuitously attempted to conjure the impression that my first encounter with Anne Osborne left me with on the very night it occurred.

What is attractive beyond resisting to one, is a matter of great indifference to another. What in one culture and place will be considered beauty, is subject to local matters of taste and habituation. However, what we are *told* represents beauty can on occasion be contradicted by what we *find* to be attractive, directly before us. Nothing could have persuaded me to accept this night what the Greenwich Coven had often expressed: the belief that Black Humanity lacked the aesthetic beauty of the European. My rare encounters with black women had not given me sufficient ammunition to fully counter this foolish notion – until today.

That love blinds the eye of the observer-in-love, is painfully true. There will be many examples where a man of seemingly low prospects finds a woman willing to sacrifice her freedom to his desires, though all her circle cry 'Foul!' at her choice. What she sees, no other can perceive, and one would have the devil of a time convincing, say, the bride to an ogre that he was deformed beyond repair, so powerful an ocular delusion does love administer. In this case, I need make no excuses, for only a man blinded from birth and without the knowledge of what is considered human beauty, could be oblivious to the charms and graces of this extraordinary creature: Anne Osborne.

She sat with an easy poise that belied her nineteen years, and spoke with an economy of gesture and movement that was at once free and decorous. Her skin was the colour of milk-drenched cocoa and her complexion remarkable. It was as if a light glowed from within that rendered the skin on the surface radiant and bright. Her clear, brown eyes, so peaceful and gentle behind her long eyelashes, were mesmerising to me. I became lost in them from time to time, before I shook myself and tried to engage in the conversations happening around the table. I took in very little of the subjects under consideration and could only nod encouragingly to the speaker every so often to at least give the impression that I was engaged. At one time, when I had forgotten to pretend to be listening, Anne Osborne turned her full gaze upon me, and I burned from within.

I had the sense of being in the presence of a great person, a person with a large and generous heart, who knew kindness as a fixed virtue of her personality. I felt that I could talk to such a one for many hours and that I would, like Othello, receive from my Desdemona, 'A world of sighs,' so sympathetic was her look to all around her.

As the band started up again and the dancers were rising around the room, I thought it was time I did something other than sit and stare, and so I requested a dance from the pretty creature. She refused. I had barely asked the question when John and Mary leapt up and the pair immediately started swerving and dipping and swaying as if they had danced with each other a hundred times before – which assuredly they had. I turned away from them – envious – left alone with the woman who had just rejected me. I tried to affect nonchalance though I felt anything but. She sipped her wine for a moment, observing me, then gracefully moved into the chair that her father had occupied and leant in to address me – and now I could catch the flavours – so many flavours – of her accent. Hints of London, yes, but Jamaican too? And was there something of a Cornish tint to her beautiful alto lilt? My ear drums vibrated deliciously as she spoke – directly – into my ear:

'I have heard much of you, Sancho. I cannot believe you intend to ask me only once to dance. Father spoke of your determination to succeed in life. I see little evidence of that tonight.'

And, with a look so mischievous that I was struck dumb, she took my hand and led me out to the roiling dance floor. The jig was bouncing along in a jaunty fashion when we first stood up, but shifted – to my relief – to a more romantic mood once we had stepped onto the floor. Only tabor, French horn and flute played this stately minuet-like tune. I hesitated to know what to do for a moment, and so I took my cue from the Clarke-Osbornes – holding each other very close while they moved as one in a graceful dance – making them appear to be moving through thick air. It was sensual in the extreme – I confess to finding it a little salacious to observe. I accepted the admonition to imitate the Romans when in Rome and took hold of Anne's tiny waist – pulling her to me. The heat that rose between us was unmistakable ... Her body was firm and lithe and her movements delicate and minimal. For a precious few moments, she let me hold her to me – I felt every pulse of her form and noted every turn of her fine and articulate feet as she pulled away from me to dance – alone – facing me. It struck me that this was a mating ritual – one in which I had never been initiated. Anne glided like a *danseuse* – I know that I was not the only man in that tavern to think she the most graceful and beautiful woman there. This mating music had no firm time signature and seemed to be made up of a series of romantic musical phrases, spliced together to make a whole. The result was a piece full of twists and turns – the rhythm ephemeral – unless one listened carefully to the percussion that continued rumbling gently in the background. Anne returned to me – let me hold her once again – her body relaxing under my tentative leading – we moved across the floor as one. I smiled at her and was gratified to see that she found me amusing. The look she turned up to me at that moment had me lost for words – thought – action. I barely registered the end of the delectably long tune and was surprised, therefore, to see that folks were preparing to leave the establishment. The instruments were being tidied away, even as we arrived back to our seats. Anne curtsied to me as she departed with her mother and I was left wondering if I would ever see her again. Clarke-Osborne took me by the arm and led me to the counter, where he bought us two final glasses of whisky. All Mr Clarke-Osborne would offer the lovelorn swain was:

'Ah, poor Sancho – I see which way it lies with you. Take heart, soldier, you might see her again, once she returns in the spring from Scotland with her mistress.'

Spring, I thought. Far off, spring . . .

*

Little did I know, Billy, that your mother and I would have to endure many obstacles and several years before our second encounter. What follows are the edited letters we wrote to one another in those intervening years.

Book Three

1752–1757

*In which we find the Letters of
Anne Osborne and Ignatius Sancho.*

Friendship is a plant of slow
growth, and, like our English
Oak, spreads, is more majestically
beautiful, and increases in
shade, strength, and riches, as it
increases in years.

CHARLES IGNATIUS SANCHO

1752

7 December
Saint John's, Barbados.

Dear Mr Sancho,
I have no words to say.
Anne ?

1753

❖

1 January
Holborn, London.

Lady.

The ? was unnecessary; your name is not a mystery
to me. In fact, it is no mystery at all that you jest so
readily, in the way you do here. The true mystery is
how you have the audacity to write in monosyllabic
brevity to a man you roundly ignored for more than
a six-month. Sending said scraps halfway around the
globe in the bargain. Kindly explain.

Yours, as you behave.

Charles Ignatius Sancho

PS It is good that you wrote. Thank you for
your trouble.

Codrington Estate, Barbados.

Dear Sir,

I offer my apologies for the lack of communication you have had of me. I thought to amuse you with the brevity of my message. A misfire, clearly.

However, I beg to differ with you on two counts. (I read between your lines: observe.) Firstly, it was not, as you report, 'a six-month' since our encounter. By my rough calculations – mathematics not being a woman's natural bent? – we met on 2 July, and my first letter to you was dated 7 December, making that – by my poor female mind – no more than five months, five days – and approximately fourteen hours by the clock in the master's hallway. Secondly, in the rush of travelling to Scotland, I had no time to send you a letter conveying my hopes of renewing our, all too brief, acquaintance on my return. This, I fully envisaged occurring no later than September, when circumstances took a most unfortunate turn. In Antigua and Barbados we have near relations who reside on those islands. One of these is an old aunt, Glenda, at present unwell and without kin about her to care for her in her infirmity. The Codrington Plantation – where she has worked as cook in her master's kitchen these forty-eight years – is, perhaps, not the most brutal of these places, but that is not to say much. This old aunt, Glenda, I say, is in need of help, and my mistress, Lady Stoke, kindly agreed to let me nurse her back to health – if God will spare her. This only, was the reason for my silence.

*I jest . . . because it pleases me to tease. But what
of that, observer of men? Do you have no ear for the
language of women? Then you must needs be schooled.*

*With down-turned lip I offer my apologies and then up
again, to promise you regular missives,*

Anne Osborne

Holborn, London.

Anne,

Where be my rage? My righteous indignation
of yesternight, at the vicissitudes of fancy?
Where lie those reams of odes to a broken heart?
Nowhere. Evaporated into air, into thin air, at
the opening of your last missive. It fell as the
truest arrow from the truest bow of the truest
archer – accurately – Cupidically?

Brief. Madam, may I suggest we use the remaining
ink allotted to us in this life to write of our conditions
as we see them? Painting a picture of your life would
please me enormously. I would feel your company,
which I doubt not would be near as pleasant as the
genuine article. Lest I stray into the territory of
the lover –

Sighing like furnace, with a woeful ballad
Made to his mistress' eyebrow.

– to work. I will play the gentleman and say,
'Ladies first.' Where do you reside this very

day? What surrounds you? And . . . When will
you return?

Your curious and growing – belly upwards – friend,
Sancho.

Codrington Estate, Barbados.

Friend, *Sancho.*

*Less beef. More walks. Less port. Less . . . insinuation,
my growing friend. There. A remedy to cure every
ailment of the epicurean. I marvel how much I smile when
I come to write to you. I took an age poring over your
letter, over and over, to see if there was anything missed.*

*You cheat me, Sir. For, while I have given you an
account of my circumstances, you do not return the favour
but instead lavish one with sugar-cream who wishes
first to taste the cake. Poetry has its place, to be sure,
but when one soul is far from another, might not we take
this opportunity to speak from the quietness of our spirit,
where we are told is heard the still, small voice of God
himself? I will not scold, but lead by example, as it were,
and tell you more of the setting, here.*

*The Codrington Estate is vast and cannot be walked
in one turn of the sun, I'd hazard. As far as the eye can
see along this part of the south-east coast of Barbados, it
belongs to Sir Christopher's heirs. This generation are less
kind than the former, I'm told – though never by my ever-
loyal aunt – and leave the running of the estate to a Mr
Wilson, a wicked man by all accounts. But we see little
of him here, those of us who live near the big house. The*

family is not large and the overseers only about a dozen or so in rotation. The poor, enslaved souls number two hundred and eighty-five and are mostly men, with about half being children, women and the odd elderly soul. The practice of throwing out Negroes who have outlived their usefulness is not in force here, I thank the Lord. They keep a kind of peace with the Negroes that way. Auntie Glenda says she was taken from her mother in Antigua at five and sent here when the settlement on Barbados had just experienced an uprising; whether caused by Spanish infiltrators or native agitators, no one could ascertain. The rebellion was soon quashed and the leaders, such as they were, were hanged and their heads cut off and placed on spikes, then left on the four corners of the estate, to be eaten by birds and ravaged by sun, until they fell to dust. Wickedness. But the Lord sees, Ignatius. Now, things changed with old Mr Codrington, Sir Christopher as everyone called him. Though he kept his slaves, he did not ill-treat them. He husbanded their good will to great effect. So much so, that he is sung in praise even now by those who worked on his land. Although I never know if Auntie is simply speaking true, without fear, or if the fairy tale is not quite so bright. His son, another Sir Christopher – less competent and not a saintly man – is never seen, and so Mr Wilson is the one to watch for. Whenever I see Wilson, he seems to my eyes to embody the description some who have seen the man give of Jonathan Sill. You know of the slave-catcher, I doubt not. A version of him, then – but smaller and cowed from within, rendering him more spiteful – like a little man with great power . . .

See how freely I write, already? I fancy myself a
Fielding! What will the weaker sex do with all our silly
knowledge in such a delicate shell?

I note here in Barbados, that despite the slaver foisting
their birth names upon them, a parent will secretly call
their Negro child by a memorable name – differentiating
them from the Johns, Jacks, Tobys, Thomases et al.
Kofee – Kizee – Malindi, etc. I will call you – Sancho –
for there are Charlies enough in this wide world, do you
not think?

I must leave off. The post-boat leaves at midnight and it
is already thirty minutes and more past eleven.

My . . . good wishes to you, Friend *Sancho.*
Anne

Holborn, London.

Anne.

The mention of Sill sent a shiver down my spine, I
must tell you, for I have had to do with him. Recalling
this disturbs me, still, though it is many years since I
was last in close proximity to the beast.

Only the positive circumstances – at least, the
positive *outcome* of the circumstances I am about
to relate – will alleviate any feelings of bitterness
or disappointment you might feel towards me,
for neglecting my pen these three months. I have
converted to Methodism! After many weeks of solo
contemplation, I followed your father to St Margaret's
Church nearby his Bond Street home. While much

pleased me there, I have taken to a kind of Methodism
in my domestic living, and a kind of mild Anglicanism
in my tolerances abroad. This way, I hope to strike
no pious figure; for a man who has thrown stones in
glass houses all his life, must not cry out on another
who tosses out the odd one. *(Insinuation?)* Practical
faith – as your charitable parents John and Mary have
taught me – is my aim – for faith without works is,
indeed, dead.

I ran into the chaplain to Montagu House, White
Hall, the Reverend Mr Cutts Barton, outside the
Hay Market, as I delivered my first piece of music for
the stage – an opportunity that came via Mr David
Garrick, for his friend Mr Samuel Foote – manager of
the Little Theatre in the Hay Market. A light piece
for one of his sock and buskin entertainments – most
pleasing – as I have desired to write for the theatre for
many years. Reverend Barton greeted me so warmly,
and the sense of my own confidence was so elevated,
that I invited His Worship to take some chocolate with
me at Slaughter's. We talked of my itinerant life – he
suggested that I seek solace in the Lord. Guidance
could be found in seeking His peace, he said. To which
I unburdened my already religiously tenderised heart.
About you we spoke too, Anne, but that is another
letter entirely. Suffice to say, when he was joined by an
American man – a politician I believe – named Mr Ben
Franklin – I made my excuses and left with a heart
made more certain of my God. And for that, I have
you to thank most explicitly.

You write –

'You cheat me, Sir. For, while I have given you an account of my circumstances, you do not return the favour but instead lavish one with sugar-cream who wishes first to taste the cake.'

Cake, am I? Jam roly-poly, no doubt? Are you answered, now? I long to hear your voice again. I have forgotten your accent – its colourful tones. Who do you converse with and in what language? I know so little, you see.

'Poetry has its place, to be sure, but when one soul is far from another, might not we take this opportunity to speak from the quietness of our spirit . . . '

To contradict you somewhat, Poetry is everywhere, Anne. Even you are not immune to its charms, I see. My favourite lyric of all the notes you sang to me in this letter was '**when one soul is far from another**' – which I inscribe in (the expense!) double the ink of all else.

Your friend from far away,
Sancho. Yours.

Codrington Estate, Barbados.

Dear Sancho,

First, a heartfelt apology, for bringing to mind a person who has had such an ill-effect on your life. You must be free to tell me your story if that would be of comfort. But if you chose to never mention Sill again, I would respect your discretion.

I write on the twelfth month after our encounter. A Happy Anniversary to you, my dancing partner.

In the quietness of my spirit, here on a simple wattle bed in the only other room not occupied by sleeping relatives, I lie, and think of our dance. This is what fills my head, Sancho. Not the smell of the ocean, pleasant as that is; or the less salubrious odours of the offal we are allotted to eat once a week; or the cries of those who have been burnt in the dangerous process of boiling the cane or extracting the molasses for rum. Painful, back-breaking and furnace-hot work, this is, Sancho. The men are not spared in the height of summer, neither. Many expire from the heat or exhaustion, for all year round they work all the hours and more the devil might send. Forgive my ungodly anger, but at times Mum is not the Word.

To lighter fare. Though, put up your guard, Sir, nonetheless. Your letter left out several points from mine and I would beg you to give my missives more than a cursory glance. You write:

'My favourite lyric of all the notes you sang to me in this letter are "when one soul is far from another" ...'

What caused you to gloss over my poetic turn of phrase, then, to ignore the turn of phrase that had a call within? You, who cries his erudition from every roof; you, who most likely adores Pope and Dryden and all those old, white men? (May a jest be taken so far and not cause offence?)

What accent? *What* tones? *Tones and Accent, yourself! I'm a Londoner born and bred but, to say*

*true, my mother and father's accent lies strong in me.
Especially Mother's own, for she spent much of her youth
in Barbados. I went back and forth to Barbados twice,
as Mother's master or mistress desired, but spent most of
my time in the streets of White Chapel. Truth be told, the
accent – which resembles a warm Cornish burr, roiling in
the mouth – is very hard not to* catch, *here. I fear you will
think me very foreign indeed, when next we meet. There.
In a pot. My history. And you? Tell me of you? I recall
you had a trick of the lips that made you seem much
younger than your years. It complimented your honest
articulacy in relation. You did not flirt with me using pert
and strained remarks, nor did you treat me as prey, but
spoke and addressed yourself to me as if I were your sister.
Though – the way you looked upon me on the floor of
that hall . . . will stay with me for ever. But – in my* only
language – English – Mum!

Yours?

Anne.

Montagu House, White Hall.

My Anne,

There. It is said!

My 'trick of the lips' – as I write this, there is a
smile of pure bliss on those lips. How kindly you
describe my little impediment. As kindly as Duke
John was when first he noted it. Sweet company,
indeed. Happy am I above all others, yet also crushed
in spirit, for I know it will be many a month before I

might dance with you again. I have not forgotten you entirely. See . . .

Your voice was like a waterfall; coming from so high and plunging so low, the tones were – yes, tones – harmonious from top to bottom of the scale – you had a lilting rise and fall of emphasis that was most certainly foreign – clearly Barbadian – now I have thoroughly scanned your missives, as sternly instructed – by my *Mistress*. You had a perfume that reminded me of a chocolate beverage for a child, and was that coconut I detected? Warm and pungent and solid and so very homely. Oh, My Anne, may I wax? Ha! I scarce know what I say or why I write. I suppose it is to fill the time until we can know each other in more ways than through our penmanship. But, on.

'Old, white men', sums up very well those who have been my tutors in life. Having a black tutor might have served me well, though I think my ignorant young spirit may have militated against learning by the hand of a fellow black. I was once guilty of supposing there could only be room for one Negro in any situation I found myself in. That is the small shame of my life, so far. I once had a Cause, Anne. *The Cause.* To be my African Brother's Keeper and to find out who my people were. I failed on both counts – until I met your father. When a black scholar, Francis Williams, and I first met, I felt him arrogant and above himself. I, a Negro, felt that another Negro was behaving *above his station*. I was never able to find

dry land with Francis after that. I did not know *any*
Negroes as intimates and none with such learning and
authority as Francis.

I long to hear you laugh – to know what it is that
tickles your fancy and what subjects are beyond the
pale of your sensibilities. These missives are a boon,
but they are the slowest method of torture, too. One
does not want to stop writing, for fear there is too
much left unsaid – but one needs to hurry, for one
does not want to delay the recipient's joy in receiving
one's letter. Madness! And endless, in my case, it
seems – you do not attempt to answer my question of
many months ago:

When will you return, think you?

Your Sancho?

Touché dans son cœur.

Codrington Estate, Barbados.

Your Anne, indeed, My Sancho.

*Was there ever any doubt in your mind, that a lady
who had been transported halfway round the globe
and whose days are spent in her aunt's home mopping
her aunt's brow, cleaning, cooking and serving, and
sometimes helping to launder for seven souls, all the
livelong day and night ... Do you think that lady could
then spend time each evening, rather than surrendering
to the sleep she so dearly lacks, on her cot, reading your
letters and writing her reply, if there wasn't a modicum of
affection of the romantic kind in it? If you do, then I must*

*refund my tuition fee since you have surely learnt nothing
of women from me.*

*How comes it that you write from Montagu House,
White Hall? Have you secured employment, as is my
daily and nightly prayer for you? Your* Mistress *approves
of your critique of her voice. She smiles, demurely, and
says nothing. How mere words can soothe and move . . .
if spoken in the right way – by the right person. You* wax,
Sir, *and I am not immune to the treatment. However,
I would urge caution. When once we know a thing we
crave, does it not lose its flavour with surfeit? Perhaps
this separation, and the thread that binds us over many
waters, will be made weak and flaccid by proximity. I
seem to see you smile at that. (*Insinuation *is assuredly a
two-edged sword.)*

Continue to fight for the *Cause, wherever you see it.
I cannot know what you mean by this entirely. I can
imagine it is to do with your kind heart wanting to help
your fellow Africans. Do not think that all that glisters is
gold. Sometimes gold is not gold to a man who needs a
coat, and riches are not riches to a woman in need of milk
to feed her young ones. You are the keeper of the Cause,
as you call it, Sancho – it is your duty before God to
maintain your course till the end. (You see, I can turn my
hand to punning, too!)*

*Writing and waiting on your letters is a kind of
pleasing torture, it is true. I would not want this sweet
torture to end, however, for my life here becomes
increasingly problem-laden, and these snatched moments
are my only respite in a house of tension. You ask when*

I will return. That I cannot begin to say. The living
conditions of my aunt, with a large group of fellow slaves
and visitors in constant rotation, is not conducive to
her recovery from what looks like a cold in her chest,
exacerbated by damp living quarters. Other blacks, from
the other slave households, and even an overseer today,
were asking about my status. I appear to be a Free Black
on a slave plantation, nursing an old slave – possessed
with an attitude like Betty Smith of Bermondsey and a
little learning thrown into the bargain. Like you, I sense,
Sancho, I confuse many. Not least myself. Still, I am here
for Aunt Glenda, and the Lord will not see me harmed.
Tomorrow, I will ask in the big house if my aunt may be
moved to a less fraught environment, while she continues
to make progress.

Your Anne.

Touché dans son cœur, elle-même. *(Had to ask a*
Frenchman.)

1754

Holborn, London.

My dear Anne,

I write as soon as the Duke's post to the Caribbean
would allow. This may be arriving to you via St Kitt's,
but I pray God it arrives soon. Anne. My fear of your
next chapter is palpable, but I must have it. I sense a
danger I am not safe in believing you feel as strongly
from your light tone. These places, according to my
recent conversations with Francis Williams, have a
reputation for arbitrary cruelty and the flouting of the
law of the civilised world with impunity. The horrors
he has both witnessed and heard tell of would beggar
belief, if we did not know that man's heart is wayward
above all things and desperately wicked. Please allow
me this passion so soon after our acquaintance, but
I feel you to be a part of my family already. Part, if I
may, of my flesh. I *insinuate* nothing, but reveal the
fullest content of my heart . . .

I now write from Holborn once more. My sojourn with the Brudenell-Montagus only lasted while the valet had leave of absence to nurse a sick relative in Scotland. Sick relations abound in the world, it would seem. I make my way in London as ever I did – gaining monies as a very erratically employed musician and teacher of music – the rudiments, mark you – and the odd errand either from the Inns of Court when the clerks are overcharged – or from the Academies and silver workshops around Covent Garden. It is not the worst life, and I avoid the beadle and the likes of Sill in this way. Carrying a package in the city as a Negro affords you a shield of invisibility that one would do well to utilise. My bulk and deportment give the game away, somewhat, but I believe that keeps the merely curious at bay. Hiding in plain sight of all, as it were. I continue to eye a position at Montagu House, but the mere suggestion that I was looking for any such would arouse much envy in the staff and such suspicion in my erstwhile patrons, that I risk losing all credit in that place – my best hope of a secure living. Patience is one of those gifts of the Holy Spirit, is it not? Let me exercise it, therefore.

I am sworn to see the glories in my life and not the ill – for what is my suffering compared to those not far from you. How far? I wonder every waking moment. Are you within the sound of the lash or within earshot of the harsh cry of the overseer? I cannot imagine it is an environment without menace. Violence – or the threat of it – is known to me – when

one feels so unsafe that even sleep evades the tired
and anxious soul, until the body can resist Sleep's call
no longer and one drifts into unconsciousness, only
to be roused on a regular basis with dreams that end
with a shock of disaster or threat. Sometimes, I dream
of the people and stories Francis Williams and others
have told me, of the horrors of West Indian slavery.
Those have always haunted my dreams, like history.
Not my history, but that of many, rendering my own
sufferings a distant memory of nothing more than
petty meanness. An easier life by far than many, and
pray God our children will have a still better one,
Anne. I have left off all *insinuation*, as you see. Indeed,
all coherence. Almost mad with worry.

Write me.

I continue to pray in my impious way,

Sancho.

*I did not hear from your mother for almost a year, Billy, as
there was a long season of violent storms in that region, and
no ships were able to sail for several weeks. Her letters ceased
as she could not spare the time to write. The Codringtons
became preoccupied with the reparations on the plantation – not
with supplying writing materials for the unpaid nurse of their
slave, Glenda ... I practically gnawed my nails to the bone
with worry.*

*The following is an extract from my letters – a dozen or so sent
out without reply. Nevertheless, I kept to my task of telling Anne
of my daily life. The saddest of my tales follows.*

There is, in the city, a house of ladies who are of
African origin for the most part. This house is run
by one Black Harriet. I waited in this very house for
John Clarke-Osborne to rescue our friends and fellow
Africans – the wayward James Kisbee and Charles
Lincoln – from an altercation arising out of a disputed
payment. As I waited, I saw a lady, though clearly one
for hire, as it were, who appeared close to collapse
from hunger. I approached her to ask if she were in
need of assistance, and it was as she roused herself to
play the game of her profession, that we both stopped
and stared ... Anne, will it not horrify you, though
you see and hear more brutish things, I fear, but will
you not be horrified to know that behind those gaudy
rags of a dress, in such a faded blue it was almost
white, and disguised beneath a layer of face-paint that
would disgrace the sock and buskin entertainments at
the Little Theatre – that beneath all this I say, was the
green-eyed friend of my childish years, Tilly Grant.
My Tilly. We stood, frozen, in the hallway of this
gaudy house of flesh – its garish red drapes and the fug
of bodies and tobacco smoke that drifted through the
air giving it a dream-like quality, as if all the senses
had been brought to their highest pitch; colours were
brighter, the sounds of music and laughter shriller,
and the look in my Tilly's eyes, deeper and darker.
I threw myself on her instantly and felt her shrink
back in discomfort. Of course. I had breached the
necessary protocol she must have chosen to protect
herself. To separate what she did from who she really

was, or at least, wanted and longed to be, once more. But that Tilly had died, I could see – she had slipped her moorings and drifted out to this sea of debauched desperation. I stepped back from her, just as your father and our friends exited to the street, doubtless looking for me.

'Tilly . . . My Tilly.'

She shied away at that, almost wounded. I decided to be practical.

'Come now. Allow us to get some food for you – for you look as if you might faint.'

And so saying, I led her gently by the arm out to my surprised friends – Mr Kisbee, naturally, thought me a customer for an instant. My pious reputation of late helped convince him that my intentions for the lady were honourable and he confined himself to a questioning look. We left your rather bemused father to travel alone to Bond Street and Kisbee, Lincoln and I walked to the Black Tar Tavern to see my dear Tilly fed. Shame to say, I almost clean forgot my mission to get Tilly fed and warmed when I saw the tavern for the first time since *we* were last there. I have not been able to bring myself to revisit the scene of the crime, where you stole my heart. It felt comforting, however, to be back – to remember where we were sitting at the end of that distant and transcendent evening – to see the tavern, subdued now – with just a few clients at this time of night, and a feeling of calm industry as people, mainly men, drank and quietly smoked and talked. I ordered some steak and potatoes for poor, emaciated

Tilly and sat us down in a snug, on the opposite side of the bar and from where we could see the kitchen-boy when he came out – usually confused and lacking proper instruction for whom the food was destined. We rescued Tilly's supper for her, hot and unmolested by passing customers – and then I asked her to tell me how she came to be in this plight. Her tale is as awful as it is cruel . . .

After relating the details of my early life, and my subsequent incarceration in the Sisters' cellar, I began to tell your mother the tragic epilogue: Tilly's Story.

Through her intermittent tears, Tilly told me how the Sisters – especially Miss Abigail – the Hecate of the Coven – had assailed her with question after question about my whereabouts. Facing all enquiries with a denial made the honest Tilly's heart break each time she uttered an untruth – not only that, but it did not help her cause when the Sisters discovered a scrap of my notebook under her bed. She must have stored my papers there before putting them in my carpetbag the night of my escape, and a scrap of that accursed notebook gave her away. To add to the danger that was already so close at hand, Hincham, angrier than ever, had accused Tilly straight away, for who else would have unlocked the cellar door from the outside? To which accusation the loyal Tilly had lied, royally, telling the household that she feared that Hincham's drinking had gotten the better of his efficiency.

Hincham seethed, looking for every way to wound her, even telling her beau, a footman from a house on that street, that she had been seen out with another. A lie. This skittish lad was undeterred at first, but shortly before the next disaster struck Tilly, he vanished before she was able to appeal to him for help. The cruel Hincham felt it was insufficient to have destroyed her chance of happiness, and clearly wanted Tilly to suffer for more than just her own betrayal of him and his loss of credibility in the Sisters' household; there was also the matter of the loss of his earnings from Jonathan Sill. Tilly had seen them together too many times to escape the surmise that Sill and Hincham had been plotting against my person for some time. Her intervention had thwarted their chances and could not go unpunished.

Hincham pretended one evening to be about to receive money from Sill, for the knowledge he possessed of my whereabouts in White Chapel. His trap was sprung, when Tilly was caught in the act of reading the note on the subject, a letter Hincham had ostentatiously announced was to be delivered to Sill that night, and that the wily footman, that jack-of-all-evil, had purposefully left on the kitchen counter. Truth be told, Mellor's flour-covered hands were also all over it, according to Tilly, so it was just a matter of 'waiting for poor fool, Tilly, to touch it. It was made to seem as if I was a spy for you and would warn you of the hunt,' she told me. These lies held sway and poor Tilly was dismissed to the Oxford Road to fend for herself – with not a word of reference after her many loyal years of service. Tilly, like myself before her, was only too aware how much of a burden a grown mouth was, in a family that struggles at the best of times, while offering no contribution. She did as I. She fled. Leaving no word that she was going to seek her fortune in town ...

The road to legitimacy closed on her very rapidly, as I have witnessed in my own life, and she fell, rather than entered willing – fell – into that bargain with men that gives and takes at the same time.

I'm sorry for relating these dark events to you, my dearest Anne. I cannot tell why but I feel compelled to tell you of my life, honestly. The horrors of poverty, Anne, in London are hard indeed. Although, not as hard, I'd wager, as imagination paints of the conditions you endure ... ?

After giving up my bed to dear Tilly that night, your father and I duly returned her to the Oxford Road the next afternoon, to the only home she knew ... But the welcome was far from warm. Barb, her otherwise kindly mother, kept eyeing her as if a total stranger had entered the house. One of the older siblings who works for the Courtauld family, silversmiths, were also hostile to her presence; as if her life had sunk so low that she was no longer welcome even in that most welcoming of families. Tilly spent the best part of two hours in a state of such confusion – an admixture of joy and fear. She could not settle in any one place for very long, and that was all the more apparent when

we sat to eat, with the help of a little leg of lamb that
I had brought with me. During the repast, she kept
on darting up to fetch items no one had asked for, but
that she insisted were needed for the table. A glimpse
of the old Tilly, the one who knew how a table *should*
be set out. Her family quietly ate and observed her out
of the corners of their eyes. It was most discomforting,
Anne. To the surprise of all, she rose, suddenly – with
great energy – declared that she was very grateful, but
that she must make her way home, now. It was then
that Barb and her eldest brother began to roar that
she had disgraced the family; that they were ashamed
of her, where once she had been their idol; that she
would die alone, for the things that she had done . . .
and no sooner had the storm risen – with these two
barracking poor, statuesque Tilly – than it subsided.
First, into a violent embrace from her suddenly tearful
brother and then a quiet wail from her mother. Barb
dissolved on Tilly's shoulders, then Tilly on hers; and
all were in tears as I stepped into the courtyard to join
your father.

I have not seen her these last three months or so,
but it appears that she is thriving in a position that
suits her quiet nature in a French tailor's establishment
on the Tottenham Court Road. We will check on her
from time to time, your father and I, kind soul that he
is. Tilly is not the only body in London whose life is
but one remove from great trials. Your father has led
me into the ways of the almsgiver, and we continue to
visit the souls in Seven Dials who have had their share

of bad luck and straitened circumstances. The poor are always with us, as the Lord declared.

True friendship had eluded me for some time until I met your dear father, Mr John Clarke-Osborne – I sometimes like to give him his full title, which makes him smile that broad grin that charms so. For what he offered me and found for me, the greatest of all gifts – companionship – family – I will be forever grateful to him, my African brother, indeed. Before your father, my relationships with blacks had been brief, or awkward, due to the perception of my exalted position. I could not tell them any story from my life that would match their own – my pampered cage-bird life was no match for even the mildest of their tales.

Take Zachariah, whom I met on that first week when I was introduced to many strays by Luke Sullivan, Mr Hogarth's assistant, in one of his sober seasons. Zach was a Virginian by his accent. He lived with two Irish giants, brothers Dillon and Cíaran O'Malley. Standing about five feet three, Zach had a hunched stance and a look of tired alertness about him – with a long scar down the left side of his dark face. He told me that he was always on the lookout for his *ol' massa*, as he called his former owner. He knew that in London many runaways had been recaptured and returned to their masters in the colonies – only a *little battered and bruised* from their capture and subsequent journey *home* in shackles. He had been brought up on a farm in West Virginia and had accompanied his master on a voyage to England for the purposes of selling tobacco. Having set foot in London, Zach wasted no time in absconding from his master and hiding himself in an area so fraught with danger for the authorities – with its Irish Catholic paupers, like the O'Malley brothers, and former soldiers – nay, rebels – co-mingling with diverse nations who had been blown here by one wind or another – that it was the safest haven in the whole of London.

You will recall that in the squalid streets behind Covent Garden's flower-scented square – to the north a little – lies a seldom-visited pocket of London known as the Seven Dials. The narrow streets about this dark scar of brick and piss are as dangerous to the eye as they are in reality. Murders happen here, some unreported and most unremarked. Here, a man or woman could disappear and never be found. It elicits a wry smile to think of those who boldly assert they have the precise numbers of Indians, Irish and Africans there be in London on any given Tuesday. Who here would volunteer their story to a man of the government, even if one might be found brave enough to venture into these environs? A city within the city of London. Impassable. Unknowable.

So, there Zach remained; gaining his strength and the knowledge he needed to navigate the new world in which he'd found himself. Like Lemuel Gulliver, he quickly rose in general esteem – attaining the decent position of a clerk's runner, delivering messages to clients in London who had concerns at court. He

tells me these were his happiest days, going about his
business, feeling a sense of purpose and rightness with
himself. Many weeks into this golden time, he was
accosted in the churchyard of St Mary-le-Bow, and
apprehended by two men – slave-catchers, who had his
description from his old master. It appears that many
a poster had been erected with his likeness clearly
depicted – a mere word in the right ear could secure
a princely sum. Zach was thrust before his owner
on board a vessel that was bound for Virginia the
next morning. Berating Zach in the strongest terms,
his owner declared that he would not shackle him,
but keep him locked in the larder room below, until
sufficient water had been put between the ship and
land to allow for his freedom and usefulness on board
the vessel. It was to his great credit that Zach's time
had not been wasted amongst his companions in Seven
Dials, and the lock of the ship's larder was no match
for the skills of breaking and entering that Zach had
imbibed from Dillon and Cíaran. He stole ashore and,
returning to Seven Dials, persuaded one of the scarred
African men to disfigure him, so that he may never
again be recognised as Zach Monroe. That scar was a
testament to the desperate straits that fear of capture
held for those who knew slavery's horror first-hand.

I visit with Reverend Barton on a regular basis these
days. I do not mean to be venal, but this is perhaps
a way that I may be kept in the minds of my dear
Montagus. A few months ago, at Montagu House, I

found Francis Williams poring over a manuscript of
music that I could not see at first. I greeted him in our
usual, formal way and sat down to read a book on the
Theory of Music, as I fancied I could write a simpler one
that would suit the youngest royals. He interrupted me,
to ask if I had read the decree from the King of Kongo,
which was to be found in a high shelf in the library.
At first, I thought he was joking with me, making up a
kingdom to entertain himself. He was deadly serious,
I realised after a short time, as he went to fetch said
manuscript. Francis handed me a leaf from this book –
if we may call this loose collection of writings that.
Doubtless, this was one of those books that Francis
had always hinted of, and the Duke of Montagu had
kept from me. Books about Slavery and Africa. Books
designed to drive a young man mad with rage, I thought
then, and had avoided looking at them all these years.
This sheet of paper was handed me, and I read:

*From King Mvemba of the Kingdom of Kongo to the
Merchants sent by his Majesty the King of Portugal:*

*Each day the traders are kidnapping our people – chil-
dren, sons of our nobles and vassals, even people of our
own family. This corruption and depravity are so wide-
spread that our land is entirely depopulated. We need
in this kingdom only priests and school-teachers, and no
merchandise, unless it is wine and flour for Mass. It is
our wish that this kingdom not be a place for the trade
or transport of slaves ... Many of our subjects eagerly
lust after the Portuguese merchandise that your subjects*

> *have brought in our domains . . . After having taken these*
> *prisoners to the coast secretly or at night . . . as soon as the*
> *captives are in the hands of white men they are branded*
> *with a red-hot iron.*

From his reading and his conversations with those
that have but newly arrived in the Caribbean, Francis
Williams had this defence of the African slave-trader:

'They may only be called a slave if they are captives
from a local war with another tribe, none of one's
own people are to be subject to this status. Another
cause of being enslaved, is if someone has repeatedly
offended the law of the land or they are orphaned,
though this is savage enough. However, slaves can
often gain status in the household and rise to being
a family member. Some become beloved heirs to
those they have served, and others have risen to
great prominence in the lands they were captives in.
Witness, Joseph, who became a great ruler in Egypt.'

This led to his concluding that the slavery that we
see practised in the West Indies and the Americas was
a purely European invention, and no blame should
be attributed to the natives, who were trading with
the same mind as the Europeans because that is how
the Europeans – including the English Christians –
chose to trade. However, once they had heard of the
conditions of these black captives, some began to
say that it was not right that black people should be
transported to foreign soil to toil, for no remuneration,
in a land that is not their home. The dissenting voice

is not strong in many African nations that know the European economy, Francis tells me, because the lure of European luxury items is too strong. Africa, he said, would never be truly free to do what it might for its own future until it could 'stand as England or France, Prussia or Spain – and even if the expulsion of these could be managed somehow – would there be anything remaining from the plunder – for the greedy, petty kings have given much away already.'

I marvelled. So, there were rules of enslavement in Africa, far superior to the European philosophy of inhumane greed for profit. Francis, seeing me enthusiastically engaged with his selected reading, began to first hum an air, then walking into the adjoining room, began to play the tune he was humming on the harpsichord. It was a masterful and disturbing performance, as ever with Francis Williams.

> 'Traverse the Globe and you'll find none,
> Who is not addicted and very much prone,
> To a black joke and a belly so white.
> The Prince, the Priest, the Peasant do love it,
> And all degrees of Mankind do covet
> A Coal black joke and a belly so white.
> The rigid recluse with his meagre face,
> From fasting and prayer would quickly cease,
> For a black joke and a belly so white.
> Let the Clergy Cant and say what they will
> They stop the mouth and tickle the Gill
> Of a Coal black joke and a belly so white.'

Finishing, he gave me one of his enigmatic smiles. Francis confuses me greatly. One moment he is as serious as a judge and the next as foolish as a stage comedian. The words were wicked and the smile so saucy, that I doubted not this time that he was mocking the sensibilities of the English and the religious. It was as if he was taunting me, daring me to object to his lyrics or the choice of song that he offered me, for I believe the performance was intended to cause me discomfort. Yet, behind it lay, perhaps, a desire to . . . educate me? Then he played 'Country Gardens'. Gentle and light, but in a strangely sarcastic tone. He really is the most ingenious player.

And now, I wait. I will not write until I hear again from you, my heart. Wishing this to be as soon as I send this to you from the hand and heart of your friend, forever,

Sancho

Your mother's tales – excised for brevity – follow. I will not interrupt these often with my worried and sympathetic interjections. You can imagine my thoughts or read them in the letters I leave out of this collection. The tales she tells are harsher than any I have presented to you before now, be warned. But you are a man now, and a man must know wickedness if he is to avoid its snares, must he not? See the world as it is, son, and fight the good fight, regardless. This too, is the Cause.

Codrington Estate, Barbados.

At last, my love, I have ink and paper.

This was the reason for my silence, for unless I wrote this in molasses there were no means by which I could send the reply you so dearly craved. I can only imagine how much you must have fretted. Doubtless by now, you will have had word from father that all is well with me, so you need not be concerned on that front. I do not mean you not to care, only that you would not worry yourself unduly on my account, for I am determined to return to you in the very near future. I am yours as surely as you are mine, and it will appear in time to be a sort of joy to be separated in this way. For these letters allow us to speak clearly to each other. Perhaps our honest declarations would have taken many more weeks or months, if we had been in proximity.

Many have perished or lost the little that they had in these dreadful, sudden and relentless rains and storms. Barbados was not the worst hit, but I fear the islands that lie to our south and east were subject to the full fury of the tempest. May the Lord aid the poor and destitute there. Many habitations, and a large portion of the crops, were destroyed. Down below the fields is where the slave huts are located. These are not badly kept, and the blacks grow crops in the little squares of dirt each property has in front of it. There is an orderliness on this plantation and a level of near comfort that many tell me is rare in the Caribbean. Francis Williams will have told you what the usual conditions can be in these cruel hovels. However, despite the relative care that the people receive at the hands of the master, if not all the overseers, the habitations, such as they were, had not been made of any materials designed to withstand so many weeks of relentless storms and rain. I visited one of Glenda's friends who had been taken ill with one of the many fevers that raged through the island during and after the storms. She lived in one of the only surviving structures on the edge of this small shanty town. The mud had slid down the hill and rested just feet away, to the back of the property. The interior was basic in the extreme, with very little to show of the sixty years this seventy-year-old woman, Wanda, had been working here. I spent the day with her – boiling the ginger roots that she had hanging from a nail above her small stove – and listened to her many stories.

There was a little girl called Ata there, who would play in the mud at the back, and whom we would have in for tea and one of Wanda's famous fruit cakes. Perhaps, nine years old? She never spoke a word, but listened attentively to our conversation with the widest, brownest eyes and a glow to her deep-brown skin. A veritable Black Cherub. A mere rag of a dress, or old undershirt with the sleeves cut away, was all she wore – one of the shoulders bare as the sun-bleached, sand-coloured dress collapsed completely on that side; the other was puckered with moth-holes, but held the dress up for decorum's sake. Her ashy and hardened feet were bare, yet she walked as if she wore thick boots, in comparison to my dainty step when on even the smoothest pebbles.

*A most beautiful child and such a quiet spirit, Sancho,
that one's heart was broken to learn that both Ata's
parents, and her two siblings, had drowned one awful
night in the tempest. She had no other relatives, Wanda
informed me, and was due to be taken to Antigua to work
the plantations there – where the vast majority of deaths
have taken place amongst the blacks. I would with all my
heart that I could adopt this little angel, but I fear her fate
is sealed and her life prescribed. But God, who sees all,
will protect her, I pray.*

*The vast fields of cane are lying on their backs and only
the little shoots of new growths, the ratoons, are standing
tall and erect. Mr Codrington sent word through his
overseers that the work of clearing and replanting, if
necessary, must begin as soon as the worst of the storms
had subsided. That was a week ago, and the men and
women who work the field have been out there both night
and day, gaining little sleep and only a little relieved by
the fact that the cloudy weather protects them from the
relentless heat of the day. The undergrowth of the cane
stalks is largely undamaged; hence no need for the back-
breaking task of replanting. They work just as hard to
restore their homes as they do to restore their master's
cane fields, and in just a few days the slave village was
less impassable – even having an air of order about it.*

*All the more incongruous then, when a man was
whipped on the post in the middle of the village for not
resurrecting his hut after the storm. This, despite his cries
that he had no family surviving to build for, and that the*

ground where he must build was buried under mud and perhaps bodies, for the smell did not leave the place for many weeks. His pleas fell on Mr Wilson's deaf ears and the man received forty lashes with the cruellest implement that I have ever seen. Two overseers took their turns in the whipping of the poor soul, with a score administered by each to keep them fresh. *From where I stood and witnessed this punishment, I could tell that the whip had been specially modified to cause the maximum level of laceration without causing bruising, or the breaking of any valuable bones. The fine ends of twine saw to that. Once the first twenty were administered and there was some fuss about which of the overseers was to perform the next twenty lashes, I took my chance to walk away swiftly, while the others were corralled to watch, like spectators at a hanging at Tyburn. They are not willing gawpers, however, but forced to watch, in order to set an example before them in blood and cries for mercy. We were not permitted to pull the wretch from the post for several hours after the beating, despite the sobs and the blood that had escaped the victim. Imagine this cruelty perpetrated by two overseers, whom I heard by rumour to be the laziest and most inebriated of supervisors, often to be found sleeping off their stolen rum in a corner of the cane fields. The man survived and was taken in by another household, where one hopes for his full recovery – from the physical brutality, but hardly from the loss of his whole family.*

Those of us in the big house are not so unfortunate. The master's family were not in residence when this occurred – they were on their holding in Antigua. Now they have returned, Mr Codrington and his wife, and two of their grown children, Mr Peter and Mr John – the boys returning to England soon after. Mr Wilson was put in charge of the house for several weeks, and his manner was exactly that of the little man, as I described him, being given great power. He seems to fear me a little, and I maintain my distance, as I suspect he would try to take advantage of my lack of status in the house, otherwise. My Aunt Glenda has been given a room at the back of the house which was the late housekeeper's room.

The house itself is not as spacious as I had always thought when passing by it on the way to the river to wash the clothes. A veranda wraps around it, from where the plantation can be viewed, at least the part that abuts the house. The staff are small, but extremely loyal and seemingly content. Molly is the new cook; a chestnut-brown Negro woman of great humour and fierce autonomy. I suspect that her skill in cooking has given her the license to contradict white people with impunity, as I have seen her do with Mrs Codrington when she disagreed with her mistress about the correct way to cook a joint of venison, so rare here, but brought over by a cousin of the family. To my surprise, the mistress, a frail and not unkindly woman, pale of pallor and prone to headaches that cause her to have to lie in a darkened room for many hours in the day, conceded without the least fuss. Molly was perfectly, deliciously, right, of course. Molly and Glenda know each other from the weekly church meetings that take place in a clearing by the river, north of the estate. It has been a boon to have such a great cook helping me to keep Glenda fed and cared for. She begins to sit up a little now, we praise our Father for it, and is eating more solid food. This bodes well, does it not? Perhaps, April will not be impossible for me to return to see my Sancho, again!

Just now I felt a shiver of longing to see you roll through me. Would you believe that last night I danced to the music I remembered from our first dance? I hummed it so softly that I thought none would be able to overhear me. Auntie only told me in the morning that she had seen me dancing in the light of the moon that shone through the window. I was pleased to hear her say that she approved greatly of 'dancing for our ancestors', as she put it. To be free to dance, she told me, is a thing that the slavers cannot take from us – she told me that she once, as a very young girl, danced by the river at night with her cousin, Maggs. She began to cry and told me that her cousin was used sorely by the master after that, and he had taken her as his mistress from the age of twelve. She became pregnant and the master had her sold along with the baby, when his wife discovered the truth. The baby was not sold to the same slaver . . . These people will answer in this life or another, Sancho – we all have to answer at the final hour for our deeds in life, the wicked and the good.

I pray that our children, if God will bless us so, will not lead a life without parents and love, as so many children in this degrading and inhumane system of bondage do. The crimes against these orphans – orphans, though their parents live – needs must be answered, Sancho. I see

*them every now and then passing by the big house, with
the look of strays that belong everywhere and nowhere.
The heart must turn away, I say to my shame, for it is at
times overwhelming to think on the injustice of children
robbed of their parents for reasons of commerce. Family
life is unstable and fidelity can be a rare thing, in a
system that instructs one in the futility of making strong,
human bonds, when the master or mistress on a whim
or for profit might remove a slave from his family and
relations in an instant. It hardens the heart of even the
most delicate of souls.*

*I am yours. For now, and for ever. May we know each
other's arms much sooner than we think.*

Your only Anne.

Your future Mrs Sancho. If you'll have me?

1755

Codrington Plantation, Barbados.

It is only a few busy days since I wrote to you, but I wanted to answer your missives before you sent another, and I fell behind in my studies. These are moments that bring me the most happiness, sitting under a small piece of tallow candle and writing to my love. My aunt sleeps much these hot days and has begun to gain weight at last. I have confidence that she will recover fully from this in a very few months. Be patient, I can see the end of the long road we have been on. I hope you will not regret your admonition to write to you after too many of my letters, with too much and nothing to say, arrive. I hazard you are a patient man, or so you have shown me in your forbearance of my extended absence.

You commit an error, if I may, my heart, to seek to compare lives of Negroes in the Caribbean to those in London. It is not the same world; as the world of the plantation in the southern regions of America – reported more barbarous still, with summary hangings a veritable policy for the plantation owners there – is different from the life in Barbados, though that is brutal enough. We all have a different story to tell, and telling them will highlight its own horrors, too, but not all of them will be of the same nature, precisely. There are millions of stories from the hundreds of years our people have suffered. You belittle your story, and your suffering, at your peril, for it was this suffering that bred your spirit. It is your genius for surviving the barbs that come your way that is the best part of you. The part I already love . . .

I heard today that we might be moving to the family's other plantation in Antigua for the summer months after harvest. I cannot say that I will be sorry to be leaving this place. I live in the constant fear of mischief. Mr Wilson has taken to stopping me on my way to ask me questions that have no answer, such as, 'Will you dance for us today, Anne, for you look as if you are dressed for a ball?' Or, 'We do not maintain the standards of the London salons that you are used to, Milady Anne, but will we do?' I think he means to tease me, but the look in his eyes is far from savoury when he makes these feeble assays at wit.

I danced for Glenda in her room, and she insisted we play your music on the pianoforte in the front room of the house. Please send more; and with your charming instructions. It provides a little exercise for me, and Auntie will join me soon in taking to the floor. We will have her dancing round the kitchen in no time. I

demonstrated to Auntie how we dance in London and
began to teach her, though she was seated as I did so,
her strength not being fully restored. No sooner had I
completed the Rigadoon Step, imagining I had a partner,
than Mr Wilson appeared, and I felt certain he had been
there for some time. He instructed us to leave off, lest it
upset the mistress, as she was lying down against another
headache. This was not a danger, as I knew her to have
taken a walk with her dogs not an hour before, and was
habitually away for two hours at a time. Nevertheless,
we repaired to Auntie's room, where she warned me that
she knew the likes of Wilson, and the way he regarded me
was not the way of a man to a woman he did not desire.
I kept my distance from him from that day, not that I
was in the habit of conversing with him beyond the usual
demands of politeness. I managed to avoid him some ten
days or so.

It was to my surprise that he arrested me on my return
from fetching the necessaries from town. I was already
heated by the atmosphere of menace I always feel as a
Free Black in a town of slaves and slave drivers. I am
afraid I did not answer Mr Wilson's quips with even my
usual politeness, instead informing him that I had no time
for any word games, as I had to store the provisions before
helping to prepare supper in the house. His look of rage at
being spurned by a Negress was very clear and frightened
me not a little. When one who does not smile begins to
grin for no reason that you know, it is surely an occasion
to be wary. When even that false smile fades, there is
where we may spy danger. Though I have no recollection

*of Antigua, which I visited when I was a very small girl
when my mother's mistress went to visit her cousin there,
I am looking forward to escaping to a place without a Mr
Wilson lurking behind every corner.*

*The house-slaves have taken to asking me to perform
tasks that they would rather not do. I oblige them, for
I feel my idleness at times and the day passes so much
more swiftly, I find, when I am occupied with some
task or other. Today, it was the turn of the few hogs
that the family keep in the small farm at the back of
the main house. Fourteen in all, and one litter about to
be delivered. The cycle of life continues no matter what
condition the world is in, and there is a comfort in the
regularity of these chores. I was helped by Ata, and we
talked a little. She has the sweetest broken English you
ever heard. When I asked her if she had ever been to
town, she stood upright suddenly and pronounced like a
woman of forty:*

*'Me? You fink you catchin' me in town? Lickle girl like
me? I ain't visit town yet, ma'am.'*

*If you could have seen her serious little face. I suppose,
like me, she has a keen sense of her own weakness and
feels herself safe in a place she knows. A few hours later,
I heard the master and mistress discussing her future,
though they called her Betty. It seems that Ata's time
on Barbados is coming to an end, and that they will
send her on to Antigua, along with Glenda. She may be
lucky, after all. Remember, she has no guardian except
those who have decided to help her from the kindness*

of their hearts, like Wanda. She lives with another old slave woman who is half-blind, and Ata helps her with her chores. She's a capable girl, if a little too playful for folks here. I believe that is why she enjoys my company, for I treat her as a little friend and try not to instruct her over much.

The time for play is so very short in an enslaved girl's life. Ata told me that one of the young boys who goes out to the field to help the men had told her that they should be together. She is very young, and though the boy is no more than twelve years old, I believe that she must be protected from these things for as long as we are able to. It is true that some of the poor blacks here behave in degrading ways towards each other. Slavery is a system that encourages ignorance of the rule of law, and forces the enslaved to govern and protect themselves. This is perfectly serviceable as a way of toiling together, but cannot hope to aid them when they have a serious dispute with each other. Two men had a fight over a woman in the lower cane field, last Saturday morning. One struck the other with his machete, cleaving his adversary's right hand clean off. Both men were whipped, and the man with the severed hand has been sent to the north to recover on a smaller estate where the work will be less taxing. We all know that he will be sold in time, for he cannot fulfil his tasks. Where do you go when you are not fit to work as an African in Barbados? The terror of being without a master is greater for these people than the institution of slavery itself, since with slavery there is at least some knowledge of your future, and

*you are fed and housed. I do not speak in advocacy of
slavery, of course, but tell you the truth, that the world
is very hostile to an African without a master or his
freedom papers.*

*The Codringtons have firmly decided to take Molly
and Ata with them to Antigua, and train little Ata as a
housemaid and kitchen girl; she will be raised to be a cook
if she follows a diligent path. I praise the Lord for your
suggestion, as I did inform the master of your thoughts
on Ata's apprenticeship. He felt you were 'a very clever
Negro' to have such a good head for logistical planning.
His patronising tone aside, I was quite gladdened by the
conversation. And not two days later, little Ata came
to me, beaming, and said that she was to be a cook in
a fine house in Antigua, and I was to 'Watcha na!' as
she sashayed away down to the riverbank. A gloriously
expressive child.*

*I long to see what you see in your strange life, Sancho,
to share it with you and to know how it touches you,
for good or ill. You have led such a solitary life, lost in
conversation with none but yourself – for who is like you
in this world? Let us be friends, always, and vow to never
let the other become lonely?*

*What a delight this is! Thank you. It helps to write to
you as I, instantly, forget the tensions in the house that
increase daily before our impending departure. Mr Wilson
held my wrist for some time today, enquiring after some
trifling matter. I did not struggle with him, strange to
say, but held my arm stiffly in hopes that he might feel*

my discomfort. He either did not notice, or did not care. The smell of stale rum on his breath and the growth of grey and black stubble on his sun-scarred, wrinkled skin, told of his intoxication, now near permanent, since the announcement of our departure. He seemed to be under the influence of a fever, too, for he perspired all the while he spoke to me, so much so that he was obliged to release my wrist to wipe his soaking brow with a handkerchief. I made off, then, at last, after one or two monosyllabic replies. I cannot go to war with this man, for he wields powers in this little kingdom that I could do little to withstand; although, it takes all my Christian patience not to tell him to go to the devil. The sooner we are gone from this place, the better.

Harvest time is shortly upon us, and the men and women are out in the fields for much of the day and into the evening. They rise before dawn and are not home for more than a few hours every night, before beginning the day's work again in the morning. At the same time, much leeway is given the workers during this season, and we have gatherings every Friday night, where the local fishermen bring fish to fry; and many bring a chicken to roast, and ground provisions are boiled in several large cauldrons by the older women of the plantation. There is a festive atmosphere, and the people sleep very late, but despite this, are up and working the next day, as if nothing at all had happened the night before. Remarkably robust people! The sheaths of cane have all been cut now, and it is left to the mill

workers and those who are charged with extracting the
sugar syrup from the boiling of the cane. I passed by the
mill yesterday afternoon. The heat that was emanating
from the barn must be felt to be believed. Hell could not
be hotter. The men work almost naked in that place,
but they are not safe that way as there is spitting and
spillage from these incredibly hot vats. I have heard
cries of agony too often to think that accidents do not
occur on a regular basis. The children, some as young
as five, are sent out into the fields to collect the stalks of
cane that are left behind after the first gathering. These
they bundle into stacks of about six, and then they bind
the stalks together and carry them, expertly, over to the
mill house. Mr Codrington is more involved than ever
and supervises some of these operations. Despite the
rains, the harvest will be a good one, by all accounts.
These people work hard, Sancho, if only it was for their
own benefit.

Codrington Plantation, Antigua.

Dear-one,
We are now in Antigua, as you may note with the post
mark. The whole caravan embarked for the island last
week, but it took us several days' wait before the sea was
becalmed. When we arrived, we were stranded by those
who were meant to greet us on arrival, and spent several
hours on the docks. The people here seem permanently
angry. I could elicit no pleasant looks from any of the
passers-by. At last, the coaches arrived, and we were
transported along very rough tracks to the estate of Mr

Codrington. It is many acres smaller, but very similar
in layout to the one they have on Barbados – though the
huts are better constructed for the slaves, who normally
number about one hundred and twenty. After the storms,
however, they are forty hands short, and new arrivals are
expected every week. This is the source of the less than
appetizing news I have to relate. Thinking that the training
and organising of forty new hands would overwhelm
him, Mr Codrington decided to carry Mr Wilson with
us to Antigua. He will be largely in charge of training
the new intake of souls, and so will be out of my way at
least. It is the only cloud in an otherwise uneventful and
peaceful voyage.

Molly is teaching Ata the skills of a kitchen maid and,
when she is tall enough, she will show her how to assist
in the cooking. All would appear to be well, there. The
mistress spends more time than ever in her darkened
bedchamber. She has suffered, too, with the loss of her
belovéd hounds, who were not deemed safe to travel
abroad, as a canine disease was suspected on Barbados,
just before we embarked for Antigua. Her sorrow is
only explicable when we consider that herself and Mr
Codrington share little in common but a love of fine
cuisine. I believe her dogs are her real children and
companions.

It is good that you wish to ask my father for my hand. I
cannot think he would object, for I believe he holds you in
very high esteem.

Here, I intervene, only to relate a momentous twist in my own tale, somewhat neglected by my attention on your mother's gripping story . . .

I approached your father and asked for your hand, which he, as you predicted, was happy to let me have. I am the most fortunate man in a father-in-law – as Mr Clarke-Osborne was my firm friend before I knew that you would be my wife. He insists that he should be paying some sort of dowry, but I will take naught from him but his good will. And that is the greatest gift, as I told him, that any father could give his daughter. I will enquire of Mr Barton – when I next visit Montagu House to play a little on the harpsichord – if he will consent to marry us. I'm floating on a cloud of bliss and wish never to make landfall.

I see that we will, indeed, have much to discuss when we are together, and I will make it my mission to persuade you to grow in love with the country you were born and raised in – a greatly flawed country, granted. A family may be hostile to one of its members, however, that member is still a part of the family, are they not? So, too, you, who feels the sting of the outsider, may in time come to know that you are an Englishwoman, despite the ignorance of those who do not know your story.

As from next week, I should expect to be employed, on an ad hoc basis, by the Montagus when they perambulate on the Saturdays and Sundays in the visiting season. Much work, therefore, may accrue to me. I would like a firm fiscal foundation for us as we start life together, my dearest Hen.

At this juncture, many more than the usual two or three months passed between our letters. I learnt from your grandmother that the letter her daughter sent in January of 1756 was somehow lost in transit. Therefore, our first communication after this news of the missing correspondence is Anne's disturbing letter from Antigua, which follows.

1756

Dearest Sancho,

I write to you at last, though not with any joy, for the first time that I can recall. It is tragic news I relate, indeed. Father informed me that you knew of my circumstances through him. However, not all the details in that lost letter could be conveyed to him in my necessarily brief communication. Here then, is my tale.

It would have been during the Easter festivities that the appalling events took place. I hardly want to begin to tell you what occurred, but fear that I must. We had promised each other the truth and with great pain I tell it. As you know, I was in much fear that Mr Wilson would press his advantage home while we were in Antigua; I did not like his increasing attentions and avoided him as ever. However, about a month after our arrival, when I had foolishly forgotten to be cautious in my movements, I encountered his sudden presence as I hung the mistress's

*garments out to dry in a secluded garden – one identical
to the one in Barbados. He emerged, sweating and yellow-
eyed, from the surrounding shrubs, and I near jumped
out of my skin with a little cry. The cruel laugh that
emanated from this toad of a man sent a chill down my
spine. He and I both knew that I was not safe, certainly
not here in Antigua, where my usual companions were
busy rebuilding the neglected plantation and the workers'
accommodations. 'How radiant you look, my dear,'
he began, then seemed to lose all confidence in his own
approach. He saw that I was determined to ignore him,
and despite my fear rising and my eyes surreptitiously
searching the horizon for help or escape, I remained calm
the whole while he was staring at me. This awful man
made the very air heavy around him, as if he carried the
weight of his cruelty with him. I foolishly turned my back
to him, like one might do to a wild beast, in order to show
how nonchalant I was to the danger. It might have worked
with a wild beast, but a wild man is not so easily ignored.*

*I felt, rather than saw, him charge towards me; I heard
an animal grunt come from him, a noise that was at once
involuntary on his part and expressive of what was in
his heart. You are a man, Sancho; you do not need me
to describe the feelings that I mean. His broad, stubby,
calloused and dirty hands were around my waist and
on my breasts before I could register what was unfolding.
His breath was redolent of whisky and rum. I wanted
to cry out, but knew that it could go worse with me if I
did, so I contented myself with attempting to escape his
grasp. His grip on my waist tightened, and I could feel*

*his desire to press himself most forcefully on me. I turned
from his attempt to kiss my neck – just then, little Ata
appeared, wide-eyed, in the clearing of the garden. Wilson
saw her too, for he released his grip on me immediately,
and laughing his flat laugh, sauntered, unafraid, back
into the shrubbery from where he had surprised me. I
was perspiring and breathing heavily, and tried to smile
at Ata, to allay her fears and confusion. She merely
regarded me, silently, and despite my friendly greeting,
crawled back into the bushes and disappeared. I stood for
some time trying to calm my breath and my hammering
heart. I quickly finished the rest of the hanging, looking
around me all the while, turning sharply at every rustle
in the undergrowth, feeling afraid in this once-safe haven.
I thought to tell someone, Sancho, but who could I tell
who would take my case seriously? Would they consider
me, a single Negro woman, with no status whatsoever on
the estate, as worthy of protection from this powerful and
indispensable man? I trusted my instincts that it would
bring nothing but trouble for me. A foolish act, Sancho; a
bad decision, had I known what would follow my silence.*

*A fortnight passed between the incident in the garden
and the next events that I must now, sadly, relate. Will
you still love your Anne, once you know how culpable I
am in the following? I beg your forgiveness for the pain
I have caused through my lack of vigilance. It was in
the early hours of a Sunday morning that I heard the
hullabaloo. The whole world seemed to be outside and
shouting and crying; women could be heard wailing
and there were fierce shouts coming from several men,*

determined that the people 'Keep back!' I rose swiftly
and, pulling my blanket over me, went outside. The sight
that greeted me was one that will never leave me ... A
small crowd of about ten people, women and men and
two Negro overseers, were standing at the gate to the
main house, speaking, arguing, in hushed tones that rose
every now and then with the emotions that both parties
were feeling. The overseers looked very much afraid,
and I could not make out what the trouble was until the
overseers saw me approach and stood aside. What I saw
near blinded me with pity and grief.

Ata, bloodied from the waist down and seemingly in
a swoon, was in the arms of two Negro men who carried
her with great tenderness and care. I rushed to calm the
men, who were determined to wake Mr Codrington to
show him what had happened to the wretched child. I
persuaded the overseers to allow me to take the men and
the child into the house, and this was agreed to with the
proviso that I did not wake the mistress and master with
what they described as 'nigger business' ... Oh, these
hateful islands!

The two men, Antony and Zadok, went quietly into the
house with me, and lay the child, still in a swoon, on my
bed. Aunt Glenda was sitting up, anxious for news, and
came to the bedside to look upon the child. Glenda knew
from the moment she lifted the dress of poor Ata what had
taken place. Oh, Sancho ... Someone had violated the
chastity of a nine-year-old girl. Who had done this was of
secondary concern, but Zadok whispered the name of her
attacker to me. He spoke the name of Wilson as one might

*pronounce the devil's name. A fact. No more need be
said. Glenda drew me away from the bed – begged me to
keep my counsel – for if any heard a Negro accuse a white
man, that Negro would be subject to the most draconian
punishment. The laws do not exist to protect the Negro
here, Sancho; the law does not recognise our humanity.
It would be the word of a black child against the word of
the most powerful white man on this estate, beside Mr
Codrington himself.*

*My tears came thick and fast – rage followed. The
idea that nothing could be done kept me awake all night,
apart from watching the child, who seemed to be dreaming
fitfully, but had not opened her eyes all the time I watched
her. I was burdened with the foolish thought that if I had
let Mr Wilson have his way, he would not have sought
out an easier victim. Aunt Glenda and I were happy to
see that Ata's eyes were open and seeing when we arose
later that morning, though in truth we had not slept with
any sense of rest that whole night. To see the child . . .
We had removed her bloodied garment and cleaned her
body as best we could the night before. Nothing was said
by either of us when we saw the state of her body, but
we both knew that Ata would be in great pain when she
woke. That morning, she simply stared out to the fields,
not looking at us – keeping her eyes averted all the while –
thinking deeper thoughts than she had ever thought in her
life. I took her little hand, which she allowed, but without
seeming to really notice.*

*'Dear child. Please tell me what befell you? We are
your friends and care very much for you . . .'*

Ata turned her once-bright eyes to me, then, arresting me instantly, and the dull life that glowed faintly there was the most tragic thing I had ever seen in my life. We had not protected her – how could we – and now we could do nothing for her. We did not cease from shedding salty drops for several days. When Ata was recovered enough to walk about the room, I tried in vain to persuade her to take a turn outside. She refused, saying that she would never leave the house again, for it was leaving the house that meant she might encounter Wilson. I could stand it no longer and went directly to the mistress to see if something might be done for her. I was momentarily thwarted by the ringing of the lunch gong, and so I waited until Mrs Codrington had finished her repast; it was the ideal occasion to approach her, as she was a woman that needed her energy if one was to challenge her to make any important decision. This was Aunt Glenda's sage advice, which I thought wise to heed. I found Mrs Codrington at her harpsichord, playing 'Friendship, Source of Joy', its happy and jaunty air lending a kind of abstraction to the burden on my heart. She finished playing and looked up at me, surprised to see me there.

'How clever your beau is to have written such lively music, and so easy to – Anne, what is the matter? You look as though you were ailing for something? Are you suffering from the headaches, as I am?'

'No, ma'am, so please you, it is Ata.'

'Who?'

'Ata? The young girl who we brought from Barbados, ma'am, to help with—'

'Ah yes, Ata. Is that how she is called amongst you people? Her name is Betty.'

I felt then that it would be difficult for Mrs Codrington to act appropriately, since it was clear that she was ignorant of the child, not even knowing her given name until this moment. But I recalled Ata's melancholy and grief and that gave me the boldness to persevere.

'She has been violated, ma'am, and we believe we know who the culprit was who committed this despicable act.'

'"Despicable . . . ?" You are quite the curiosity, Anne Osborne, really you are. Where did you learn to speak English so well, my dear?'

'Ma'am, this is a matter of great importance and I beg you to help the poor girl, for she has not spoken many words since it happened.'

'Since what happened, Anne? I am most confused by your speech. If there are any problems with the Negro girl, please address yourself to Molly or Mr Wilson; that is not in my purview.'

She rose then and left me alone. I stood for some time in the doorway, gazing about the room with eyes blinded by tears. There would be no help from this quarter, and the thought of trying to approach Mr Codrington presented an even bleaker prospect for redress. I realised then how alone we are in the world, we Negroes: how friendless, how powerless. I stepped onto the veranda and stood with the sun full in my face.

'Miss Anne?'

I looked up, blinking back the tears that had been

*rolling down my cheeks for some time. There stood Zadok,
with a wide-brimmed straw hat upon his head to ward
off the sun. He nodded at me and passed directly into the
house. A few moments later, I could hear him speaking to
Mr Codrington in the master's drawing room. Not long
after that, I was summoned before Mr Codrington, and
found him in a rage. He sat behind his large oak desk,
papers strewn chaotically all over its surface. His hunting
trophies were incongruously set around the walls, making
little sense, as every animal depicted – from wild boar to
the most glorious stag – was a native of Europe and not
the Caribbean. It seemed that even the master did not
wish to be here. Zadok stood, silent, and with his eyes on
the Persian rug beneath our feet, its tiger motif arresting
the eyes, momentarily.*

*Mr Codrington began: 'What has happened to Betty,
Anne? Tell me what you know, for Zadok makes little
sense to me.'*

*'I cannot tell what Mr Zadok has told you, Sir, but
Ata – Betty – has been molested by a man who I believe
to be Mr Wilson. She is but nine years old, Sir, and
should not have been used so. She hardly speaks, now,
where she was quite voluble previously – she weeps herself
to sleep every night that she has been under your roof, Sir.'*

*I tried to speak factually, but the truth of what Ata had
been through, and her current state, got the better of me
and I'm afraid I dissolved into tears. The master allowed
me the time to compose myself, then rose and asked us
both to leave, as he needed to ponder what was best to
be done about the situation. Three days passed, Sancho,*

*without a word from either the master or mistress. Three
days – in which I learnt to hate this family and this place
in ways that prevented my sleep and gave me little peace.
How could these people take such a light attitude to the
sufferings of an innocent child? Why was Mr Wilson not
also summoned to give an account of himself? What did
Mr Codrington intend to do for poor Ata? Three days,
I say, elapsed before I was summoned into the drawing
room by Mrs Codrington. She sat upright on a tall-
backed and deeply upholstered armchair, the patterns of
roses and thorny branches giving her the air of sitting on
a throne of rose-barbs ... I suppose I thought this in order
to steady myself; I did not know what to expect of her. She
calmly laid the letter she had been reading on her lap,
before beginning:*

*'We have taken your story and that of Zadok to
Mr Wilson, who denies all. Since we cannot very well
question the child, who seems to be mute, we must accept
that he is being accused by those who do not like his
ways. Therefore, we are sending Ata back to Barbados.
We cannot have a child about us who would lie to her
superiors in order to take revenge on one she could not
entice with her forwardness. Mr Wilson was quite clear
that the child desired him to embrace her, but he would
not, good man, and she sought revenge by accusing
him on this false charge. I suggest you no longer listen
to niggers and piccaninnies for your knowledge of what
happens here. You are not like them, Anne, for you have
been civilised by your happy life in England. But here,
the Negroes are apt to tell lies about each other and, if*

*they can, on their masters. We will entertain no more
accusations against an upright and useful man from a
wayward girl who wishes to entice said man to be her
protector and benefactor; that much is known to me, and
should, by now, be known to you. That will be all.'*

*And so saying, she returned to the letter she had been
reading before I came in. I uttered not a word, but left as
instructed. As I entered the kitchen, I saw Zadok leaving
by the back door, and Molly watching him go. She turned
to me then and, crossing the floor swiftly, slapped me
across the face. I was so stunned by her actions that I
could not move for an instant, and she pulled me in to her
and held me while the tears came in earnest. I felt that I
was in a sea of sentiments; they kept washing over me like
wave after wave in a storm: rage at my impotence; anger
at the white folks who treated this tragedy with so much
contempt; despair at the weakness of the Negroes; guilt at
my culpability; and finally, a deep sense of fear that we
were all vulnerable, nine years old and upward – all.*

*'Nuttin' go change iffen you shout from the mountain
top, darlin. Nuttin'. Nuttin'. You put Zadok in a bad
place with Mr Wilson by telling tales 'pon him. You mus'
learn that we niggers don' have the right. No right to
accuse a white of anytin' they doin'. Don' you know that,
yet? For the sake of the people, you mus' quiet, you hear
me? So, nuttin'. No talk, you hear me?'*

*I nodded through my tears and, leaving the kitchen, lay
in a field away from all and did not return to the house
until evening. When I returned, Glenda was waking from
a long sleep. What she told me did nothing to comfort me.*

*Ata had been taken away, already – I did not have a
chance to even say goodbye to her, Sancho, and my heart
remains, these six weeks or so since she was sent away,
broken into many, many pieces. Mr Wilson continues as
before, though they must have warned him to stay clear
of the house, as we did not see him after this and still
have not. Thank the Lord that I did not, for the feeling
that I must confess rules my heart more than all others is
murder, if murder can be called a feeling.*

*I cannot write more, for it pains me too much. Please
understand.*

Your Anne.

Holborn, London.

Dearest Anne,

I cannot begin to know how you wrestle with the
tragic events you relate in your last letter. I can only
imagine that though the tears may have ceased, the
melancholy remains. Poor Ata. Poor, lonely child.
Hateful Mr Wilson, not worthy of the name Man.
Beast, is closer to the mark. I believe you are right
to say that his advances towards you had no outlet
until he found this poor child, vulnerable and easily
overcome. He deserves the noose ... Alas, we know
that he will likely escape judgement in this life. God's
mercy, though it is just, should not extend to such
as this hell-born soul. You cannot be blamed for the
actions of evil men, Anne, no matter if your rejection
encouraged Wilson to take this desperate course. You

needed to protect your person, and did your utmost. Wilson's mind was bent on mischief and, sadly, Ata was all too easy prey. It is prayer alone that can help her now, and I pray God that He would guide her steps for the rest of her time on earth. At least she is safe from one villain . . .

I come now to you. You must leave this place, Anne, and right quickly. It cannot be safe to have such a dangerous enemy as Mr Wilson, who knows you see his guilt and his shame, roaming unmolested about his master's property. He will surely be on the hunt for an opportunity to avenge himself on you and Zadok, that brave man. If Hincham was in his position he would do to you what he succeeded in doing to Tilly, and despoil your reputation as far as he is able.

In that light, I have spoken with your father, and we agree that you must be brought home for your safety. How we are to manage this is the conundrum of the moment, but it will be done. Your father will speak to his mistress in London and urge the Stoke family in Scotland to send for you. My first idea is to gather as much money between us and the other friends we have, and try to get you passage to England at the earliest possible opportunity. Rest assured this will be carried out at the swiftest speed imaginable. You cannot any longer remain there and think yourself safe for an instant. A man that has free rein over so many will not baulk to lay a snare for one lone woman, and a Negro woman at that.

Your father will send you news, no doubt, before my next arrives with you, as I have much to do and cannot spend as much time writing as I would have liked. However, this is the most important thing I could ever do, and think the sacrifice of a few lines well worth the waiting.

With love and an assurance that we will have you home safe and sound, soon.

Your Sancho.

Codrington Estate, Antigua.

Dear-one,

I am glad that you are concerned for me, but you need not put yourself to such an expense. The cost of passage to England is exorbitant and I wonder if I might be permitted to leave, in truth. On the other hand, Aunt Glenda is almost well enough to walk about now, without the aid of a stick or the arm of a companion, which may help my case for a swift return. No news, as yet, of Ata, or from the Codrington Plantation in Barbados. We can only trust God, as you say, and hope that she has a guardian angel that will care for her there, poor soul.

See how brief our missives are now? We are grieving, you and I – grieving for the life of a young girl who had the brightest eyes and the sunniest spirit, despite the tragedies that had too soon encompassed her since early in her short life.

Glenda insists that though she would miss me greatly, she no longer needs a nurse. She urges me to demand my

return to England from the Codringtons, but I will wait
until Lady Stoke has written to them from Scotland.
This will have more authority and efficacy than any
intervention on my part.

I send this to you in the hopes that this may be one of
our last communications before we are face to face.

With love and hope,

Anne. Yours.

Montagu House, White Hall, London.

Hen,

We have much to discuss and I want to send
this letter as soon as I am able. Forgive its brevity,
therefore.

Your father has secured at least half of what we need
from your mistress, who was much concerned that
the situation in Antigua was so precarious. She hopes
to see you next year, but for my part that is too long a
wait. I will ask today if the Earl and Countess might
aid us in this rescue mission.

I had thought to distract you with a word on life in
London, Hen, but the mind, and my intent, is dulled
by this cloud of Ata, that hovers over nearly every
word I write to you. Poor, dear young soul ... Truly,
until you are back safe and sound in England, I have
no heart for writing of my trifling life. It may be,
Anne, that I never take joy in such things again, if I do
not have you in my arms within this six-month. I am
determined it will be so.

I leave off. Impotent tears sting my eyes, love. You must know these blots are a sign of my love for you.

He, who loves you.

I.S.

> Rise up my love, my fair one, and come away.
> For lo, the winter is past, the rain is over and
>   gone.
> The flowers appear on the earth; the time of
>   singing has come,
> And the voice of the turtledove is heard in our
>   land.
> The fig tree puts forth her green figs,
> And the vines with the tender grapes give a
>   good aroma.
> Rise up, my love, my fair one, and come away.
> O my dove, in the clefts of the rock,
> In the secret places of the cliff,
> Let me see your countenance,
> Let me hear your voice;
> For your voice is sweet and your countenance
>   lovely.

SONG OF SOLOMON

Codrington Estate, Antigua.

Dearer to me than life,

I greet you in the manner of one who is sure of your love. Still, I must confess, this love can sometimes seem illusory. I do not know when we shall see each other again, yet I know that we have seen each other but once. This exercises my mind greatly. I fear for the moment when you see me, ravaged by recent cares and these harsh and sun-blasted climes. These thoughts cloud my mind, and instead of looking gaily upon that day when we will gaze upon each other, I search, frantic, in any looking-glass I find, to see what would be your first sight of me after so long an absence. Pray God you will be kind to me, if you must say that I do not please you? Truth, always, we promised each other with our vows of love, did we not?

These words when read over are melancholy indeed, Sancho, are they not? This is the legacy of the last few months – perhaps, the harvest of these many years since I arrived in the Indies. The heaviness I witnessed in the natives when I first arrived is now upon me – a constant cloak of protection. One's guard is always up; one's eyes are ever restlessly on the lookout for the next hazard on the horizon. A tension rises to the shoulders by day and sits on the chest by night, weighty and inescapable. I cannot write of joyful things, Sancho, because I have felt no such sentiment this six-month, nay, not even reading your letters allays this cloud of Ata ...

I came so close to tearing these sheets apart and starting again, in a lighter vein ... but Truth, always, with us.

I am sad. I cannot say more. I long for you and to be with you. I cannot do more.

Your Anne.

1757

Montagu House, White Hall.

Hen,

Before all, your father and I have secured the necessary permissions and monies to have you home with us next month!

I wept to read your last. I rejoice to read your truth and feel the privilege of being your confidante. I do not want you to ever censure yourself, for no soul can keep better counsel than I, love. Be sad. Say no more. If you returned to me prune-wrinkled by the sun and with locks as wild as a lioness's mane, I would love you. Your gentle heart and loving look are what remain of you in my soul. The one I have lived with these past five long years in letters, the other I will enjoy to my heart's content in life! One encounter was enough to know we loved deeply; a lifetime will prove our instincts right, love – never doubt my constancy.

We will mourn together, love, and lay a wreath

of flowers for dear, little Ata, and light candles to
remember her by. Pathetic tokens, I see too clearly.
The heaviness you describe is but a form of grief and
will pass. Do not think it an indelible stamp on your
character, for you will smile again, and one day you
will laugh, too, believe Sancho.

Once more, I thank you for your trust in me. We
will not be in any danger of rupture, my dove, if we
keep to this strict rule of *Truth, Always*. No more.
Your father will write soon with the full arrangements
laid out with dates, etc. No more, for now.

My love to you, Always.

Sancho.

Codrington Estate, Antigua.

Dear heart,

*It was good to read and re-read and re-read your last.
I was assured of your love before my letter reached you,
be confident of that, but that you responded so kindly to
a moment of melancholy, is a joy to me. What a kind
husband I will know. A kindly father and a trusty friend
and confidante.*

*My mood is much mended, though we still have no
news of little Ata. She was sent alone, poor wretch –
wicked Codringtons – and the captain would be entrusted
to pass her through to her guardians on Barbados.
From there she would be sent to a plantation, or sold to
a merchant from another island entirely, to avoid her
encountering any she knew from her previous life on*

*Barbados. We may dream that one day she would be
taught the rudiments of reading and writing, as I began
to teach her, and learn to write me a letter when she is a
grown woman – we must hope, my dove.*

*You were my dove and the cleft in the rock for me these
past years. I cannot dream of you any longer, for my mind
will only settle on the* genuine article. *And at that, see,
I smile for the first time in a very long season of grief.
Perhaps, as you wrote, I will not be sad for ever – and
remember that we are a surviving people, and that many
suffer worse.*

*An hour ago, the mistress informed me that a storm at
sea was threatening the harbour, and that there would
likely be no shipping for a month as many boats had
been smashed already. I took the news with no expression
that she might read, but inside it felt as if a volcano had
spilt its contents. I sat on my bed and cried for full thirty
minutes, then pulled myself together and went out again to
fulfil my household chores. I have learnt a resilience that I
did not possess when I arrived here, husband – beware. I
am not the little dove you might recall.*

*I am neither prune-wrinkled nor lioness-maned, I
thank ye for your concern. We Black Ladies have our
vanity, of that you must not be mistaken, pupil.*

It is good to smile about you.

Soon, with you.

Anne. Yours.

And here, Billy, the letters across the ocean cease.

Dundee, Scotland.

Dearest Angel,

I have arrived in Scotland, at last, and made my first task the writing of this letter to you, my only heart, and so very soon to see.

We embarked on the eighth of May and set sail along the east coast of America as the captain supposed it would be the calmest way. Until we reached the coast of Florida, however, we were tossed about with some violence. Many were ill of the sea-sickness, and many could not sleep for several days. Myself, I slept soundly for the first time in what seems like years. I was away from Mr Wilson, plantation life and fear. I will miss Molly and Wanda, Zadok and Auntie Glenda in particular, but I was overjoyed to set sail from Antigua that morning. We sailed to New York due to our water supply running low, and to avoid the storms in the middle of the Atlantic Ocean. After two days at anchor, being stocked with fresh supplies, we set off for Portsmouth. The journey was uneventful, save for the shock of cold that greeted me on deck one morning, informing me that you and I were closer still. Arriving in Portsmouth on a clear June day was the perfect tonic for one who had feared every look and every soul about her in the harbour in Antigua. Father arrived with my young brother John, just in time to see me off, as my mistress had desired me to be taken to her in Scotland, directly. I am sorry for this, as I longed so to visit with you. Just a little longer, my darling one. My mistress has never sojourned in her Scottish home for longer than a six-month. We may see each other at Christmas-time . . .

The last few weeks in Antigua were full of tension and fear. Mr Wilson had been seen lurking about the slave quarters. The men set up groups to watch, lest he seek another victim. Usually, Zadok told me, they found him in a heap just outside the compound, a flagon of rum in his arms – like his sweetheart, they said. When I had packed my bag – one small bag after so many years – and was awaiting the coach to take me to the harbour, Mr Wilson appeared from behind the house and stood and watched me, no more, until the coach came, whereupon that evil man took to waving a soiled handkerchief in my direction, in imitation of a lover waving farewell. The sound of his mocking laughter was the last sound I heard in that blasted place. As I gazed upon the men and women working in the blazing sun in the cane fields on either side of the dirt track, I knew myself to be fortunate to be able to leave this hell and, like you, I now have a Cause. To raise sons and daughters to know a pride of person – beacons of light in a benighted world.

The setting in Scotland is pleasant if permanently chilly, even in late spring. I sometimes rise at five in the morning to breathe in the air outside. It is quiet about, for the trees are some way off from the house itself and the birds can be heard but faintly at that time of day. I look towards the horizon to the east and orient myself to the south from there, sending a prayer of love to you, so very far, but not so far from me as before. I pray you hear my

love whispering in your ear every morning. Say you do,
even if that is a pretty lie?

   With love, love and more of love than can be expressed
in words, I am,

   Your Anne.

Postscript:

When I found him, the one I love,
I held him and would not let him go.

Thus ended our correspondence. Mark how words have power
to make one person known to another – if the object of affection
reciprocates with the honesty your mother showed me.

   Never underestimate the power of the Word, my child.

Coda for Young Lovers

In which Charles Ignatius courts Anne Osborne.

23 August 1757

I hardly know what I do.

Luke Sullivan says he feels as though he has lived with fifteen different men for the last three days alone. I vacillate between feeling an unworthiness in my person compared to such an angel as Anne, and wondering if my fancy for her will have diminished with the passing years and so long an absence . . .

Even writing my diary no longer feels like an act I do alone. I have shared every deep thought with Anne Osborne for so long that I want to write to her in person on these private pages – I cannot find the motivation to speak of deep matters, it seems, until I speak them with her. My stomach lurched just then when I thought of her, and I experienced an ache neither dull nor sharp but all-enveloping, come over my spirit, as if I had passed in spirit from my body momentarily to shake off some lethargy. Tomorrow.

Tomorrow at seven o'clock at Mr John Clarke-Osborne's home, I will meet with my destiny in human form.

How will that be?

26 August

The Encounter

I slept so badly two nights ago that I rose to the sounds of Sullivan returning home from a night of frolics. He came into my chamber and sat on the bed, most unusually for him. This night he chose to sit next to my head, a little too closely, and so I sat up and enquired if he'd passed a pleasant evening. He began coherently enough but soon drifted into some indecipherable nonsense in the thickest Irish accent he had ever employed in my presence. I could not understand a word. I was about to tell him as much when he launched into this small speech:

'They come, they go . . . but the rare ones . . . the rare ones, Charlie boy, we do not throw back, d'ye hear?'

So saying, my potential groomsman lay back onto my legs and promptly fell into a deep slumber. I laid him up in my bed and went to prepare breakfast. I stood by the window that looked down on to the street below. It was largely deserted for it was still dark. I must have been staring at the street for some time as when I finally shook off my reverie the sky was a bright blue. I stoked the dying embers of the stove and made some tea for Luke and myself. For the first time in an age – I smiled. I would be seeing Anne Osborne this very day.

I was breathing so heavily when I arrived – ten minutes late!! – at the Clarke-Osbornes' home, that I forced myself to walk slowly up and down until I was becalmed somewhat. To economise, I had run all the way from St Martin's Lane to Bond Street, but now found I had debilitated myself rather, as I had not taken such vigorous exercise since . . . our dance, perhaps.

Standing before John's house and wiping my perspiring brow, I felt overwhelmed by the moment. I could not shake the fear that all would be lost if I had only imagined an Anne that could not be found in truth. The door was yanked off its hinges by John himself who rushed past me while reminding me – unnecessarily – that they had the first floor, adding that he needed to fetch his wife Mary from the post-house. And with that he was gone. I duly mounted the steps to the right of the narrow corridor. Turning from the landing, I saw the door to his chambers ajar. Sitting by the window in the gentle evening sunlight was Anne Osborne.

If I had felt unworthy yesterday, I felt doubly so now, for before me sat a veritable angel from the skies. The light played on her caramel brown skin, so glowing, so redolent of sun and the outdoors. She wore an exact copy of the outfit she had worn when we met that first night at the Black Tar Tavern – but this was no young girl who sat here, patiently waiting for her parents to return – knowing her lover is soon to walk in through that door – this was a woman of experience and great powers of resilience. Just then, the angel looked up.

Anne stood up immediately and my legs – which seemed moments before to have lost the knowledge of movement – carried me to the threshold of the door. I took in nothing but the woman before me. Slighter than I remembered, and just the smallest sign of strain around the eyes and mouth, where she must have allowed many tears for dear Ata to wash away her sorrows. It was fitting, then, that I began our first proper conversation with this:

'How I longed to know this moment, how many hours and words and thoughts and dreams and daydreams. But now that you are before me, my heart fails me – and I can only think on Ata. Dear, sweet child.'

Anne walked towards me purposefully and drew her arms about me – I held her to me.

'It is good to be home.'

'Yes', I agreed.

We two strangers wept then, for a girl I had never met nor was ever likely to, who meant the world to both of us. We wept for our missing years, the carefree years that we imagine we might have enjoyed. We wept for gratitude in our fortune – in Divine Providence – in being reunited after so many years and over so many, many miles.

We were cautious with each other. Patient. Observant. We were two strangers – really we were – in a strange room mourning a stranger, and yet I trusted already – hoped – that we could agree on the most important thing which was that we were both home. At last.

Anne and I held each other for a long time. I could feel

her body relaxing into mine more and more. I felt a surge of self-awareness at my girth for an instant, but I pushed that aside swiftly for vanity had no room when comfort was required. We were both consoled by this embrace, I think, and held on to each other for a while longer than was perhaps normal for a pair that had spent so little time in each other's company.

At last, she pulled away from me, and taking me by the hand, just as she had that fateful night five years ago when she led me onto the dance floor at the Black Tar Tavern, she drew me down to the settee beside her, smoothing down her skirt as she did so, in that graceful way I had noted the night we met. The light was golden through the lace curtains behind our heads, and the motes of dust that gathered in the shafts of evening sunlight leant the room a dream-like atmosphere. The pungent aroma of lilies in flower which sat in a vase on a long side table across the room suffused the air with its sensually rich heaviness. We could hardly believe it to be true: we were together at last, after five long years.

We sat rather formally at first, while she poured the tea that had been prepared by her before my arrival. I apologised for my tardiness and began to explain myself when there was a door opened downstairs and we thought it must be John and Mary. I rose with her and waited for their steps on the stairs when another door slammed downstairs . . .

We realised it had been a neighbour arriving home. We turned to each other then and smiled shy smiles, for we could see we were both nervous suddenly. John might have helped with his easy air of social affability and Mary was a kind and pleasant conversationalist. But we had almost too much to say in order to commence our conversation and that fact kept us mute for some minutes more.

'Delicious. Thank you.'

'Good tea. I have missed it, so.'

'Did not you find it drunk in the West Indies?'

'Sometimes. It is more popular in India, perhaps, for they believe the heating of the blood causes one to perspire, which cools the body . . .'

'You really are a mine of information botanical, geographical and biological.'

Her easy laugh was a joy to hear. I had only imagined her laughter all these years and it was nothing compared to the music that emanated from her chest when she was greatly amused. A ringing tone that rose and fell swiftly with a smile as wide as the ocean. A joy to behold. I silently vowed to make her smile my daily reward for demonstrating my love to her. We sat, again, this time more easily. Her eyes were bright with tears shed in the last few moments, giving her a faraway look for a moment as if she were not of this earth. This sense lasted only a short time for we smiled anew at the proximity of the other.

'So much was said in our letters that so little need be said when we meet. I am happy with that state of affairs, Charles, are you not?'

'I am. Though I pride myself on being lyrically rich, silence in the presence of great emotions is wise . . . if dull.'

That smile, again, and a lowering of her head that has me glowing with affection. Mary's harpsichord, given to her, she had said, by her mistress when a newer model was purchased, stood in pride of place next to the entrance door. I rose and sat at the low stool and began to play. Whatever instinct had led me to do this was a good one for after a few minutes of warming my fingers over the keys, Anne came to stand beside me, her delicate hand resting lightly on my left shoulder. I thrilled to her touch.

I played a gentle minuet but slowed its pace to a legato, softly pressing the keys to keep the sound simple. It was a moment of peace after the maelstrom of emotions we had both felt on seeing each other after our five-year separation. As I played and lost myself more and more in the music, I felt Anne move gently behind me and hold me close, drawing her arms across my neck and leaning on my shoulders, her face pressed next to mine.

She was so affectionate that I found myself challenged to reciprocate. I turned my face to hers as she gazed into my eyes with a look of such gentle love. I was kissing her before I knew what I did. That warm aroma of cocoa and coconut came from her whole body. I stopped playing and drew her down to me on the low stool, kissing her gently all the while. Her lips were full and soft, warm to the touch of my lips and welcoming. We explored each other in this way for several minutes.

Recovering somewhat from our unexpected passion, we took the time to rise and sit at the window, once again. We tried to sip our tea but even that which she'd kept in the pot was lukewarm at best. She rose to make a fresh infusion and I followed her into the tiny kitchen that gave on to the side of the main room. Though the space was as narrow as a corridor, it was neatly appointed and had all that might be required. Anne filled the kettle with water from a large pail and set the kettle on the stove to begin heating it. I watched her as she bustled efficiently from the living room to the kitchen, gathering the cups we had used and washing them in the basin they kept on one counter.

A small window at the end of the kitchen poured evening light into the room, bathing the space in a heavenly glow. She was angelic. Her small movements, economical, graceful, her habit of gently smiling all the while she toiled over our refreshment, had me intoxicated, hypnotised. Heated. She turned to me as she waited for the kettle to boil our water and that look had me reaching for her, again. The steam from the boiling kettle had almost filled the room by the time we could disengage ourselves from such a sweet embrace.

Returning to the settee with our steaming cups of tea, we sat very close to each other and talked freely, like the old friends we were. That laugh. That smile.

'Did you receive any news of more employment with the Montagus?'

'No. Not as yet. But fret not, Anne, I have sufficient to start our life together. I have saved a fair sum that I take to be enough to secure a set of rooms. And I will find work that—'

'You mistake me, Charles. I do not concern myself with your financial credentials.'

She hugged me briefly, then: 'It is too late for this poor soul-in-love to worry about solvency in her chosen. Did not you write that a wife to an ogre may not see his faults?'

It was my turn to laugh, almost spilling out a geyser of tea in the act. We smiled as she handed me a napkin with that shy nod of the head, pleased, I could see nevertheless, that she could make me laugh in her turn. A moment of pleasant silence between us. Then: 'I hope to hear of more work soon, for Montagu House is short of staff, as ever. Bessie and I will ply our trade in Hampstead next week, I trust.'

'Ah, dear Bessie. I wish you had brought your mandolin to meet me, too.'

'Oh, she is too timid a soul to meet one so exalted as you are in my esteem. I feel she may become a little jealous, too.'

'Well, then you must tame her, Charles, as you must tame all your mistresses.'

'Why the plural?'

Laughing at my theatrical indignation we both jumped slightly at the noise of the front door being opened and slammed shut, and the sounds of Mary and John mounting the stairs. It was only at that moment that we realised in what proximity we had long been in upon the settee. To look at us scooting away from each other, you would think we two had been in a fond embrace.

John entered with a flourish, clapping his hands, and dancing around the space, even playing – badly – a bar or two of gay music on the harpsichord; Mary greeted me with her usual kiss on the cheek and an affectionate embrace for her daughter – then proceeded to push her husband from the stool and began to play for us. It was a joyous moment that made me feel included in the Clarke-Osborne family in a way that I have never forgotten.

Anne's smile was permanent and broad, and as she danced with John to the lively jig her mother was playing, I marvelled at my great good fortune to have a creature such as this in love with me. I felt like a made man, at long last.

Book Four

1759–1780

In which Sancho tells all that remains –
We bid farewell to our hero.

Taking leave of those we esteem
is, in my opinion, unpleasant;
the parting of friends is a kind of
temporary mourning.

CHARLES IGNATIUS SANCHO

Chapter I

Sancho and the last things

1780

I am fifty-one years old, Billy – my time is short. My life seems like the sand in an hourglass, increasing with speed as it draws to a close, where I see each grain as a breath. Once it is released it can never rise again. Those grains can be numbered, and that is frightening to me. Not the undiscovered country, but the life I leave behind for them that loved me. How much of my task remains that can never be done?

I ask myself, now, what can usefully be said in these pages that I have not said before, and that you cannot find in the memory of your mother and your sisters. For, like one of the writers of the Gospels declares, we cannot hope to relay the doings of a man's life in a few pages, but would need an entire library to note even the few years of a person's journey on earth. And who would spend a lifetime reading the lifetime of another? Only a very great fool . . . or a dying man who thought he might live to read to the end of a long tale?

My lad, let us to business here. I will only tell you that which may aid you in recognising good friend from bad – worthwhile labour from profligacy of time. I have learnt that you cannot please all, and most of the time you please very few. Do not waste your efforts winning over those who would discount your worth before they ever see the product of your genius. Of that I know too much, in that I have wasted precious grains of life in the effort to impress some soul for whom my life's blood spilt in the quest for equanimity would be so much water cast into a London ditch.

I have laughed so this morning with you, my Billy, as you ran in and out and up the stairs and round every corner of our home. The girls could not get you to sit still so that they might draw your likeness. You cannot be stopped, I say, for you have much to do ... You have done much for my spirits and your mother's, my sweet hero. For, though you be only five years old, your hands have helped your father to secure the future of his children. I will end these final pages with your act of heroism, lest your siblings neglect to relate this story to you, thinking you recall well enough. Not all of us have cause to remember our life before the age of five, and it is the comfort of my last days that only a traumatising incident would cause any child of ours to remember those days too vividly. Mine are full of Sills and Abigails, and looming violence ... Yours, of much laughter and the love of a close family.

I sit in the peace and quiet of the afternoon – in my bath chair – in the store, which used to be a little less cluttered – a little more peopled with clients – and search the shelves for objects to hand that might help me tell my story of the years since the felicitous wedding day your mother and I enjoyed. And what do I see first, in the early morning light? Your sister Fanny's little theatre, made from an old sugar box ...

Chapter II

*Sancho, the actor versus
Sancho, the father.*

1759

When Mary Ann was born, Anne and I had what we called 'the golden days' – days we both believed were inimitable. How could you reproduce the moment you two become three; or the smell of your baby's skin as it sleeps so profoundly beside you; or count the hours you can spend just gazing at them from toes to marvellous crown? Mary Ann was born at a time when I was gaining some ground in regular concerts, but not enough of those to make a living for three. I set to scheming . . .

I had not visited the Ivy Lane Club for about a year and was happy to see that nothing had changed, except the notices on the slate board the little post-boys would chalk up, swiftly. I met John Clarke-Osborne in Mr Hogarth's favourite snug, but found the latter's absence convenient, as what I had to say to Mr Garrick – Davey – once we had eaten and drunk a little – would be best said with the most optimistic of advocates around me. Hogarth could be a sneery bastard when it came to other people's artistic pursuits – he fancied himself a musician of the first order. He was not. It was this night that I had chosen to fulfil a long-held ambition of mine and – despite my girth and despite my intermittent gout – I meant to do it. I would become an Actor.

The statement rang strangely in my head, suddenly, as Davey joined us and – while we allowed him to be assailed by every member of the 'bar' who had ever seen him perform – or merely gazed upon his immortalised figure in the plague of prints of the famous portrait by Joshua Reynolds – we gorged ourselves. Mutton stew, Mr Horseman's speciality, and the thickest gravy that ever was, together with more potatoes than in an Irish acre, and cabbage chopped roughly and boiled in wine and water. A feast. We sat back for a few moments and lit our pipes, puffing contentedly.

Clarke-Osborne disrupted the tranquillity: 'Y'all ever see young Mr Henderson act?'

'Yes, naturally, Mr Osborne.'

'And what think you of him ...?'

'Am I to hang up my breeches and let the younger man have the stage? Is that what you mean to say?'

'I never say anything of the sort, Sir, though you seem to have given the matter plenty thought, already.'

We were silent for a moment more before Garrick's gentle laughter began, followed in crescendo by John's, and then my own braying guffaw punctured the air. I stole a glance at Mr Clarke-Osborne, who was watching me with his *unseeing* eagle eyes. By that, I mean he appeared not to be staring at you, but he seemed to be, nonetheless. A sort of side-eye trick. West Indian in origin, I'd hazard. I cleared my throat before my father-in-law might intervene with a question to me.

'Davey!'

'Good Lord, dear boy. I nearly jumped out of my skin.'

'Sorry. I had a thought that excited me, somewhat.'

'Well, spill the beans, as the Bishop said to the Houseboy in Milady's larder.'

Clarke-Osborne chuckled, unhelpfully.

'I ... I wanted to ask you what you thought of my desire to ... to become an actor? You've said many a time how talented you thought I was in recital. I know how to deport myself on a stage, I suffer from no stage fright, and my voice is as loud as any minor Roscius.'

I immediately wished I had not mentioned *Roscius*, the greatest actor of antiquity. It exposed a hint of immodesty. Davey's face was not helpful. Neither was my father-in-law's closed-eyed visor. Neither looked at me. After too long, Davey leant back in his chair and took a long suck of his pipe. *Suspenseful* doesn't near describe it.

'We must begin slowly, you understand?'

I bounded off my bench and embraced him before he could say another word.

'What think you to this, John? I am an actor!' I said. Turning to Davey, then: 'Or very nearly. We'll start slowly, of course. I have much to learn, I know. There is a world of difference between performing in the music room at Montagu House, or in the little interludes of my mistresses when a mere child, and acting upon the stage at Drury Lane. I cannot expect to simply—'

Garrick suddenly interrupted my glossolalia with: 'Now look, Sancho. There can be no thought of appearing at Drury Lane. One must audition to be an actor in my company – I hope this does not offend you?'

'Offend me, Sir? Why, I'd give my eye-teeth for such a chance as this. And so, I'll leave you.'

I couldn't wait to surprise my Hen with this news. I embraced Davey anew and it was only as I pulled the curtains closed behind me that another thought struck me and, turning on my heels, I whipped the curtain open, making my two companions jump with mild surprise.

'Othello? No, Oroonoko, Prince of Angola? Which? Or will we attempt a new piece?'

'Well . . . I—'

'I have it! We will invite His Majesty the King! I've met him several times, you know . . . Now, that would draw a crowd, would it not? I must home again to tell Dame Sancho that all I've ever dreamt of has come to pass. Farewell, friends – and thank you.'

And with that, I was gone. I believe they would both have taken a breath before confirming my insanity to one another. At the time, it seemed the sanest scheme I had conjured up in my long life of schemes.

I was right to be optimistic, for that summer, during the usual hiatus in the theatre, Garrick offered me the chance to rehearse and perform – for one night only – Shakespeare's Othello.

'Fifteen rehearsals of two hours' duration should see it roughly standing.'

Around that time, dear Anne was as happy as I had ever known her, and I wanted to maintain this state in her if I was able. The night I rushed away from Clarke-Osborne and Garrick to tell Anne all, ended with a long walk home to assess my course, and the conclusion that informing her of my doings in the theatre would not have been conducive to her calm.

My strategy for rehearsing *Othello* without the knowledge of Anne went thus:

I crept out of the house three days a week, shortly before eight o'clock in the evening, announcing that I was going for my daily walk – returning late at night, especially after we had begun to rehearse in earnest. In addition to rehearsals, I had a few hours each week alone with Davey, for what he called *refinement*. *Refinement* consisted, in the main, of Garrick trying to lessen the sibilant effects of my persistent lisp. Patient soul.

We began one evening in late June by gathering in the rooms behind the Theatre Royal stage. When I entered the large, airy space, I had the distinct impression that Davey had not mentioned the fact that their Othello was none other than the man who had from time to time composed a comic ditty for interludes between the company's acts. What exactly was I doing here, I could hear some say under their breath. *What say you, the Black Fellow? – A Singer, perhaps? – An Actor? – What? – No – surely not?* Other blacks were to be found in Garrick's company, to be sure, but their roles were only to be stock characters who spoke little or not at all – dancers – in a scene set in some imagined, exotic land. None of those performers were given a role that could be called prominent. I had certainly pulled back the curtain to another world, and all the occupants were flummoxed by my presence there. I stood, politely, to one side, while they gave each other fond embraces and related the events of the previous day's performances in their various other shows. I felt very alien of a sudden; an amateur. Just then Garrick entered, fresh from some crisis or other, and very casually introduced me to his shocked company. The looks I saw on the faces of the ensemble were not encouraging. I was as incredulous as any in that room. Why was Garrick doing this? Was this some sort of experiment; to see if the cleverest Negro he knew could imitate the great European tradition? Once again in my life, I pushed these unhelpful and ungenerous suspicions to one side – determined to show that I was worth the risk to Garrick's Public reputation; those members of the Public who style themselves Critics, that is. A terrifying thought – to be judged by the harshest Critics in the land – London Critics are a species of predator who can take down their prey with a word from their quills. Brutal. Again, I wondered, why was I here?

Almost immediately it became clear how much work I needed to do. Garrick had asked me to read one of Othello's earliest speeches out loud. I did not read well. My voice was too quiet and when I tried to raise it, I found myself stumbling over every other word. I broke into a discomforting sweat and had the sense that I had disappointed my friend, who kindly asked me to cease after some time and politely applauded my efforts. It was not a rousing endorsement from the company to hear the weak smattering of hands that followed Davey's benevolence.

Rehearsals. Days of stumbling over my words, perspiring at every turn, added to which a new affliction – the inability to look another human person in the eye – and I knew that I could bear it no longer. I had to tell someone whom I could trust just how badly things were proceeding. My good friend,

Davey, would lose a little lustre from his shining reputation if he took a risk with an unprepared performance. He would be accounted an ill judge of talent if I could not improve, and that right quickly, as we would present our show in three weeks' time. By my quick calculations, there remained a mere eighteen hours of rehearsal before we would be exposed to the Baying Public, alias the Critics. I tried Mr Clarke-Osborne at first, but he did not want to know the ins and outs of rehearsals as, he said, it robbed him of the magic of attending a play as an ignorant consumer, not one of its cooks. He spoke plain, did our John.

'Why d'ye not ask y'Madame?'

'Because, "m'Madame" is not inclined to approve of the acting type, nor my close association with them.'

'But you are working. Not playing. Although, to see you all in your silly costumes ... One might say you're playing, all right.'

Once he'd recovered from his own witticism, he set to pummelling me with his homespun wisdom.

'You will be on that stage. You might do it many times after; you might do it just this once. You really mean to allow this opportunity to parade your talents before the people – before Anne – to go unseized? You may have your eccentricities, Sancho, but foolish you are not. You would regret that for a very long forever.'

Of course, he had a point, and I resolved to tell Anne all. I found her that night in her bed clothes, laying sweet Mary Ann down in her crib. I stoked the small fire in the grate and we sat on the edge of the bed, side by side, in companionable silence, watching our little angel's chest move up and down and listening to her gurgles as she slept. It was a moment of peace that I guessed belied the storm ahead. Before I could confess, however, Anne turned to me and declared that she had news of her own. But before she could begin, I barked out:

'With child! You are with child!'

There was something about the way she looked before she announced child number two that reminded me instantly of the time she had announced the coming of number one ... She nodded. We held each other for a moment or two, then:

'How was your constitutional this evening? Did you note anything of the works on the square?'

'Works? I really hadn't noticed. I'm afraid I've been a bit distracted of late.'

Anne turned her attention to me with her penetrating honesty and everything, as ever, poured out of me in a torrent of words. I told her of my lie; why I wanted to try my hand on the stage; of my life-long desire to be an actor; I told her what a privilege it was to have David Garrick sponsor me; I told her of my disappointment that the company were not as enthusiastic as their employer; of my inability to be reposed while I portrayed the great general – I stopped. Anne had a look of the most tender care on her face – it was all I could do not to collapse into her arms as though I were her child. She placed a hand on my face and told me softly of her concerns for our family, our precarious fiscal situation, and the coming addition to our ranks. She then surprised me by saying this:

'But your dreams are the map that have taken you so far, Sancho. I do not wish to stand in the way, for I have chosen to travel with you.'

She kissed me tenderly. We talked for some time after that,

until she fell asleep, lying across my chest. I had not the heart to disturb her and my round belly made a soothing pillow for her beautiful head. Her headscarf – of light blue silk – gave off the aroma of the coconut oil that she combed through her hair from time to time. I still have not visited the West Indies, but I have always imagined this intoxicating aroma is to be found everywhere on those islands. We rested well that night, and Mary Ann slept like the cherub she is, until almost eight o'clock that morning.

When, at last, the day came, I could barely breathe with apprehension, and the sure knowledge that I had ruined the reputation of the great Garrick – and disparaged the art of acting to boot. I felt a charlatan and a fraud of the highest audacity; to think of assailing the stage, when many greater than I have failed? Utter madness. I could see the orchestra was assembling and Mr Bagley, a black cornet player, was just taking his seat. He looked nervously toward the stage, and although I was certain he could not see me peeking through a crack in the stage curtain, his look told of one as anxious for my success as any. And then I saw them: the Critics. They were lined up across the front two or three rows of the auditorium, much like carrion crows perched over a carcass, and all wore the same look of disapproval before the curtain had even been raised. They talked amongst themselves and appeared to the observer to be smiling – exchanging pleasant-ries – but, when one heard a word or two emanating from this murder of crows, one knew that they were merely sharpening their talons on each other, only to turn with lethally honed blades to the stage. A musical overture was struck up – my heart leapt out of my mouth and died a shrivelled death outside my body. I stole one more glance out to my executioners and caught a sight that blended comfort with terror. Mr Clarke-Osborne and Anne were making their way along the middle row of the house – taking their places among the people already in their ground-floor seats. There would be no escaping her presence, now, and I cursed my good eyesight for the first time in my life. I would see every grimace my performance elicited in her. I took the time to curse my good hearing too – honed in those Greenwich days – as I could now hear the most appalling comments coming from the Critics about Garrick's fading star and other such nonsense. The man himself stepped out to greet the audience and as the hush descended and the orchestra fell silent, I pulled the curtains to and stepped to the stage left wing, ready for my entrance.

'Ladies and Gentlemen, distinguished connoisseurs of the theatrical delights that our great city has to offer – I welcome you heartily and gratefully to this audition of our play. As you are all no doubt aware, in the normal run of things I like to avoid any preamble to a play in this theatre. In my opinion:

'"Prologues precede the piece – in mournful verse,
As undertakers – walk before the hearse."

'But it is not a death scene we enact here this evening – rather, the dawning of a new day. I present to you a spectacle never before witnessed anywhere else on the globe. A Black Tragedian, ladies and gentlemen! The likes of which come only once in a century.'

The gasps of surprise were loud and numerous. I simply

could not let Anne down now, could I? Humiliation was a valuable lesson in life, I recalled Duke John once telling me, for with it you can learn to behave better. Praise and success, he suggested, renders the victor cocksure and arrogant, at times. I was not in any danger of falling into the latter camp this night. After the murmurings ceased, Garrick continued:

'And, no, not a false Moor, an actor in black-faced make-up, but the genuine article, my friends: a true-born African. He is our very own and dear friend . . . Charles Ignatius Sancho!'

The silence that greeted this crescendo of a speech confirmed every fear I had had in the weeks prior to this day of *execution*. Garrick seemed discombobulated for an instant, looking into the stage wings to his right. After peering into the dark for a few moments, he turned at last to his left and spotted me, frozen to the spot. He gestured, gracefully at first, then made a couple of impatient gestures to beckon me on, and I moved forward. Few have written about life on the stage in a way that can convey the sheer terror of walking before a group of strangers and demanding their attention. I could not remember a word of my rôle – I barely remembered the name of any character in the play – I certainly had forgotten where and when my first entrance was. I found myself standing stiffly beside my brave and foolish friend. The long robe I wore covered the goutish limp that had returned that morning in earnest. I began to feel it was coincident with my anxieties surrounding my debut. The mind can play tricks with our bodies. I felt faintly ridiculous, on top of all the other emotions that battled within me. I was dressed as we imagined an African prince might dress, but the garment caused me to feel I was closer to an imitation of a pre-Restoration actor playing a female role. To my mind's eye, I resembled an overstuffed Lady Margaret from *Richard III*, and I wanted to disappear more than I have ever wished for anything in my life. It was then that a comforting thought occurred to me – as the audience dutifully applauded my appearance – that once again I was in a position of great honour. I knew very few blacks who were as free as I had been for most of my life – none who were privileged enough to perform like this upon the stage. It may have been a mere audition of a play, but it was a landmark in my life that I knew I must relish with all my skill and enthusiasm. I was not shaken out of this more optimistic attitude by one or two spots of suppressed laughter that I could hear scattered around the auditorium. I saw Anne shoot a look – that would do physical harm at closer range – to two fops in the seats in front of her. The dandies adjusted their behaviour accordingly, but continued to sneer behind their lace handkerchiefs. Davey, undeterred by all these distractions, declared:

'I'll leave you now in the very capable hands of my fellow actors, as they present to you Mr William Shakespeare's great tragedy – *Othello, the Moor of Venice.*'

When Davey looked to me over the applause his speech encouraged, I had no idea for an instant what his look meant. Then I jumped, in a rather unlikely way for the Venetian army general, realising the look meant, 'Goodbye – you are on your own from this moment.'

Davey bowed to the audience for a final time, encouraging me to do the same. I duly, stiffly, followed his lead. I froze, again, not knowing what was expected of me. Garrick gestured for me to leave the stage and we rather comically exited into the opposite wings. I collapsed onto a stool at the side of the stage as soon as I had escaped into the wings, and noticed my hands were shaking. My Desdemona passed by at that instant and gave my arm the gentlest squeeze, before heading off to prepare for her own entrance. I took a deep breath and returned to the downstage-left entrance for my first cue. My final memory before stepping onto the stage was the sight of Garrick mopping his brow with a large handkerchief, and a young stagehand handing him a glass of port, which he downed in one relieved gesture.

Much of what followed is an empty space to my recollection. These blank canvases of memory increase with age, it appears to me. I can recall the odd sensation of hearing my voice echoing around the space. I thought the accent I chose was going to make comprehension difficult, but it had the benefit of slowing down my usually rapid speech, and the clarity with which Othello pronounced his words gave him a dignity and power that I revelled in. I only remembered to search for Anne once – in the madness scene – I hoped to impress her with my execution of this tricky moment. I shivered, then fell awkwardly to the floor in a theatrical faint (epilepsy, some say was Shakespeare's intent – ridiculous and clumsy, if one asks the actor). My descent to the stage floor was greeted with laughter in some parts of the auditorium – a few cries of dissent were heard – the laughter ceased. The next time it happened was much later, as I asked my Iago, 'How shall I kill him, Iago?' To which one of the fops Anne had tried to censure cried out, 'Why not merely sit on him?' Again, there was some general laughter at their quick wit, but for the most part I heard voices raised in disapprobation of those foolish fashionables.

'Let us have order, gentlemen. This is not the English way; silence! Let the Negro speak, for shame . . . '

The voices of my advocates were winning out, I discerned, and turning to Iago, a short and wiry man called Arthur Steele, I saw him subtly nod, encouraging me to concentrate on our next moments. I recall very little else, save a short interlude where the musicians seemed to miss the mood of the play altogether and played the most inappropriately jaunty tunes all the while. I held my own temper in check while I pronounced the final words of Othello over his poor murdered wife's corpse. After all that has passed, and all the insults imputed to the dark races of the earth being hurled at Othello's head – by some who exalted him at the beginning – comes a moment of quiet humanity. I forgot where I was entirely, and gazed upon my dead wife on the bed, admonishing the men present to speak:

'... Of one that loved not wisely but too well;
Of one not easily jealous, but being wrought,
Perplexed in the extreme;
... of one whose subdued eyes,
Albeit unuséd to the melting mood,
Drop tears as fast as the Arabian trees
Their medicinable gum. Set you down this;
And say besides, that in Aleppo once,
Where a malignant and a turbaned Turk
Beat a Venetian and traduced the state,
I took by the throat the circumciséd dog,
And smote him – thus.'

The violence with which I plunged the dagger I had hidden into my breast caused some audience members to gasp; one or two screams were heard. I thought – strangely – of my father, then, for the first time for many a year. Perhaps it was not strange at all ... I sank to the bed and almost whispered my last:

'I kissed thee ere I killed thee. No way but this,
Killing myself, to die upon a kiss.'

As I lay, heavily, upon Mrs Sarah Daniels, who took it manfully while the last few lines were spoken, the hush in the auditorium descended deeper still. The silence that met the final lines had us all holding our breath on stage. Had they brought the curtain down at that moment, we may have stolen away without the faintest inkling of their opinion. Then, brave John Clarke-Osborne stood up in his seat and began the applause, accompanied by piercing whistles made with his fingers on his lips. The audience joined him immediately. They appeared to have been in some kind of shock. Anne, whose eyes were full of tears as she stood beside Clarke-Osborne, applauding passionately, gave me a look of such pride that it was all I could do not to burst into tears as we took our first tentative bows. Audience members turned to their neighbours and whispered their opinions, I could see, and many were nodding and smiling in encouragement at what was said. The applause continued to crescendo over time, if anything. Then, Davey came on to raise the note still higher.

I walked to the edge of the stage, as instructed by Garrick

and encouraged by the ensemble behind me and the cheering crowd before me. I bowed low, grateful and moved, feeling not a tinge of pain from my receded gout – Theatre really is the greatest physician. There were many more people in here now than when we first began the performance, I could see; almost half the seats were occupied, and the back stalls had folks standing to see what all the fuss was about. I will never forget it. Nor will I forget that look on Anne's face. I – we – had triumphed . . .

I knew, as surely as I knew I loved my Best Half and my Sanchonettas, that I could never walk this way again. I would never hear applause like this again and I would never take a bow like this again. I left the stage knowing that a lifetime's desperate wish need never be repeated. As rich as the moment was, as accepted as I felt at that moment of finale – it was not life itself – it was but an imitation. I left the stage knowing that I would never act again.

My ever-discerning Anne said little to press for my thoughts when I returned, for we had greeted each other but briefly as I went to noisily celebrate with my fellow Othellites. My Hen had learned over the years how to tell when these moments of contemplation were upon me – she discerned that I appreciated time. Later, however, lying in the dark beside her unsleeping spouse, she turned to me as I sighed anew. I thought she had been asleep, so still she was, until she whispered: 'Was tonight a disappointment to you?'

I paused for only a moment – gazing gratefully in the half-light at this Partner – the Help that was always meeting me in my greatest need – before whispering my words like a child at her private practice – whispering them, softly, in a way that helped me hear their meaning:

'I thought it would be full of a kind of lasting joy.'

'And it was not . . . ?'

'No. It fled the moment I left the stage. Strange. I gazed on my own reflection in the mirror of Garrick's dressing room for quite some time – so very quiet – though I could hear the others chatting – laughing with happiness in the busy hallway – joyful sounds – a kind of relief that it had not been disastrous, I suppose. But, much like when I was a child, my heart held a sort of fear. I felt near the same as the little boy in Panza's garb before that terrifying crowd in Greenwich. Foolish of me . . . '

'Not foolish – never foolish, you. Though, recall things aright – you were but a child – doing as you were told. Fear was your daily bread. Those women used fear to keep you timid – obedient. Now, why do you call this fear a foolishness? It is clear to any that they kept you fearful, to chain you in terror of the whip and the plantation – compliance to their every need would follow – as the lamb his mother – and a cruel manipulator "mother" at that. It would be strange indeed if you did not feel fear, and that hourly.'

As she softly kissed her teeth, in contempt of them – a thing she learnt in her time in the West Indies, and how I adore this trick – as she made this sound, I say – pulling me to her as though she felt a chill after she had spoken with such loving wisdom – my Best Half – Anne Osborne – I realised, of a sudden, that a door had been unlocked.

'See, that's what strikes me as strange. I do not need what I needed as a child in the Sisters' drawing room: approbation, compliments, treats, favour. But I felt that same emotion today – a grown man, willingly performing – but that same fear, nevertheless.'

'What was this fear, my darling?'

'I suppose ... it was becoming lost, somehow, in all the pretending – constantly dressing-up – changing – disguising myself. I feared today that I may not – in the end – be able to find my person, my true person, again, under the face paint and the costumes ...'

I fell silent, I could say no more. I was emptied in some way, not altogether unpleasantly. Anne embraced me and we lay that way until the bright morning sun woke our precious baby. Our first Sanchonetta.

Chapter III

Sancho, the valet.

1780

A great career in the theatre was smothered – albeit gently, and with love – in the womb. Garrick demurred, but he could see it was of little use trying to dissuade me. The whispers from some critics afterwards, was that my figure and a 'gross deformity of the tongue' rendered me – though competent – too distracting for my many eccentricities. I was happy enough. I had made the decision myself to relinquish a life upon the stage rather than be left out of it altogether by my true fault – a rotundity of person and the hue of my skin. Those critics would never have let that alone, I knew.

A melancholy coda but, I'd lay my life, a wise decision. To sustain that life – those four lives – Frances Joanna, Number Two, was a busy, hungry baby – I redoubled my musical engagements where I was in demand, and limped with more purpose about town, carrying letters and small parcels of lace from the tailors near our home close to St Martin's Lane. One rare, less occupied afternoon, I visited Mr Cutts Barton at Montagu Villa in Richmond to petition him to christen Frances as he had done for Number One, Mary Ann. He seemed in low spirits, and I suggested we walk along the river where passable – for both our constitutions and humours. It did more than the trick.

1761–1766

Arriving at the water's edge with the barges busying the ripples a few yards from where we stood, looking out towards the east in mist, he spoke. Mr Barton confessed he was in urgent need of a chaplain's assistant as of that morning – 'For Gregory has suddenly decided to train for the priesthood in a Catholic seminary in Dumbarton – or was it Kilmarnock . . . ?' His worried voice died to a whisper.

I had no knowledge of who Gregory was – 'I'm sorry,' was all I offered, save an appropriately sympathetic look in my eye – before, to my complete surprise, he offered me the role, there and then. Ha! After all my years of scheming and making myself subtly – and unsubtly, I'm sure – known to the Montagus, in order to be taken into their household by some means – I would never have guessed an act of common sympathy would open the door as easily as if its hinges had been a decade in the oiling. And that is where I stayed, secure – a light clerk's role – very few burdensome chores – save learning the liturgy for various primitive rituals of the Anglican Church. There's hocus-pocus in these incantations, of that I have little doubt.

My weekly nights no longer filled with gatherings and entertainment, meant that I could set my eyes on composition, to supplement the adequate, but by no means luxurious, remuneration of a chaplain's assistant. I revelled in the title, as well as the stability and recognition it afforded me. I was called *Mr Sancho* and *Sir* by more people than had ever called me so before – I began to think *this* the cause of venality in great office. I merited little of their approbation, truth be told, for all I had done was survive, thus far. For, while the position of chaplain's assistant carried said perquisites of civic favour, the role itself was not my desired, final, prey. I eyed the valet. I wondered at his state of health – constitution – wine consumption . . . None of these observations satisfied my patience and all of them left me with a sense of having sullied myself a little in the act. My patience had waxed and waned in this way for many years, and I hadn't fully realised my desire's ultimate aim, until now. I had thought it was merely to be part of the whole – rather, it was to be that major cog in the Montagu Machine – keen ear of the master of the house – trusty right hand of the Earl of Cardigan, himself: valet. Butler was out of my reach, I knew, and its responsibilities too burdensome for one with other duties: viz. father to two young girls – husband to one young wife – keeper of two gouty knees. Meanwhile, for extra resources, I printed several songs and dances; some of them very popular, indeed. I listen to them now and wonder at my joyful spirit – clear within them. True, I had begun to teach the youngest members of the Royal household the rudiments of musical timing and scales, so the tunes were simple and playful. But something else was in these seemingly light and airy jigs, reels and cotillions – and it was mostly dance music – something of the stubborn – something of the refusal to be sombre or pessimistic.

The Royal children asked so frequently for me that it was all I could do to prevent *Their Miniscule Majesties* from breaking centuries-old palace protocol and giving me their pennies when they heard that I was not paid for teaching them and had to work elsewhere one afternoon. Cherubs. It was my diligence in the small matters of small peoples that brought me to the attention of, first, Her Royal Highness the Queen, and then King George the Third, himself. His compliments to me were probably what tipped fortune in my favour; that, and a death of the smallpox in the valet's family. I was hired with immediate effect – and was, at last, valet to the now officially titled George, First Duke of Montagu, of the second creation. On informing Anne, she merely nodded and said no more. But I knew that mischievous look in her eye – she may as well have danced a minuet and sang, ''Twas I that told you long ago . . . ' We smiled for a week.

The task of a valet is to be the right hand of his master – to be constantly available – to care for his sartorial needs – his food and drink – his toilet and his appointments. Sometimes, in the Duke's role as Governor of Windsor Castle, we spent days at a time there. My first day at the castle was memorable not so much for the sense of history surrounding one, but because I was given a room to lay my affairs in whenever we had to stay overnight or longer at a stretch. I adored the room from the moment I saw it. It was on one of the highest floors of the north-west tower. The walls – to my utter delight – were curved in a near-complete circle – like Duke John's magical library. I was in a space not much bigger than would afford me room to place a bed, if the door could be negotiated, and a small table and chair to write by. A small window to the right of the space where I might lay a cot, gave sufficient light to dispel some of the natural gloom of a room built for security, not country vistas. A few candles and one or two drapes and *couvertures* hung over walls and over the window for when it became cold, and the space was as comfortable as any monkish scribbler could desire. Much of this very diary has been written in my many hours of repose in that room. I dressed His Grace for supper most days, but he did not always require me for luncheon. I gave that time to my óverburdened angel, Anne.

I love my hen above all creatures. Her bouts of melancholy have all but ceased this last year and the happy trio play all day, it seems to me – laughing with an abandon that pleases me. Her charitable work – which she insists against all medical, nay, conjugal advice on continuing – exhausts her – carrying one child in a kind of papoose, as they say the Indians do in America – another in a small carriage on wheels. Ingenious. She insists that the girls love to help and to play with the children of St Giles, and it is good, she says, for them to see what privileged lives we live. I find I have little time to play Mr Good Samaritan, however. The exhaustion of continuing to run the odd errand for a little money and to play music with a group of friends for love – and a little money – is almost too much to sustain some days. I have even found myself asleep at my post in the pantry while Cook prepares Duke George's refreshment. I feel a tremendous sense of embarrassment when she gently nudges me awake with a, 'Sorry to disturb you, Mr Sancho, Sir, but His Grace's tea will be cold in a trice.' Exhaustion ... But, Number Three is coming whatever the weather – and milk must be had. I began my search for decisive action to fulfil my desire to be the captain of my own destiny, the week Anne informed me that three-year-old Mary Ann and two-year-old Frances were to be joined by a nought-year-old – name unknown. I sprang into action and went about to look for work that might be done to further supplement the Duke's wages – generous ones by any standard – but, when one has known great poverty, no cushion seems plump enough to break the fall – should one take an unexpected tumble.

When Number Three – Ann-Alice – was born – I had the oddest sensation that I had met this dear sweet creature before. Ann-Alice had a smile on her face from the first day of her life, and that smile never seems to leave her countenance. She had a dark complexion as deep as mine, and the clearest whites around her bright, brown irises. I thought of Ata as she was described so well to me in Anne's letters. Ata, who had been so mercilessly attacked – violated – left nearly dead – by the wicked Wilson – poor, bewildered child. And here was this little one, reminding me in ways her sisters had not, how vulnerable the little black girl is in this world. I fretted on this for many a week until I saw a moment when I could ask Mr Barton's opinion on my concerns.

'All fathers worry for their children, Ignatius. See how Our Lord, the Father, worries over us, like a mother hen, the Good Book says? Alas, it is more true than we would like to admit, that African women are highly sought after for the sexual pleasures of sailors and the like. Depravity breeds depravity, surely. Slavery is depravity writ large, and it is this institution that will need to crumble before your girls be safe. But, the Lord will protect them, I trust in His grace.'

I nodded, as if satisfied with his answer, but something in it left me searching for the nugget of truth within his speech that might lead me to an *action*. I had tired of talking and worrying and waiting for divine intervention to change my course, or alter the circumstances of my life; each time my life had truly changed for the eventual better, I had taken steps myself. Running from the Sisters Three – smashing Sill over the head with the bottle – even shooting myself . . . and missing. I would do more than just pray, I resolved. It remained to discover what that 'more' would be, however. Mr Barton took pity on my continued look of valiant defeat, then rose, abruptly, and came back with a small brown book in his hands: *The Life and Opinions of Tristram Shandy, Gentleman* by Laurence Sterne.

Chapter IV

Sancho, Sterne and Gainsborough.

1766–1768

I wrote to Mr Sterne at once, the very day I had devoured his
wonderful story of Tristram, his uncle Toby, Trim et al. I read
until the early hours of the morning, for it was impossible to
cast the book aside until I knew all. I laughed, I cried, I was
in raptures at his depth of knowledge of the human condition
and marvelled at – nay, vowed to imitate – his writing style.
His heart was clear – his sermons, with which I had long been
familiar, betrayed a spirit that I felt confident could speak
for the many black souls held in bondage, particularly in our
West Indies. I began thus:

'I am, Sir, one of those whom the vulgar and illiberal
call, Niggers.'

Urging him to take up the Cause on behalf of my black
brethren caught in this barbarous trade, I went on to
describe – in too ornate a tone, no doubt – the state of Black
Humanity and its supplicating pleas for equanimity as sons
of Adam and daughters of Eve. His swift reply, informing
me that he had been at that moment of receiving my letter,
writing a description of a poor Negro girl who refused to kill

a little fly, though she herself had suffered at the hands of those who cared not so much about a member of their *own* species – raised my spirits to a height hard to describe. The coincidence gave me the bold confidence to visit Mr Sterne some time later on the way to Scotland with the gracious Duke and Duchess of Montagu, securing a few days' leave from their service to accommodate the encounter. I would join them in Dalkeith in a few days and my friend, James Kisbee, would take my place.

I arrived at Mr Sterne's modest little vicarage on the edge of the North Yorkshire Moors – in the shadow of the church he presided over – on a sunny afternoon in the spring. Laurence, for so he insisted I call him, was all his written words promised he would be. He was a much slighter man than me, with a kindly face and a strong, aquiline nose, which seemed designed to smell out hypocrisy. And, that is what we spoke of: the lie that African Humanity was not the equal of the European; that this excuse was acceptable in the eyes of neither God nor man, for the barbarity of chattel slavery. We ate scones – I need not say how this delighted me – and drank near a gallon of tea served by his housekeeper – sitting in his sunlit study in that modest home – most befitting for this generous heart – this humble soul. He urged me to secure a subscription from Their Graces for his next printing of *Tristram* – assuring me that my letter and our visit had settled his mind on including the passage on the *poor Negro girl* in that new edition. I gladly accepted his commission and doubted not to obtain the favour that he had so timidly asked of me. The most significant moment came as dusk settled over the small valley that surrounded us, and I was about to make my way to the coach house in that quiet village of Coxwould. Lighting his evening pipe, Laurence arrested me on the threshold of his little cottage and urged:

'If you seek to influence the great to any acts of kindness towards your brother Moors, you must yourself appear a figure of some significance. Like magpies, they are drawn, inexorably, to that which shines brightest – shallow and fleeting as that interest may be. How you achieve this is in God's knowledge, not mine, but this I would say: your name – "Sancho" – may already be known to some for your music. You might do well to profit by that. Adopt that name at all times and make of it what you can. Then, perhaps, you will achieve the ear of those who may do much to save your people – Sancho.'

And I never did use *Charles* again – insisting – without opposition – all address me as Sancho from that moment. I contemplated Laurence's words all the way to Scotland and never left off meditating on them for the months that followed. A way to fulfil his suggestion became clear to me almost by chance, some two years later. Duke George had been urged by Duchess Mary to have his portrait rendered by the most celebrated of English painters of that day, Mr Thomas Gainsborough, now residing in Bath. I took the side of Her Grace, as subtly as I was able, and we succeeded at last in persuading him to write to Mr Gainsborough to request a sitting. In the April of 1768, we took to the road and headed for Bath. I would have taken Anne, but she had just given birth to Number Four – my first son – my darling – Jonathan William Sancho – named in memory of the late, dear, William Rio Montagu ... She was aided *in the straw* by her brother

John and her parents. I should perhaps have stayed myself, but I saw a clear way I might make that mark Laurence had so compellingly urged. The journey – which I will not describe here, for its details are not relevant to this account – was pleasant and rapid as the weather disobeyed the season and remained calm and clement. We arrived at our lodgings on the Royal Crescent – and after partaking of the waters for three days – made our way to Mr Gainsborough's studios. My plan – executed to perfection, if I may say – was to casually show the Duke and Duchess portraits of beloved servants, already adorning the walls of Mr Gainsborough's house, on the quiet Circus in that beautiful Romanesque town. The always reticent Duke had cold feet and sought to avoid his own portrait being painted, asking, instead, that Gainsborough paint both his wife – and myself. An *idea* of great genius that came suddenly to Duke George. This being accepted – *reluctantly* – by me – was agreed to by Mr Gainsborough – though the Duchess insisted that Duke George agree to have his likeness rendered at a later date – to allay any feelings of disappointment the change of plans would elicit in the great artist, known for his sensitivity to such matters. All was agreed to with good humour, and I dressed my hair as best as my gout-ridden hands would allow on the morning of our sitting. It really was becoming a nuisance, this debilitating condition – its frequency increasing by the month.

Though the Bath day promised fair, and intermittent bursts of sunlight would break the clouds, we were in a room that appeared gloomy to the eye of all but the artist, it seemed. Placed strategically around the space were candles, low and tall – imbuing the space with all the atmosphere and pungent aroma of a church – and sacred work was afoot. Thomas Gainsborough – a most affable man and completely without affectation – greeted us warmly on our arrival, then seemed to disappear *into himself* once the work on the canvas had begun. He would rise from time to time to extinguish an unnecessary flame with his tongue-wetted thumb and fore-finger – all the while gazing upon his subject – sometimes so closely that I could smell the liver and onions he had enjoyed for luncheon. I had observed him in action for the first time that morning, as he started and executed to perfection the portrait of my Patroness. I could barely see by the light of the candles, though they were many. How Mr Gainsborough is able to capture such vivid colours – as we so often see in his works – is a mystery solved by none. In this half-light he must have conjured dreams, for the magic on his canvases was not evident in the unpromising gloom of his quiet painting room. The curtains billowed out every now and then, affording us a reminder that it was a bright day outside. We were not alone. The folks who gathered – about a dozen in total – were riv-eted by his skill and speed over the canvas.

Strangely, though I was flattered by my employer's decision to have my likeness taken by Mr Gainsborough, my mind was very much elsewhere. I had come so far in my turbulent life to this point. Gazing upon me in my finery (a costume, after all), these folks could have no idea how I came to be in this fortunate position. My image, forever held in time, immutable, near perfect, rendered immortal by the hand of the greatest portraitist of this or any other epoch.

Chapter V

Sancho, the grieving father.

1780

Dear, sweet Billy, as I write this on a quiet and gloomy day – custom in our store all but ceased – I gaze upon the portrait bequeathed to me by Their Graces and wonder at the joy – evident to me – in the eyes of that 'stranger me'. I could not know that but two years after, tragedy would strike us all and that light – caught so brilliantly by Thomas – would dim from my eyes for some considerable time. Haste dictates that I must not waste time on useless mourning, but tell you directly how we survived this blow. My body weakens, son – my hands cannot write with the stamina of even a year ago. Therefore, let my account of those dark days be taken from the pages of the diary I bequeath to you. Is it a bequest, I wonder yet again, or a burden? Recalling such awful times brings the sentiment back in force, I see, and your poor father's eyes are fogged with tears, once again.

1770

To describe the short illness and demise of my first son, is a thing I have neither the desire for, nor the power to undertake – even in diary form. I do not mention it in my letters, for it is not a fit subject for fireside readings. His casket was unfeasibly small, yet his death leaves a great, gaping chasm in our lives. I can say no more.

The fame that I had sought to fan into a blaze, that might save many of my Black Brethren, was not forthcoming from the painting, even by so great a genius as Thomas Gainsborough. And now, it seemed to be the most insignificant of quests, when another little soul could not be saved under my very roof . . . dear Ann Alice . . . Dame Sancho wept for a six-month and I could do naught but hold her arms up, as it were, by taking over all the duties of parenthood for our girls. Only sweet Betsy, her late brother's favourite, seemed to rally quickly, and though not the eldest, held all our hands with her determination to see what we still had – a family that loved and cared for one another. That smiling angel was the reason we survived that dark period and I believe she has something of the divine in her constitution. Four years old and with the sensibilities of an abbess, she became the family's trusted confidant when we did not wish to burden the rest with the sudden waves of grief that pounded our broken hearts. The Montagu family allowed me leave-of-absence, and Kisbee took permanent root in that household, much to my delight. He did not supplant me, but as his was the liveliest of constitutions, he has been made much use of in the perambulations of Their Graces. I did not begrudge Kisbee his rising status and indispensability in the Montagu household, but I could see that his fitness for the physical duties of valet led the Duke to realise how inadequate my service had been these past few months. I began to think it would not be long before he saw that I was more hindrance then help in his increasingly active duties as both Governor and Constable of Windsor Castle. My gout-ridden fingers could barely button the tunic of his ceremonial outfits. Naturally, this often proved more testing still for the Duke who – even when such a chore was done with alacrity – did not like to be *trussed up* in this manner. That I took many more minutes than a valet ought, only added to his controlled irritation. The strain was untenable – as it turned out – and this next describes best what took place just before the final straw was laid on that reluctant camel's back.

Chapter VI

Sancho, Sommersett and Slave Goods.

1780

I had promised you the portrait-in-word of your father, Billy, and a defence of his actions, questioned still by many, in having a grocery store that sells – when poor custom allows – slave goods. I do this not to appease my conscience – which is clear – but to obviate any feelings in your older self that you may have gained advantages over your Black Brethren on the backs of those very members of your own race. It is not so, for how else could I have sustained the life of my Sanchonettas if I had not engaged in this trade? Perhaps posterity may answer this question to the satisfaction of all dissenting voices, but I do not seek to lay out a case for that here, rather to reveal the truth of the circumstances that led me to take such a momentous decision.

'Know thy father – and forgive him.'

1771–1772

In the summer of 1771, Number Five – dear, sweet Lydia – was born. She appeared to be made all of bones, poor child, and was never out of a fever it seemed, for the first months of her life. Her complexion – paler than all her siblings – spoke of a weakness in the blood, and like many parents we knew enough to consider that her life may not be prolonged. By early September, however, she had turned the corner on these bouts of fever, and we were delighted to see that she began to smile and giggle at the antics of her solicitous sisters. Our hearts were lifted, then, and we worried less. A respite from cares and grief that had been a long time in coming.

In the spring of the following year, Zachariah introduced me to a fellow runaway slave, Mr James Sommersett – late of Boston – and we dined – at my expense – at the Ivy Lane Club. A tall man, of chestnut brown complexion, he ate most ferociously of the fare – putting me in mind of my own devouring hunger here when I first met Dr Johnson's circle. James told us in his small voice – most surprising, in a man so strong-seeming – of his life as a slave in Boston and his subsequent bid for freedom two years after his brutal master had landed in this Kingdom. Whispers of the haven that is Seven Dials had come to him from a white servant in one of the houses he and his master had visited, and – brave soul – he had absconded that very night. This was James's first outing in the city since his escape – and after some time he became more reposed – ceasing to stare about him as if expecting the slave-catcher at any moment. I confess we were all quite drunk by the time we left and said our fare-wells as the bells of St Paul's pealed ten o'clock. Perhaps the ale had loosened not only James's tongue but his vigilance, too? For it was a few weeks later that I learnt from Zachariah the tragic coda to this happy night. Some spies of his master, a Mr Charles Stewart, had captured him and incarcerated the poor fugitive on board a ship bound for Jamaica – following a brutal beating. There were instructions to have him sold there, according to Zachariah's account. Fortunately, his godparents – who had stood for his baptism some months before – were informed, and the great Thomas Clarkson, together with his friend Granville Sharp – two men well-versed in the law, it seems – had him off that ship. Now, he was nursing his injuries and awaiting the bizarre trial that ensued. That this Stewart could feel justified in the eyes of God in bringing such a case – as if this man's freedom was nothing at all – is the shame of his race. That it was allowed to come to trial – a shame to this nation. Lord Mansfield's deliberations were longer than seemed feasible for a man who we all knew to have a black niece living with him many years in Kenwood House, above Hampstead Fields. What was his household like – that could harbour a loved, black niece – yet treat her black brother as one would a prize cow escaped from a field? The minds of those who support the institution of Slavery – yet baulk at its excesses – can never be fathomed by those of us who see in this only the cruelty so often inferred to the so-called *barbarous* nations of the East. Anne was unequivocal in her condemnation of the Lord Chief Justice's procrastinations:

'Who does he listen to when he is home at Hampstead? The voices of those greedy merchants who assail him with their fears of losing revenue, if their slaves were to demand and receive their freedom? Or that poor girl who must be kept from other blacks, for she would surely speak in advocacy of Mr Sommersett? Do you still think your England the best of Christian nations, Sancho?'

'It is not a matter of that, Anne. I have no love for these niceties of the law they say that Mansfield espouses in the court. They smack of accommodation. But I see the pressure that great men bear when their hearts sway one way for Humanity, and their need for obeying and being led by the letter of the Law compels them to swing another.'

She was silent, then. Not in a sulk, but in that quiet contemplation that sometimes led to her pronouncing – with such clarity – on a dispute we might have – as now:

'Then, go you, see and hear what he says. Tell me if you note his heart, you who are so kind and good a judge. Tell me if he speaks as you say, like a man caught between frying pan and fire. I will trust your judgement above all others.'

I resolved to do as she wisely counselled, and begged leave of Duke George to do so one afternoon in the early days of May 1772. We were in his dressing room at Ditton Park when

I put this request to him, which he acceded to immediately, only adding:

'But, do you take no faction, Sancho. I would not have my household – and therefore, by association, His Royal Highness – involved in legal dealings, be they never so pressing and poignant.'

I closed the door to him and stayed in the corridor, contemplating precisely what he might mean by this admonition. Was I to remain silent if I saw an injustice at work – to keep my counsel in order not to muddy the name of Montagu? I felt the compromise then, and I knew that this would be a difficult path to tread. My heart was all enraged for the injustice that was being perpetrated by such a trial, and my anger turned then to Duke George and his concern – his first concern – for the sensibilities and name of the King. I resolved to see for myself, as requested by my Hen, but not to think of the consequences of my support for poor Sommersett if this led to a rebuke from the Duke.

The afternoon I visited, the chamber was unusually warm for that time of year. The crowded visitor's gallery, packed with black humanity and not a few white men and women, mostly in support of James Sommersett, was heavy in atmosphere – legal, temporal and emotional. The entire gallery rose when the judge came in and – wearily, it seemed to me – sat at his seat in the centre of the far wall opposite the gallery, where we all turned our eyes to him. I felt his pressure then and wondered, though he did not look above but once for the three hours we sat there, if he felt this, too. The only time he did glance upwards was the moment that Mr Sommersett was brought to the bar and seated. The crowd in the gallery rose, in silence, as a mark of respect for him, and Sommersett raised a small, brave smile to us in thanks. Lord Mansfield looked up to us – momentarily – then at Sommersett. I believe I saw a fleeting glimpse of the man, then – a man who could feel the palpable, yet silent, support of a tribe of witnesses. How could any man not feel the weight, I decided, as I leant forward to hear the *Arguments*.

Nothing of what was intoned by the supporters of Mr Stewart would surprise one; reiterations of the arguments of the Black Body being not the equal of the White abounded; lies about the laws of Christ allowing slavery in circumstances like these, despite the man – Sommersett – being a baptised Christian these eighteen months. The defence case rested on the truth of Sommersett's humanity and his right to freedom in a land where slavery is not officially recognised. The hypocrisy of this was not lost on the many in the gallery who had either run away as slaves in England, or who well knew others who were indeed of that status in London and elsewhere. My attention was caught by Mr Stewart's defence, that of the thirty thousand known blacks in London, all would think themselves free indeed, if the ruling were to go against him. I thought this number to be an exaggeration, but perhaps not so if we counted the entire Kingdom – and those many, many runaways ... He wished, clearly, to paint a fearful picture of black people running amok in a Kingdom made for the freedom of whites, only. I seethed with a rage I had not truly felt since I was very young, and there rose in me a need for air.

Escaping after those three hours into the streets of the city, I gazed at my belovéd capital and saw her with new – and not loving – eyes. This idea that blacks were free was merely notional, it seemed, for the laws of England said nothing about my people. How then could I be sure that a real and living slavery might not come to this land after I had gone? That my children, my Hen, would not be enchained with no one to speak for them – not even justice? I drank an ale at Slaughter's, feeling the heaviness of these thoughts, after which I left and headed home slowly – hoping the walk would dispel the gloom that had descended upon me. Anne was just putting little Lydia to bed when I returned, and we sat up a while – her taking a little soft candlewax to massage my aching calves from so much walking.

'I will not return to court until the ruling, Anne. It is too much to bear. To see that soul, who I knew free and jolly, have a look of such resignation to a negative fate, was too much to support.'

'Perhaps all may be well, Sancho. You say Mansfield had the air of a man who had noted for whom this judgement mattered most? Then leave it to God to prompt his conscience to act according to the good tenets of Christian faith.'

For the first time that I could recall, I did not feel assuaged in my pessimism by Anne's faith in divine promptings. A most un-Christian sentiment, indeed.

On the day of Lord Mansfield's decision – the twenty-second day of June 1772 – I did not inform the Duke that I would attend, but feigned an inflammation of my gout. This little lie was to disguise the truth that may have caused an irrevocable rift between myself and my employer. I am not proud that I could not boldly state my support for Sommersett, but I had to think of my only source of regular income and the security of my family after my passing. Remaining in the Duke's employ would surely mean their continued patronage of my family – as they had done for many a beloved servant before me. Young John Osborne and his wife Phyllis, were deputised 'parents' for the day while Anne and I ventured forth on an outing that was rare for us these many years. We obtained a coach to carry us to the Oxford Road – now more usually called Oxford Street – growing in commercial bustle and popularity by the day – stopping frequently for Anne to admire the shops there. We took tea and refreshments near Hanover Square before making our way back towards Westminster Hall. That bright June day was blessed with a gentle breeze that cooled us as we strolled arm in arm. A few looks – one or two comments on our colour – were met with disdain, and our usual pride in deportment – but we refrained from comment, as we considered this beneath our especial notice. We made a fine couple, I knew, and jealousy of our obvious freedom and elegance was increasing, I had found, lately. The city had become a general hotbed of animosity to all who showed any degree of wealth – and though we had but little money to spare, we always deported ourselves and our Sanchonettas with a fierce pride of carriage and dress. We would not concede in that – though it offend some – to the devil with them that would have us covered in dirt and clothed in rags.

Arriving at the Court of King's Bench in Westminster Hall, we were pleased to see that the crowd of mostly black witnesses was large and dressed as smartly as we – to the close limits of their household budgets. Whatever the outcome of today's verdict, we would be a spectacle for everyone to marvel at. A truly surviving and proud people, as Anne so wisely said ...

The courtroom was heavy with anticipation. We rose and applauded when James Sommersett took his seat at the Accused's bar. Lord Mansfield chose to come in after him, no doubt aware that there might be some disruption to the usual protocols if he had been first to arrive. The hush returned and the Lord Chief Justice began his lengthy summation of this complex and trying case. A pin might have dropped and been heard when it bounced a second – quieter – time. Lord Mansfield cited two previous cases of *trover* – the property rights held by the owner of said property. Two judges – Yorke and Talbot – in a case of 1729 had sought to protect planters who brought their slaves to Britain, fearing their escape, or their baptism, rendered them free. That *Opinion* was held as common law and was not reviewed until a case some twenty years later brought that old fear to the fore – a fear allayed by the then Chancellor, Lord Hardwicke. This Chancellor's sickening argument was that planters were avoiding baptising slaves in the belief that this conferred a freedom on them – a freedom not, in fact, supported by law. Lord Hardwicke then solidified the Yorke-Talbot *Opinion* – citing an ancient law, long abolished under the reign of Charles II, of *villein-age* – the right of any man to have 'ownership' of another in England – this Hardwicke suggesting that the abolition of *villeinage* did not apply to slaves, since their owners had not *granted* them their freedom. Once again, many in the gallery were restless with this appalling use of the law to deny a person their Christian right of freedom. The murmur caused Lord Mansfield to pause while it subsided, though again, he studiously avoided meeting the piercing gaze of many in that upper level. The obvious – odious – contradiction in this

Opinion – made to appease the skittish planters – was clear to Lord Justice Mansfield, for he went on to summarise his decision thus:

' . . . no master ever was allowed here to take a slave by force to be sold abroad because he had deserted from his service, or for any other reason whatever; we cannot say the cause set forth by this return is allowed or approved of by the laws of this kingdom, therefore the black must be discharged.'

Pandemonium ensued.

For many hours after that great moment of eruption in the chamber, we embraced and laughed and sang and danced. So much so, and for so long, that the Lord Bailiff was called to see if this was not *Riot in a Public Space?* It was not. The joyful band repaired to their respective homes, where it quickly could be seen by many that celebrating alone – for something that made *You*, *We* – well, that needed *Us* all to be together. To accommodate so many souls, a large hall was hired near Parliament – the numbers attending surprised many.

I could hardly rise from my cot the following morning. But, the message requesting me to see His Grace sobered all other thoughts into submission. An interview – in my experience of them – nearly always ends in disappointment for one of the parties involved. I held no *hands* in this affair – and could only hold my arms out in surrender to my fate. And it was all as I suspected, as I tried to stand throughout Duke George's lengthy pleas to be understood that he regretted:

' . . . this momentous and sad decision – based primarily on your . . . condition and your deportment about town. I warned you not to take sides in this dispute over these primitive laws of human chattel, and this particular judgement was more about the freedom of all blacks and not just Sommersett – this I feel you know.'

'Of course, Your Grace. I had expected this, truth be told.'

'How so?'

'When you asked me to be circumspect in my support for either side of this shameful trial.'

'Ah, I see . . .'

'I must be my own man, at last, as your late father-in-law, His Grace, the Duke of Montagu, would have had me be. I wish you long, good service from Kisbee, or whoever has the very great pleasure to serve you, Your Grace. I have been fortunate, indeed.'

Her Grace came in then and asked to be alone with me, whereupon she wept profusely and did not cease to say her 'sorries', while I intoned acceptance and understanding. Serving, till the very last.

'What will you do, think you?'

'Ah well. A delicate matter, for which not a little expenditure may be demanded of Your Graces . . .'

'Speak, Sancho. We will help, if it be a scheme liable to success.'

'Of that, I will give no guarantees. If life has schooled me once, it has a thousand times: I cannot speculate on future stock, for it does not exist till past – eh, what?'

She giggled, as we used to in the music room, at my impersonation of her dear father. Would he have put me out like this? What would he think of this action were he here? I saw Her Grace thought the same, for she gazed at the settee opposite us as if she faced the ghost of her father; his spirit, disapproving – disappointed? I held her hands and told her that a near neighbour, a Miss Lydia Leach, had enquired if we wanted to purchase a shop premises near Parliament.

'I immediately thought of my skills learnt under your dear mother, as butler. The buying of provisions from the best sources and knowing the price of a pound of butter. So, Grocer I will be. It rings truer than Actor, eh?'

I left her with a sorrowful smile on her face. Explaining the idea of a shop to Anne was straightforward enough. It was as she asked that searing question – one that I had avoided any deep introspection into – when I had won her over with so many of my arguments for family security – that I was arrested by the contradiction: I must sell goods to survive – and the goods that make the most money? Not vegetables or expensive fruits – and ours should be expensive, to suit the class of clientele I was expecting. Beef, eggs, blue, nuts, bread, milk and dried pork and grains etc., would do well enough, but not help me afford the costs of running a house and a business. Sugar, tea, tobacco ... These were the commodities a grocer was expected to provide his community. How to resolve this, was the conundrum of my every waking and sleeping thought. I determined to find the least cruelly made sugar from the plantation with the greatest reputation as regards its treatment of the labourers. This was not – as you can imagine – an easy task. Asking a sailor to compare one draconian regime with another is not science by any definition. Eyewitnesses among the hidden runaways were good sources of information – some islands already experiencing pockets of freedom, even some states in North America? – well, perhaps I could trade with these.

All those ideas were swept away in an instant, when I first set foot in the Royal Exchange in London. Vast halls of produce, coffee-drinking, spice stalls, bales of hay, some livestock in the outer courtyards – though this is increasingly frowned upon, as London tries, again, to beautify herself. But where should I begin? Just then a large, white – bordering on burgundy – man, with flaccid cheeks and a red-mottled nose, clapped me on the shoulder and greeted me as one would an old friend:

'Ah, Sancho, just the fellow. Barons, broker-trader-helper! Come with me. I hear from good sources that you have decided on the Noble Trade and are to become a purveyor of foodstuffs and necessaries, and the like . . . '

'Er . . . yes. Mr Barons . . . ' His vague suggestions of what I was about seemed uncannily perceptive. And so, I listened, as he led me through the belly of the hall, gesticulating where necessary to point out this spice or that fig – this sugar or that rum. He spoke without interruption.

'Now, it's not the spices – like those there – that have us drooling – it's the sweet stuffs of the Orient. Spices do not match sugar – tea – rum – and yes, it needs considering – as I've heard you have – but try Trinidad. Their tobacco may be in its infancy, but if you do well by them – why an upstanding citizen – a voter, now, eh? – you might be one of the members of some kind of Trade Board – what? – and you may say what is to be said . . . '

A degree of nonsense is acceptable in business, but one thing his words convinced me of was that there was no way around having a successful grocer's store in London, without the sugar, tea and tobacco so craved by a populace semi-ignorant as to how it is produced. I moped through my day when I got home. I collected the rags and old garments from my usual more affluent acquaintances – getting to see folks who I had not visited for some time. Like dear Dr Johnson – whose Francis, 'Frank', had decided for the sea. A risk for any lad, but for one of the colour ...? The doctor had aged at his absence, I could see – but this generous heart gave me plenty of Frank's clothes for the poor of London.

I had taken Number One, Mary Ann, a tall and elegant thirteen-year-old and a fine lady, indeed. We braced ourselves for abuse until we reached the city, where we would simply blend with the populace – rare, but not alien. We received none. Some, even friendly, smiled. We last arrived with our little cart of stuffs to Seven Dials, where I met dear Zachariah and Dillon and Cíaran. We ate a stew that Dillon had prepared and, afterwards, I took Mary Ann by the hand as we waved goodbye. I was on the cusp of a final decision regarding our future – a conclusion, at last, to those endless thoughts in those days when – just as it became clear that I had the answer – out of the shadows – older – no less huge and menacing – and with him one who matched, and more, his ferocious air of menace – Jonathan Sill and his apprentice. The scar above his eyes had deepened and become livid with age – he must have been sixty-five now. I instinctively pushed Mary Ann behind me, as she screamed when these two loomed over us in the shadow of the slaughterhouse. I gazed to the left and right but saw no egress; they had blocked the only two alleyways that led into this quarter. I decided to speak first, to try to take control with authority and not lead with fear as on our every previous encounter. I would speak in a loud and clear voice – as taught by John Montagu on the night we met. I thought of what I would do if they rushed me – and, once I had gotten Mary Ann clear, I would do to them – my cane held a sword within, and my bulk was enough to withstand a few blows from the cudgels they held.

'I always said I'd have you yet, butterball. I really had begun to doubt that myself, eh Christopher?'

'Yah, Dad.'

So, he was his son. A family business. And – in-temporally – I decided there and then that I would be a grocer and save my family – use the proceeds to fund writing materials – alerting friends and politicians and newspapers – gathering support to wipe this scourge of slavery from the English statute books. I stood tall, ready for the fight ahead – when the head of Sill was yanked back, off his neck – as if he had looked up, suddenly. I saw a flash of metal slide across his neck, before his entire body was dragged back into the shadows. And before Christopher Sill – a name, at last – could perform any act to save his father, his legs were bound together in one brisk movement – pulled violently from under him – and the boys pummelled him for some time.

I do not know when Zachariah, Cíaran and Dillon stopped, for I had swept Mary Ann away – my hands on the hilt of my sword-cane. We reached home soon enough, where the shaken Mary Ann was given a little cocoa and rum. She slept soundly, and for the first time that I could remember . . . so did I.

Chapter VII

Sancho, the voter.

1780

Number Six – your immediate forerunner, Billy, was born in '73. Katherine 'Kitty' Margaret Sancho – a bonny lass, indeed. Serene and altogether lovely. Her prized possession: a pewter cup that she always drank milk from, even if another were to hand and clean. We scratched it with a 'K' for her, as she dreaded it becoming lost somehow amongst the other wares in the kitchen.

My eyes were then on the vote, for the first time. I felt the need to voice my concerns as an upstanding and full citizen – as Mr Barons had implied I was. I determined to raise my hand for Earl Percy and the youthful Lord Thomas Pelham-Clinton – candidates who spoke my language as far as our injudicious treatment of the American Colonists was concerned. I had no truck with war against our nearest relatives – what though they have chafed against the yoke of their Mother Country and natural superior. A child – as I have found – needs as much carrot as stick, and we have whaled on the American backside for far too long, without the soothing touch of care. No child enjoys discipline, but discipline administered with love and a concern for the future welfare of one's offspring, is soon submitted to, when once the child understands the cause and motivation of the punishment. From my diaries, then ...

1773–1775

The wooden structure before me resembled a pavilion hastily erected for a pageant, and indeed this is precisely what a Husting is: a place where theatre meets politics.

Perhaps these rituals may fade with time. For posterity, a brief description of a Husting. It dates back too many years to count, but before the advent of gentlemen's breeches, no doubt. Decisions of local concern were decided there, especially if there were factions involved in the dispute. It has since come to mean the whole circus of the Poll. Men gather in town squares or parks, a farmer's stables or a landowner's cottage and declare, publicly, who they will vote for. There is a simple show of hands by those present to hear the assembled candidates' speeches, and thus the candidates can decide to continue their campaign, or abandon the cause in the face of visible apathy. Many stubbornly continue, despite a tepid showing in these spectacles and – such is the class of modern politician in our House of Commons – those that do so persevere, are usually found in time, running the country by one means ... or another. This wooden stage or scaffold, hastily – flimsily – built by the Mayor or Sheriff of each district, has a platform where the electors may stand to declare their vote; an air of theatre surrounds this circus. One would think the best and most worthy of any kingdom should be given the honour of declaring their choice there in the public square, but alas, we find it is not so – no, not by a country mile. Every man here owns property and that is all the requirement the law desires or allows. A public show of hands ends this spectacle; no secret ballots, here. The very idea would appal these fine, upstanding gentlemen. Besides which, how else would one know who to bribe or threaten after the first vote?

These thoughts did not sour the small triumph I felt in this act. A sense of belonging undiluted by equivocation – I voted as any man of any shade may vote.

Unnecessarily holding my Property Papers in hand, I stepped forward with the rest of the men at the Husting in that pig pen of a square ...

Then you came, Billy. And, here we are. Almost at the end. I excise those days of mourning for my sweet Lydia – her mother's mirror image, as Billy, you are mine ... Then, my darling Kitty ...

There remains but one chapter – omitting those that deal in dark things – for death is not the stuff of endings, eh what? We will end with the Triumphs of Billy Sancho. Our next, and final, tale.

Chapter VIII

Sancho, and the last things

1780

The reasons for this violent conflagration before me are almost negligible, compared to the devastation that these events have brought to the capital. If Lord Gordon had known that his belligerent protest against the Papists Act, allowing the Irish Catholics to be recruited into the British Army without swearing allegiance to the crown – a small matter, for some – a reason to burn the City, for others – would bring this destruction, I would hope he would have never begun his campaign. That the British Army needed troops to supply their wars on many fronts – and on at least two continents – was not in doubt by any. The French predilection for eyeing the necks of their Monarchy, caused some to shiver with the shaving blade in great houses in the United Kingdom. And so, the ban that had existed for years against the Irish soldier was on the cusp of being lifted, when Lord Gordon announced a Protestant Association rebellion, including a petition to be delivered by himself. The crowd that gathered behind his train grew in size and heat very quickly.

All I saw, as I peered from behind my well-boarded

windows, out of my well-darkened shop, were gangs of thugs – beating suspected Catholics – destroying one Catholic butcher's store – making away with the produce – Irish or not. The word came today that the Clink was broken down and many prisoners absconded. They too – some of them known felons, indeed – joined in the violent skirmishes against the authorities. The clash outside the store was horrendous, but the Guards took charge of the street in just a few minutes and now all is relatively quiet. Writing a letter to friends on what I had just seen, I saw clearly what my fears amounted to all these years. Who is to say how safe we are, if whites can seek to destroy whites? For want of a soldier? What of slavery which thrives today? If my portrait, my fame, my letters, my music, could not convince those who think Africans less than human to give up this lie, what would?

I thought the best way was to find the candidate who spoke – be it ever so little – for my Black Brethren in bondage. Charles James Fox, being that candidate, had my support from the start of his campaign in 1780 and – since he promised to bring a motion against slavery – I trusted his word on the rest.

The day of the final vote was odd. I woke with that tremendous gout that presaged a hard day – but also a more ominous inkling that something had gone wrong in the world, yet again. My first confirmation that all would not be straight and narrow today, was arriving at the Husting and being asked by some rather uncouth and thuggish-looking chaps where the proof was of my right to vote. I had never before been asked that and neither had any other man. I knew better than to begin a quarrel with these louts, and turned back for my papers. I could not find them. I ransacked the store, the dust choking me as I moved sacks and papers five years undisturbed. I could not find those papers . . . I sat forlornly – unable to move. Anne tried to rouse me to continue my search, but two hours of this had near exhausted my force. You came to me then, Billy, to ask what was amiss. I told you – you swore to find it, or your name was not Oroonoko, Prince of *Angolaaaa*! And off you screamed, followed by your faithful companion Nutts, the dog, yapping at your heels. A tonic, my boy. I roused myself, once again. I would go to the Husting and demand my vote; surely, I would be known and vouched for by some about there who might overhear the argument.

But they had me fooled by their nonchalance when I passed them without hindrance, and entered that square. I found myself needing to take refuge on the stage itself, along with several others for whom the throng had proved too pressing. I took out my handkerchief to mop my perspiring brow, when up stepped the fattest man I believe I ever beheld. One body he made, from neck to toe – and a face of thunder plonked on top. He bellowed, rather than spoke, perhaps not out of volitional aggression, but because of the force the words needed in order to emanate from this planet of a man. This Walrus – the Returning Officer, the Sheriff – was flanked by two men, one of whom I recognised as the ruffian who had demanded my papers, and another, more thuggish-looking still. The Walrus stood too close to me – breath musty as an old lady's night cap – breathing the evidence of his fishy luncheon into my nostrils, forcibly.

'You there, Blackie. I don't know you. Where go you, there?'

'To vote. As I did – not ten weeks ago in this very square.'

'That's all as it may be, but it was the first day perhaps – and it's the Mayor presides on those ceremonials . . . '

He spoke *ceremonials* like it was a dirty word, and with such menace – implying that today was the Real Thing. I froze, then, realising that there would be no kindness, no Humanity to be found, here. Attack was the best form of defence, I saw, trained as I was by the master of Defensive Attack – John, Duke of Montagu:

'That I stand out, Sir, from the common sort is true. Then, it is best you speak more civilly to an "out-standing" gentleman.'

The hush of what I instantly considered my *audience* was immediate – a trick one learns in great houses when Royal Persons are about.

'I am Charles Ignatius Sancho – Proprietor of Sancho's Grocery Store, at Number Nineteen, Charles Street, Mayfair, in the Borough of Westminster – a Londoner, Sir – a shop-keeper, therefore, a land-holder, therefore, eligible to cast my vote – my Black Vote – the first such you have seen, perhaps, but pray God, not the last.'

One or two 'hear hears' – but not nearly enough to deter the man before me. Our position in the centre of the stage and above the heads of the spectators made me see the non-sense of my quest, and this whole theatrical game. What was this circus? The Vote. Did it alter anything? Did it change one mind or realign one heart? It was nothing then, but an act of faith. It was a message of hope for change that this act represented, not the assurance that it would change the world by the end of next week. A gesture of hope. Alas, when even that coin in the wishing-well is denied you – then you really are no one at all. My Irish friends and their runaway lodgers – Tilly and her like – Young John Osborne. They had no say in how their lives were organised and here was I – for want of my papers – shortly to be arrested for trying to cast my ballot to the wind. As I watched the Returning Officer turn to his flunkeys and seem to decide my fate – I saw you – Billy.

Running, weaving through the crowd below – so small, you appeared a little man amongst giants – a Gulliver, a Sancho Panza – and my brave boy ran – despite the looks and cries and general confusion erupting all around him – he ran. Now, what was in your hands, my dear child – your sister Kitty's pewter cup? Dear sweet boy, I love your heart. But, as you reached me, the men stepped forward to arrest me – I thought it most unjust, Lord, that my Billy – at five years old – should witness this shame on his father. And then you were wrapping your arms so tightly around my calves, as a man who has grasped a raft in a stormy sea. All eyes were upon you. I reached down to you and held your darling face in my hands.

'You have done well, Billy. Thank you for this.'

I reached to take Kitty's cup from your little hands. I saw that there was something at the bottom of this so late abandoned vessel – it was almost a year to the day we had lost dear, sweet Kitty – crumpled, wedged so tightly, so securely to the bottom, I found ... my Property Papers. I wept a little – but held – until I could show not only my accusers but my supporters in the throng – I held aloft my papers and declared – with my darling boy in one hand – and his future, fluttering in the wind in my other:

'I vote for the anti-slavery candidate. I vote for Charles James Fox. I vote . . . for Freedom.'

AFTERWORD

There is always a degree of personal speculation involved in the telling of any history. Whilst I have written a fictionalised version of Sancho's life, I based it on the bare facts offered by the threadbare archive. I pulled together these fragments and have attempted to paint a clearer picture of the life of a man of whom much has been speculated, but very little known for certain. Was he, in fact, born on a slave ship? If so, why did his owner send him to England? Who were the mysterious Sisters Three and where in Greenwich did they live? Also, how can we authentically piece together a life from such poor archival material?

Author Saidiya Hartman calls this method of imaginative storytelling 'Critical Fabulation', which I interpret as the piecing together of a life or an event, based on archival material and contemporary cross-referencing – adding the crucial elements of logic and imagination. Clearly this method of recounting history is hugely subjective. After nearly a quarter of a century of investigating eighteenth-century London life, I increasingly feel that every recounting of history fits that description. Frankly, I have little problem with that. It entirely depends on who is doing the speculating and what their attitude is to their subject, right?

Scientists say, 'We just don't know . . .' Historians should perhaps admit, 'We simply don't know everything . . . yet.' For example, in the case of Charles Ignatius Sancho, despite his myriad correspondence, contemporary anecdotes and the Gainsborough portrait, despite the years I've been investigating his story – as well as the groundbreaking work of Brycchan Carey, Vincent Carretta and Gretchen Gerzina before me – I had only very recently been informed that Sancho and Anne had two children previously unknown to me, as well as to the aforementioned scholars.

The first discovery was Mary-Ann Sancho, born in 1759, followed by Frances-Joanna in '61 and a possible newly uncovered son, Thomas-Johnson Sancho born later that same year. Mary-Ann died in 1805 and Thomas-Johnson in 1815. Nothing more is known of these two siblings despite their forty-six and fifty-four years of life, respectively. Crispin Powell, the archivist for the Duke of Buccleuch (Montagu) and the wonderful History Sleuths at Northeastern University London, led by Professor Nicole Aljoe and Professor Oliver Ayers, are busy trawling through the archives at Boughton House, the London Metropolitan Archives and elsewhere to unearth more nuggets from this fascinating seam.

Two more pieces of information that recently stirred my heart were the discovery that Billy Sancho became a kind of librarian to the Duke of Montagu and bought and sold books in a shop in Mews Gate, a street that is now buried beneath the site of the National Gallery in London. For many years, Sancho's portrait which always hung in the store, would have lived where the gallery is now. There's heavy irony here, as the portrait now, inexplicably, hangs in the National Gallery of Canada, in Ottawa ... Billy also assisted at the newly opened Vaccine-Pock Institute in nearby Soho where they were experimenting with using cowpox to inoculate people against the more virulent killer, smallpox.

These fascinating snippets on the life of the second generation of Sanchonettas, reminds us that with history, the 'story' is never really over until all the facts are in. I would love anyone who finds anymore gems like this to contact me on social media and let me know what else you find.

Keep an open mind and, happy history sleuthing.

Paterson Joseph
June 2022
Cricklewood, London

Acknowledgements

The roll call of people who helped me on the way to the creation of this novel is too long and not long enough. From those who listened to me talk about my dream of writing, to those who accepted my work and published it. Success or failure – those people who encouraged my efforts deserve my deepest gratitude. My confidence as a writer has grown in many ways – and the following people are in part responsible for that growth. My teachers have been those friends who read the first drafts, and my editors at Dialogue/Little, Brown.

I'd like to thank: Lucy Briers, Richard Leaf, Irene Levin (friendliest of neighbours) and Felly Nkweto Simmonds – who sacrificially read an undiluted version – giving me comments and encouragement that I found invaluable. Gretchen Holbrook Gerzina – who made me believe I belonged in the world of historical writers. I owe you everything – you started my journey off with *Black England*. Gaia Banks, my agent, whose input and marathon reading stamina is astounding, and who championed my book even in its earliest form. Richard

Laws – gone, but never forgotten: thank you for believing I was a writer before I did. Lucy Fawcett, literary agent and stalwart friend – my first professional writing colleague. The brilliant Nikesh Shukla has my eternal gratitude for helping me out when every publisher in the UK we sent the manuscript to rejected it. Nikesh tipped me off to a most wonderful publisher – Sharmaine 'Lovely' Lovegrove. Sharmaine, thank you for being such a ferocious advocate of this novel. (May I consider this our love-child?) Millie Seaward, Emily Moran, Maisie Lawrence, and all at Dialogue/Little, Brown. Josephine Lane was indispensable – her editing notes, addictive. Copy editor Gabrielle Chant, it was a pleasure to work with you, and thank you for teaching me how to fine tune my work. Crispin Powell, archivist to the Buccleuch (Montagu) family, who gave me access to their private archive. To Richard, Duke of Buccleuch, my gratitude for the warm welcome.

And lastly, not least-ly, my friends and family who have put up with my lack of graft at life, while giving my life to this novel: thank you.

My especial thanks to my patient partner: T x

Bringing a book from manuscript to what you are reading is a team effort.

Dialogue Books would like to thank everyone who helped to publish *The Secret Diaries of Charles Ignatius Sancho* in the UK

Editorial
Sharmaine Lovegrove
Amy Baxter
Josephine Lane
Adriano Noble

Contracts
Anniina Vuori

Sales
Caitriona Row
Dominic Smith
Frances Doyle
Hannah Methuen
Lucy Hine
Toluwalope Ayo-Ajala

Publicity
Millie Seaward

Marketing
Emily Moran

Design
Sophie Harris
Nico Taylor

Production
Narges Nojoumi

Copy Editor
Gabrielle Chant

Proof Reader
David Bamford

Audio
Louise Harvey
Sarah Shrubb
Jessica Callaghan

DISCOVER SANCHO'S LONDON
In partnership with VoiceMap

The most observant among you may have spotted a QR code languishing on the back cover, alongside the barcode.

Scan it using the camera app on your smartphone – or go to voicemap.me/sancho – and you'll start out on a self-guided audio tour of London. This immersive experience, voiced by Paterson Joseph, brings the Georgian city to life through the eyes of Charles Ignatius Sancho. It was created exclusively to celebrate the release of this novel.

You can do the tour on location or virtually. For the best experience, we recommend installing the VoiceMap app from the Apple App Store or Google Play.